ADVANCE PRAISE FOR *Albatross*

"Fallis writes from another time,
when Wodehouse and Leacock and Twain roamed the
earth. May he never become extinct."
LINWOOD BARCLAY, New York Times bestselling author of
A Noise Downstairs

"Booklovers, rejoice and buy this book!
In *Albatross*, Terry Fallis has found the antidote for what
ails our sorry world. May millions of you benefit!"
ALAN BRADLEY, New York Times bestselling author of
The Sweetness at the Bottom of the Pie

"It's hard not to get excited about a new Terry Fallis novel,
and it is equally hard not to fall in love with Adam Coryell,
the big-hearted, sarcastic, fountain-pen-obsessed hero of
Albatross, a young golf prodigy who just wants to write
short stories. In his inimitable style, Fallis has crafted a
tender, funny, and compulsively readable novel about what
it means to stay true to your dreams, and to yourself.
Do yourself a favour and pick up this book—you won't
put it down again until the final page has been turned."
AMY JONES, author of *Every Little Piece of Me*
and *We're All in This Together*

ALBATROSS

A NOVEL

TERRY FALLIS

McCLELLAND & STEWART

McClelland & Stewart and colophon are registered trademarks of Penguin Random House Canada Limited.

Library and Archives Canada Cataloguing in Publication data is available upon request

ISBN: 978-0-7710-5096-1
ebook ISBN: 978-0-7710-5097-8

Book design by Five Seventeen
Cover art © leonardo255 / Getty Images
Typeset in Joanna by M&S, Toronto
Printed and bound in Canada

McClelland & Stewart,
a division of Penguin Random House Canada Limited,
a Penguin Random House Company
www.penguinrandomhouse.ca

1 2 3 4 5   23 22 21 20 19

James Coryell Fallis

(1929-2019)

In memory of my father,

who passed on to me an abiding love of language.

"Ah! well a-day! what evil looks
Had I from old and young!
Instead of the cross, the Albatross
About my neck was hung."
"The Rime of the Ancient Mariner"
Samuel Taylor Coleridge (1834)

Albatross: A score of three strokes under par on a hole.
Oxford Dictionary

"That, young Adam, is an AK-47," Bobbie said. "I'm sure you already know this, but the Kalashnikov, as it's affectionately known, was designed in 1947. 1947! It's older than I am!"

I tried to ignore her little assault rifle treatise, but after years alongside Bobbie, I knew resistance was futile. Oblivious, she prattled on with her little biography of a firearm.

"I mean, that weapon has played a defining role in so many revolutions across the last seventy-five years. It deserves credit and blame, in nearly equal measure, for most of the coups, terrorist acts, territorial skirmishes, insurgencies, and armed conflicts from one side of the globe to the other!"

"Bobbie," I whispered.

"A few years ago, I read a fascinating account of the Kalashnikov's pivotal place in world history, and . . ."

"Bobbie," I said a little louder.

". . . it would not be an exaggeration to say that governments were toppled and born, wars were won and lost, and national borders were drawn and redrawn, all on the trigger of the same gun that guy standing in front of us is holding right now."

"Bobbie!" I snapped in a voice that quite accurately reflected just how freaked out I was at that moment.

"What?" She looked genuinely puzzled.

"Bobbie, that's all very fascinating—actually, at this precise moment, it's really not—and I'd be pumped to learn more about this historically significant firearm were it not for the complicating fact that he's pointing it directly at us . . . on purpose . . . with malevolent intent and little chance of missing us should he decide to squeeze off a burst."

Bobbie fell silent for a moment, but not nearly long enough. "But look how the sun glints off it," she continued after a moment, shaking her head. The faraway expression on her face seemed somewhere between admiration and awe. "Quite stunning."

I lifted my eyes to the man standing about thirty metres away. He wore an expression that balanced rage and anxiety on a knife edge while brandishing what I now knew to be an internationally celebrated assault rifle.

"Yeah, and look how angry he is," I replied. "Quite frightening."

While his gun was pointed our way, his eyes were not. He just kept staring into the clouds.

Bobbie ignored me and turned to scan the horizon.

"Man, what a view from up here."

By this time, she seemed completely at ease. I was not. I was terrified—all-in, flat-out, and full-on. On the fear spectrum, I situated myself somewhere well past freaking and heading fast to fainting. If I knew of a stronger word than terrified, believe me, I'd be trotting it out right about now.

"Aren't you scared?" I asked.

"Quite," she replied. "But so is our friend over there."

I looked over at Mr. Kalashnikov, who kept his weapon trained on us while taking furtive glances into the sky and tilting his head like a dog hearing a sound we could not. Bobbie and I sat next to each other with our backs literally, and in every other sense of the word, against the wall.

"These things are so much more effective than handcuffs," Bobbie offered, examining the plastic tie-wrap that bound her wrists. The one that secured mine was too tight and dug into my skin. It hurt.

"I mean, they're strong, light, easy to carry, and just as effective as over-built steel cuffs against the modest power of the human forearm," Bobbie continued. "Plus, the pièce de résistance, there's no key to lose. Brilliant!"

She actually chuckled as she said "brilliant." I'm not kidding. With a bad man training an assault rifle on us, she chuckled. I felt like I might pass out, but Bobbie didn't notice. She continued her enthusiastic, even fawning, dissertation on the advances in personal restraint embodied in the lowly plastic tie-wrap, but the sound of my own pounding heart nearly drowned her out. Yes, I know. I plead guilty to the charge of cliché. I'm a writer—or at least I want to be a writer—so I'm programmed to hate clichés. But sometimes they're clichés for a reason. I had never really believed that old adage—that old cliché—that your life actually passes before your eyes in moments of dire peril, in that little space that exists between passed out and passed on. But you know what? It's true. Perfect memory fragments, intact, whole, pristine, flying at you almost faster than you can take them in. And with more detail than you'd ever recall without the catalyst of a life-threatening event. It's true. It's all true.

PART 1

Chapter 1

"WOULD YOU MIND if I measured your extremities?"

It wasn't the first thing she said to us, but it was within the first hour after we'd met. We were in the phys ed classroom that opened onto the gym. It was my senior year in high school in Toronto, long before I became what I was to become. But it started right there in that classroom, the first morning of the first day of my final fall term.

My homeroom teacher was new to the school. She was dressed in blue track pants, white Nikes, and a white short-sleeved golf shirt with the words *Ladies' Golf Club of Toronto* embroidered just south of her left shoulder. A whistle hung from a lanyard around her neck. She was just a clipboard shy of the complete collegiate-coach stereotype. As we filed into our all-boys phys ed class and found desks, she stood at the front, leaning against the blackboard and watching us with a bemused but warm smile. I'm not being unkind when I say you could see she was a woman, but it took more than a glance. Her grey hair was cut like mine—shortish with a side part. I'd say she was in her mid- to late fifties, and she was very solidly built. If she played rugby—and if she didn't, she should have —she'd have anchored the scrum.

She wrote the name Davenport on the blackboard and then moved to stand just in front of her desk.

"Good morning, gents," she started. "I'm Ms. Davenport. You can call me Ms. D. if you're prone to efficiency and like to get to the point faster. But to be clear, it's Ms., not Mrs., not Miss, and despite the temptation, not Mr. It's Ms. Clear?"

All twenty of us nodded at once.

"Good."

She handed Mike Gleason at the front-left corner desk a piece of paper. "If you don't mind, please write your names on this seating plan and pass it on so it's a little easier for me to get to know you," she directed. "Next week, you can switch around and sit where you like. By then, I'll know you all by name, by face, by fashion sense, by haircut, by vocal stylings, and perhaps even by smell. You see, to the best of my recollection, I'm blessed with a prodigious memory. I'm not bragging. It's just the truth."

She smiled and then perched on the front of her desk.

"Anyhooo, I gather I'm your homeroom teacher. Lucky me, lucky you. We're going to have some fun in this class, I can tell. I mean, it's gym, right? We'll be doing units on basic fitness, football, rugby, wrestling—and of course I mean real wrestling, not the off-the-top-rope, hit-him-with-a-folding-chair, bite-through-the-blood-pack antics we see on television, although there are times when I find that quite entertaining—gymnastics, basketball, track, badminton, and if the lawyers don't get too antsy, trampoline." She then leaned towards us and held a finger up. "And of course, there'll be several health units as well, covering stuff that I suspect most of you already know. But we're going to make sure, because the cost of not knowing some of this material is very, very high. I'm not being too cryptic here, am I, gentlemen?"

On cue, most of us shook our heads.

"Good." She paused and looked up, perhaps in search of something. Finding it, she continued. "Oh, right, I'm also coaching the school golf team starting later this week, and then in October, the hockey team. So I hope to see at least some of you out after school. You know, there's so much more to gain and glean outside of the classroom. A very smart and funny man named Mark Twain once said, 'I never let school get in the way of my education.' I love that, but don't read too much into it. You need stellar marks to get into college and university, and I hope many of you will be headed down that path a year from now."

She fetched a stack of papers from the windowsill and started down the first column of desks, passing stapled sheets to each student along the way.

"Okay, just to start off with a bang, I'm handing out the rather lengthy release form that absolves the school, school board, and me from liability should you sprain your ankle, break a leg, lose a kidney, suffer paraplegia, or endure any other medical misadventure on my watch."

She paused at the back of the room when a few of the guys with shorter attention spans started whispering.

"Okay, stay with me, gentlemen. We're almost there," she said. "I know this is scintillating stuff, but do try to stay calm and focus on the task at hand."

The room was immediately hers again, and she continued up the aisle towards the front, talking all the way. "You're to fill out most of the form right now to spare your mom, dad, or guardian the tedium tonight, and then you're going to take it home for parental perusal and signature, hopefully without delay, for independent legal counsel."

She was funny and articulate, and talked the way I thought a writer might. She also gave off a quiet confidence that instantly placed her high on my list of people I'd want around in tight situations—you know, in the midst of a bank robbery, or stranded on a desert island. I liked her.

When she reached my desk with the form, I noticed for the first time the ink stains on the fingers of both her hands. I liked her even more. When I took the paper from her, I positioned my hands so she couldn't miss my own nearly perpetually inky fingers. She smiled and flashed me hers.

"A kindred spirit?" she asked with elevated eyebrows.

I nodded, pulled that day's fountain pen out of my pocket, and placed it on my desk.

"Ahhh, the Pilot Custom Heritage 92," she said. "I loves me a good Pilot piston-filler. And a fine gold nib to boot."

Because I'd recently perfected the art of doing two things at once, I simultaneously beamed and nodded as she moved on to the next desk. It felt good to have staked out a modest acreage of common ground with my new homeroom teacher.

While we completed the form, Ms. Davenport sat at her desk at the front, reading. From my seat in the front row I could just make out the title of the magazine. It was the *Scandinavian Journal of Kinesiology and Sports Medicine*, and she seemed quite absorbed in it.

"Mrs. D.?" said Mike Gleason from the desk beside me.

"Ahhhhh, the fires of Hades' furnace!" she barked.

It was so quiet in the classroom you could hear a pen drop. Actually, I think I heard four pens fall to the floor from startled hands.

"Um, sorry, Mrs. Davenport?" Mike stammered.

"Ahhhhh, the curse of the minuscule memory!" she shouted, her hands reaching for the ceiling in plaintive supplication. (Yes, I guess "plaintive supplication" is a bit over the top, but I'm a writer, and even back then I wasn't enamoured of the old *less is more* axiom.)

I leaned over and whispered to Mike.

"Oh, right. Sorry. I mean, Ms. Davenport?"

"Much better, son," she replied. "I knew you'd get there. Now, how can I help?"

"Well, um, I messed up my sheet. Do you have an extra?"

"Of course. I quite often botch the first attempt myself," she replied, handing Mike a second form.

Crisis averted. Pens picked up.

By this time, the seating plan had made it back to Ms. Davenport's desk, and she scanned it as we continued to fill in the blank spaces on the form. The next time I looked up, she was consumed in her Scandinavian journal. Now and then she'd nod, then look up and survey the room, eyeing a few of us up and down. It was a little odd. Maybe more than a little odd. Finally, she rose and, carrying the journal and seating plan with her, walked the aisles, stopping at certain desks and looking more closely at the occupants. I was one of them. By then, it was well past more than a little odd and heading fast for downright weird.

At that moment, the bell rang, ending first period. We all instantly started packing up and hauling ourselves out of our chairs.

"Wait! Just before you go, gentlemen, and I assume that moniker is appropriate," she started, "please guard those forms with your lives and have them signed and back to me hot-foot-tattyo, as my mother used to say. If you're still in the dark, that phrase simply means *fast*. I look forward to running you off your feet this year and improving your mental and physical fitness. Now, just one more thing before you bolt with fevered anticipation for whatever class awaits you. I wonder if four of you would indulge me in the name of science," she said while scanning the seating plan in her hand.

"Messrs. Coryell, Atkins, Sharma, and Sinclair. Would you mind if I measured your extremities? It won't take but a few minutes."

We all stopped. None of us said anything. But the four of us exchanged baffled glances before turning back to Ms. Davenport.

"Let me reassure you. I have no nefarious intent. I'm simply examining an interesting theory outlined in this periodical, and you can help," she said, waving the journal in the air. "Might you be able to return here after school for just a few minutes?"

All four of us lucky winners agreed. What choice did we have?

ALLI SAVED ME a seat beside her in Writer's Craft, our last class of the day. If it's not obvious by the warm and heartfelt way I just used her name, Allison and I were, in my parents' vernacular, "an item." We'd been together for about a year, held fast by a shared love of fountain pens and creative writing. I imagine teenage hormones may also have been a factor in our mutual attraction, but we hadn't yet covered that unit in health class.

"Hey," she said as I dropped into the chair. "What are you packing today?"

"That seems like a rather personal question," I replied. She smiled and rolled her eyes.

"Still the CH92," I replied, pulling the Pilot pen from my pocket and laying it on the desk.

"One day, I too will have a gold-nib pen." She sighed.

"Yes, you will. And I want to be there when you get it," I said.

I could never have afforded a CH92 on my own, but my parents had given me the transparent blue model for my last birthday. I had a few other pens in my fledgling collection, but the CH92 had become my go-to, everyday-carry pen. I mean, why would I write with a scratchy Noodler's Ahab when I could opt for the smooth gold nib of the Pilot?

"What have you got inked?" I asked.

She pulled a small leather sleeve from her backpack and slid out a matte black pen with a big wire clip on the cap. It was her Lamy Safari with a medium steel nib.

"That's two days in a row for the Safari," I continued. "What gives?"

"I've got it running so smoothly now that it's hard to switch it out."

"I hear you," I replied. "Oh, and happy anniversary."

"And to you," she said with a high-wattage smile that was so radiant, it had a physical effect on me. I could feel it in my heart, and in my stomach, and . . . well, let's leave it at that.

We'd met in English class exactly one year before, on the first day of school. I was just sitting there, minding my own business and writing the date at the top of my page with my Blue Pilot Prera (I like Pilot fountain pens, if that wasn't already clear). As providence would have it, Alli sat at the desk next to mine. My aforementioned heart, or my stomach, or perhaps some other internal organ, did a little triple salchow when two things happened in quick succession. First, she looked right at me and smiled. Then she uncapped a pink Platinum Preppy and started writing in her notebook. She was also very cute, tending towards beautiful. Her brown hair was short, her denim-clad legs were long, and everything in between, including her brain, was a little out of my league. And by "a little out of my league," I probably mean "way out of my league." But I was feeling optimistic that day.

I'd never met anyone else, let alone a potential girlfriend, who adored fountain pens as much as I did. Ink, too. That first day, we were engaged in writing what our teacher called a "personal reflection." I could tell at a glance she had inked her Preppy with Diamine Ancient Copper. I stole another look at her page but she caught me and moved her arm to block my view. I shook my head. I wasn't trying to copy her. Why would I do that? It was a personal reflection, not a multiple-choice math quiz.

"I wasn't reading your piece," I whispered. "I was admiring your taste in ink."

To drive home my point, I pulled a bottle of the very same Diamine Ancient Copper from my backpack and placed it on my desk, the label facing towards her. I then used my hands like a *Price Is Right* model to direct her gaze to the ink. Her eyes widened, and she giggled at my hand antics.

"Allison Clarkson, but most people call me Alli," she whispered.

"Adam Coryell. Most people call me, um, Adam."

She laughed again, and that was that.

"Do you think it means anything that we have the same initials?" I asked.

"Probably not," she replied. "But it's early days."

"Right."

If the fountain pen connection weren't enough, I really fell hard when, shortly after we met, she revealed a passion for creative writing that rivalled my own. And we both wanted to be writers. When we learned this about one another, everything seemed to fall into place.

Allison was new to the school but carried herself like she'd been there for years. She wasn't part of the mega-popular stratum within the school—you know, the "in" crowd—but it seemed to be her choice. She was just very comfortable in her own skin for someone so young.

I wasn't exactly in the "cool kids" clique either, but neither was I in the no-hopers geek society. I was average. Tall and skinny, but with good hair—not that I'm blowing my own horn, let alone hair. Think Ryan Reynolds—his hair, I mean, not his Hollywood face. I guess my face was fine, but when you see it, what springs to mind is nice boy, maybe future accountant, but not movie star, not quarterback, not Mr. Popularity.

But somehow, it all seemed to work with Alli. The constellations aligned—or whatever that metaphor is—and we became inseparable. We walked to and from school together most days, even though it took me out of my way. We'd eat lunch together in the cafeteria, hang out at each other's lockers, sit next to one another when we shared classes. You know, the high school definition of inseparable. I kept waiting for the wheels to fall off. But they never did—well, not then, anyway. We may have veered onto the soft shoulder a few times, but we somehow always made it safely back onto the road and were still together a year later.

We had a few minutes before our Writer's Craft class started. We were both quite excited about the course, but we'd learned via email a few days earlier that the teacher assigned to lead the class had unexpectedly taken a medical leave. That didn't sound promising, for the teacher or for us. Neither of us knew who had drawn the short straw, but we'd know soon enough.

"Hey, you're up," Alli said, and handed over a thick spiral notebook.

I opened the book and found my way to the start of the most recent chapter. There I found Alli's neat and slanted cursive. The ink was a light but still rich blue. In brackets before the chapter started, she'd written, *TWSBI Eco, Iroshizuku Kon-Peki*, noting the pen type and ink used. It was a thing fountain pen nerds routinely did. I closed the notebook and slipped it into my backpack.

"Okay, great. I'll read it tonight and start figuring out what happens next," I replied.

We called it our antiphonal novel. I like interesting words, and *antiphonal* usually describes a song where alternate lines or verses are sung by two choirs opposite one another. Kind of like a two-party musical conversation, or a freestyle rap battle without the attitude. Back and forth. That's what we were doing with our novel: She'd write a chapter and then I'd respond with a chapter. Back and forth. And it was my turn, again.

The bell sounded just as Ms. Davenport strode through my classroom door for the second time that day. I watched as she wrote her surname on the board.

"You're going to like her," I whispered to Alli. "She's got inky fingers, too."

Alli nodded, raising an eyebrow.

"Hello, fresh-faced literature lovers and storytellers. Apologies for my tardiness. I'm still learning the labyrinthine corridors of this school. Now that I know where we gather, I'll not be late again."

She did a modified version of the Ms., not Mrs., Miss, or Mr. thing that she'd done in homeroom that morning. We all nodded. Ms. it is.

"Ah, and nice to see you again, Mr. Coryell. How fortuitous that we open and close our day in one another's company," she said.

I was surprised and a little chuffed that she somehow already knew my name. I seemed to have been infected with her formal speaking style, for I answered simply with "Indeed."

Alli glanced my way with quizzical all over her face.

Ms. Davenport started the seating plan around the room and then faced us from the front.

"How many of you are avid readers?"

Nearly every student in the class raised a hand.

"Splendid. Now, how many of you actually have a novel in your backpack right now?"

Fewer hands were raised, but Alli's and mine were among them.

"Excellent. Finally, how many of you need literature to live?"

This time, only two hands were in the air, and you can guess whose they were.

Alli and I looked at one another and I felt warm all over. I think the right word might be flushed.

"I'm glad," Ms. Davenport said. "I fall into that last demographic grouping myself. Okay, who knows where Thessalon is?"

I looked around. Exactly zero hands were raised.

"Let me enlighten you. I grew up in Thessalon, Ontario, on the Trans-Canada Highway, a little more than six hundred kilometres from Toronto. It's on the north shore of Lake Huron, just before you hit Lake Superior. Not much goes on in Thessalon, other than a declining timber industry and some tourism. And when I say tourism, almost everyone who visits Thessalon is just passing through on their way to somewhere else. It's not really a destination as much as a place to fill up your tank or maybe spend a night after a full day of driving."

She was just telling us a story, her story, but we were completely engaged.

"My family owned a small and struggling motel right on the lake, and sometimes we even had overnight guests in some of the rooms." She paused to see if we'd caught it. A couple of us chuckled. "Yes, friends, that was a modest and clearly inadequate attempt at humour to illustrate just how struggling our motel was, and to see if you were still with me." She looked at the clock and sighed. "Oh well, I guess I need to pick up the pace a bit. Anyway, by the time I was about twelve years old, I knew every square inch of land in every direction within the radius I could cover in a day's bike ride. I was an only child and there weren't too many kids my own age in the area, so I was by myself much of the time. And for plenty of reasons I'll not go into here, it was just better for me to stay away from the motel as much as I could. Don't worry, it was nothing too serious. So when school was out in the summer, I spent a lot of time on my bike, bored and alone."

She paused and scanned the room. It was quiet. Most of us were paying attention, and those who weren't were quiet. Alli appeared riveted and never took her eyes off Ms. Davenport.

"Then I was saved. One summer morning when I was about to set off for the day, a strange-looking vehicle drove past the motel, heading into town. It looked like an old school bus, but it wasn't. It was brand-spanking-sparkling-new and freshly painted. On its side I read, *Sault Ste. Marie Public Library Bookmobile*. A happy and friendly-looking cartoon character shaped like a book with arms, legs, and a face smiled back at me from the tail end of the bookmobile as it drove down the highway."

She kind of assumed the shape of a book and moved her arms and legs to mimic the character on the back of the bookmobile. We laughed.

"I didn't know it then, but my life changed in that instant."

She paused for dramatic effect and looked at her students, most of whom were leaning forward and waiting to hear the rest.

"At that time, nearly half a century ago, there was no library in Thessalon. I'd only ever seen our sad, neglected, and minuscule school library, and I'd read nearly every book in it. So I pedalled after that bookmobile like my life depended on it. And it might well have. I prayed it would stop in town and not drive right through back to the Sault, about an hour's drive northwest. It didn't take long before I lost sight of it ahead of me. I was fast, but a bike is no match for a bookmobile with a well-tuned diesel engine. Still, I kept pedalling.

"I found it parked in front of the Algoma District municipal building. A couple of kids were piling onto the bus as I skidded my bike to a rather impressive fishtailing stop, so I followed them in. I didn't emerge for about an hour and a half. The young student who was staffing the bookmobile helped me find wonderful novels, most of which I can still remember to this day. I could take out up to five books at each weekly visit the bookmobile made to my town."

She paused with a faraway look in her eye, then shook her head and resumed her story.

"Through those books I travelled the world, laughed and cried, learned about life, good and evil, right and wrong. I came to understand how the power of words and stories could leave you transfixed, transported, and transformed. This may sound a tad melodramatic, but to me, the bookmobile was the weekly medication that kept me sane. Without it, I wouldn't be teaching English or Writer's Craft today. I might still have been a phys ed teacher, given my brute strength and obvious athleticism—that was another attempted joke, in case there's any confusion—but I wouldn't be standing at the front of this particular class."

She took a breath and sat on the front of her desk.

I could tell out of the corner of my eye that Alli was as entranced as I was. I sensed a few students at the back were restless, but they'd almost certainly signed up for this course thinking it would be an easy credit. I loved what Ms. Davenport was saying, and I think she could tell. I was staring at her with such intensity, clinging to every word before she'd finished enunciating them. So, it seemed, was Allison. Ms. Davenport was speaking to us, to Alli and me. And we were spellbound.

"This is Writer's Craft. Some of you may wish to become writers, to make a life by writing. That is a noble calling. Writing our stories is important. Our own literature is part of what defines our country and sustains our culture. But it's not easy. It's a tough slog. But something this essential, something this crucial, shouldn't be easy."

I looked at Alli. She sensed my gaze and turned to me. Her eyes were wide. Then she fixed her eyes again on Ms. Davenport. I did, too.

"Just think of it for a moment," Ms. Davenport said. "You're creating something from absolutely nothing but what's floating around in your head and your heart. It is an extraordinary achievement to place words on a blank page in such a way that, when read, the reader is moved. Is inspired. Is empowered. Is changed. No visual cues, no sound effects, no musical score, no sight gags, no breathtaking vistas, no CGI, just printed words on a white page. Now, that is the power, the challenge, the beauty, and the purity of the written word. And that's what this class is all about."

Wow, I thought. *Powerful and perfectly put.* I looked again at Alli —I found it hard not to—but her eyes were riveted on Ms. Davenport. The room was very quiet.

"Writing is hard, but it improves with practice, just like most endeavours. So we're going to write in this class, every day. You can write whatever you want, as long as there's a story in it. Memoir, short stories, non-fiction, personal essays, even a novel. The choice is yours. The only rule is that the words must move me and move your classmates. The words must count, every one of them. They must be carefully chosen and strung together with passion, purpose, power, and polish. What device did I just employ?"

Allison's hand shot into the air. "Alliteration," I blurted out. Ms. Davenport ignored me and pointed at Allison.

"Alliteration," she said.

"Bingo!" said Ms. Davenport. "Clearly your overly eager colleague, Mr. Coryell, is afflicted with premature alliteration," she said. At least some of the class chuckled. "Alliteration is just one of many, many literary devices you have at your disposal to help your words grab a reader by the throat and not let go. Hmmm, perhaps a less violent metaphor might be more appropriate in a temple of higher learning, but you know what I mean."

Allison and I nodded in unison.

"Okay, I think I've droned on enough. Let's do some writing."

She wrote a few different writing prompts on the board, then wandered the room while we all wrote. A few kids asked for clarification about the exercise and she responded patiently. With about ten minutes to go in the class, she picked a few students at random to read their work. Neither Alli nor I was chosen.

"All right, we're about out of time," Ms. Davenport said. "Your first mission, should you choose to accept it—and I suggest you do, as it will eventually be submitted and marked —is to think about the story you want to tell. Don't worry about the form yet, just the story. Your homework is to jot down the key points and be ready to discuss them next class if called upon. And I also want to know what novel you're currently reading. And if you're not reading one right now, you'd better be by next class. You'll thank me for it. I can even suggest some titles if you like. Until then, as one famous writer once said, 'Parting is such sweet sorrow.'"

"Okay, I've got to bolt," I said to Alli outside the classroom. "I'll pick you up at 6:15 and we'll subway it down to Harbourfront. That gives us plenty of time to make it for 7:30."

"Great. I'm so excited about seeing him tonight. But I'm also a little nervous."

"Me too."

By the time I stopped at my locker and then made my way back down to the gym, Scott, Ahmed, and Eric were already there. They had their arms extended horizontally and Ms. Davenport was wielding a tape measure with the practised movements of a veteran extremity-measurer.

"Mr. Coryell, good of you to come," she said.

"Sorry I'm late," I replied and sat down at a desk.

"Okay, gents, you can lower your arms. That was the last measurement I needed," she said. "You are free to go, and I shall report if anything noteworthy emerges from your numbers. Thank you for indulging my curiosity and donating your time and extremities in the pursuit of science. I'm grateful."

The three guys gathered their stuff quickly and headed for the door while Ms. Davenport crunched numbers at her desk. Eric turned to me on his way out and used his index finger to etch crazy-circles in the air next to his temple.

"Just give me a moment, Mr. Coryell," she said, her fingers flying on what looked like an ancient pocket calculator that was too gargantuan to fit in any pocket I'd ever seen.

With a cheap ballpoint, she wrote down various numbers in a table she'd created. I could see Ahmed, Eric, and Scott's names listed in the first column. Then she opened the journal article she'd been reading during our morning phys ed class, her eyes darting from the journal to her handwritten table.

"Yes, yes, okay, right, yes, yes, okay. Right, then. Nothing interesting here," she said, lifting her eyes to me. "So we come to you, Mr. Coryell. Could you stand for me, please?"

I did as she asked. "I really liked what you said in Writer's Craft," I said, just to make conversation. I was feeling nervous. "I'm looking forward to the class, and I know Allison is, too."

"Thank you, Mr. Coryell," she replied. "Now, could you extend your arms from your body at ninety degrees, please?"

She began measuring away—my forearm and whole arm, my overall height, my leg, my torso from the waist to the top of my shoulders, my waist to the top of my head, the length of my shin up to the kneecap, and then from my kneecap to my waist. She even measured the length of each finger.

"I was thinking of maybe a double-breasted suit, perhaps grey flannel," I joked. I wasn't used to being measured by my gym teacher.

"A perfectly tailored remark under the circumstances," she replied. "Now, just bear with me for a few more minutes and all will be made clear."

She took a few more measurements, for good, um, measure, and then sat back down at her desk.

"At ease, soldier."

I lowered my limbs.

"Can you sit for just a few more minutes?" she asked.

"Well, I may take a look at the dress shirts, and maybe a tie to go with the suit."

She indulged me with a smile and waved me to a desk, then pulled a very nice-looking fountain pen from the backpack that rested on the floor against the leg of her desk. Even though her hands were quite large—okay, they were massive—the tortoise-shell acrylic pen was still sizeable.

"Is that an Edison?" I asked, leaning in.

"It is indeed. You know your pens, Mr. Coryell."

"It's the Pearl, right? In Aztec Flake?"

"Very impressive, Mr. Coryell," she replied. "Here, try her little sister, the Pearlette."

She pulled a smaller version of the same pen, in the same beautiful resin, from her pack and passed it over to me along with a Rhodia dotPad. I unscrewed the cap and noted the medium steel nib. Such a beautiful pen. And it wrote so nicely, leaving a wet line in a lovely, almost plummy colour.

"Wow. Very smooth for a steel nib."

"Some of my smoothest writers are steel nibs," she replied.

"And the ink?"

"It's Pelikan Edelstein Turmaline," she replied. "If I'm not mistaken, it was the ink of the year in 2012."

"Yes, it was," I said. "I've been meaning to order a bottle now that the price has dropped a bit."

"So why the interest in fountain pens?" she asked. "Where did that come from?"

"A couple years ago I read an article online about the writing instruments of several famous writers. Some of them used pencils, but many wrote with fountain pens. Arthur Conan Doyle favoured the Parker Duofold. Hemingway liked Montegrappa pens. Mark Twain used the Conklin Crescent Filler. So I bought a cheap TWSBI and fell hard. I want to be a writer some day, and I think fountain pens give me some kind of link to writers of the past I admire. The feeling I have when the nib is on the paper is almost the same as experienced by all those great writers. I guess that must sound weird."

"First of all, Mr. Coryell, you speak like a writer. Secondly, that was one of the sanest explanations for the often inexplicable fountain pen habit I've ever heard."

"What about you?" I asked.

"Mine is a simpler explanation. I inherited my grandfather's 1946 Parker Vacumatic in Azure Blue with a super-smooth medium nib. After I had the diaphragm replaced, it wrote like a champ, and still does. And that's all it took for me."

She moved to the calculator and spent two or three minutes furiously pumping in measurements and jotting down numbers in the hand-drawn table on her pad. She then capped her pen, put it down on her desk, and again picked up the journal. I turned my head a bit to read the title upside down. *Scandinavian Journal of Kinesiology and Sports Medicine*.

"Ahhhh, yes, ye olde SJKSM," I deadpanned. "I let my subscription lapse a few years ago."

She ignored me and turned to a page about halfway through, marked with a creased and crinkled Post-it note. A table of figures took up most of the page. She placed her pad of scrawled numbers next to it and lowered her head to the data. She uncapped the pen again and as the large nib on the Edison Pearl tracked down the page over and over, she talked to herself.

"Baseball, no. Pole vault, not bad, but not really. Discus, hmmmm, no. Hurdles, not close enough."

Then she sat quietly for a moment, her pen yet again tracing the table and flitting over to her pad. Then she snapped her eyes to mine. Her gaze was quite intense and left me a little alarmed. I talk when alarmed, often attempting humour. When it works, it feels good. When it falls flat, not so much.

"I really hurt myself on the hurdles last year, if that helps," I said.

She ignored me again and went back through the figures one more time. She was shaking her head, looking from her pad of figures to the journal's figures to my figure.

"Astonishing."

"Not really," I replied. "Lots of other guys hurt themselves at hurdles. Phil Lester's voice is still slightly higher than it was before, you know, his hurdle incident."

"Mr. Coryell, have you ever played golf?"

Chapter 2

"GOLF? YOU MEAN the whole little-white-ball-in-the-hole thing?"

"Yes, yes, yes," she said. "Have you ever played?"

"I've never even held a club in my hands," I replied.

"Given that golf is best played with a club in your hands, I'll take that as a no."

She returned her eyes to her calculations and just shook her head.

"Well, you'll be holding one soon," she said.

I had no idea where this was going. *She measures my arms and legs, crunches some numbers, and arrives at golf?*

"Now you've lost me."

"I'm not surprised. Okay, you now deserve a full explanation.

Have a seat and I'll try to summarize it for you. So as not to bore you unduly, I'll give you the Cliff's Notes version of this obscure Swedish professor's interesting but not yet universally accepted theory," she explained, handing me the journal before standing up and writing PIPP on the blackboard. The journal was opened to an article titled "Body Type Analysis for Predictive Innate Pinnacle Proficiency (PIPP) in Major Sports."

"All right. Are you ready?"

I nodded.

"The PIPP theory was developed by Professor Ingemar Gunnarsson, a biomedical engineer and kinesiologist at the University of Adelaide. He hypothesizes that every human being, regardless of athletic inclination, has a body that is suited to perform competently in at least one sport, and often more. The problem is, most people never actually try the sport for which their body is optimally suited. He argues that even seasoned athletes, who are quite proficient in the sports they happen to play, might have been the very best in the world in a different sport they've never tried. Are you with me so far?"

"I think so." I still wasn't sure where this was going and how it affected me, but I had an idea a golf course waited at the end of the story.

"Right, then. Onwards," she said. "This theory took him fifteen years to develop, despite ridicule from more traditional academic quarters. His algorithm involves a series of body measurements that, when evaluated as standalone benchmarks and more importantly as a series of ratios, can be mapped against the projected optimal numbers for about twenty-seven different sports, all based on elite athletes whom Dr. Gunnarsson has studied using an advanced computer modelling methodology. His optimal numbers represent an extrapolation into uncharted territory."

My mind began to drift. I understood that a person might have a body better suited for bobsledding than basketball, but what was the point? And what did it have to do with me? But I held my tongue and tried to catch up.

"It's a fascinating theory to contemplate. Just think how heartbreaking it would be to learn, after a twenty-year journeyman career in the minor leagues of professional baseball, never having made it to the majors, that all that time you were supposed to be playing professional jai alai in the Philippines and could have been among the best in the world. More simply put, imagine if Michael Phelps was afraid of the water and never learned to swim?"

"Hmmm. That is kind of interesting, I guess," I said. "Maybe Canada could have picked up a few more swimming medals at the last Olympics had Phelps been scared of the water."

I was trying to follow and I thought I understood what she was getting at, but again, what did it matter?

"Let's forget about Mr. Phelps, and talk about you, Mr. Coryell," she said. "When viewed through the lens of Professor Gunnarsson's work, you appear to be very special, at least in theory. Judging by the ratio of your arm length to your leg length, your torso to your overall height, and the dozen or so other blessed measurements and ratios dictated by an obscure but perhaps brilliant Swedish kinesiologist, you, Mr. Coryell, should be quite the prodigy—on paper."

"Prodigy on paper?" I replied. "You mean my dream of being a writer might come true?"

"Well, I hope you do realize that dream, but that's not what I'm talking about. I was referring not to your writing skills but in part to your orangutanal arms."

"And all this time I just thought I was lanky," I replied. "I had no idea I'd crossed into the orangutanal zone. And that somehow makes me special?"

"In the eyes of Professor Gunnarsson and his theory, your numbers make you very special, son. And to think lightning struck on the fourth student I measured. What are the odds?"

"But it makes no sense. I've never really been into sports, and I'm not exactly a gifted athlete. At least, I don't think I am." I was as coordinated as the next guy but had never been obsessed with sports the way some of my friends were. I'd rather read a good story, or better still, write one. So it was hard to get my head around what Ms. Davenport was saying and what it meant.

"But here's the key. One part of Gunnarsson's hypothesis turns traditional athletic performance theory on its head. If, according to his theory, your body type scores above the ninety-fifth percentile for a certain sport, your success in that sport is not dependent on the conventional approach of constant practice and refinement. In fact, at that level, practice of any kind actually compromises performance in these special individuals."

"Wait a second," I interjected. "Practice is bad? It doesn't make perfect?"

"Hang on, son. Stay with me here," she said. "You see, Gunnarsson theorizes that for these rare individuals above the ninety-fifth percentile, it's the natural makeup of the body that has equipped them to excel. He argues practice is not natural at all. In fact, it's the very antithesis of natural. It forces your body's natural positions, rhythms, and motions into unnatural patterns assumed to be optimal for that sport, and anchors them through repetition. In fact, to reverse engineer his theory, if you require constant practice to be competent in a sport, your Gunnarsson score will fall far short of ninety."

"So the best of the best, whether they know it or not, are gifted with natural superpowers that can be hurt by practice?" I asked. My head was starting to fog up. This whole theory seemed ass-backwards to me.

"Precisely. He hypothesizes that if you score above the ninety-fifth percentile—a Gunnarsson score of ninety-five—you really shouldn't practise, but simply do what feels most natural. Let your perfect body do what it naturally wants, and you will be rewarded by peak athletic performance in your particular sport. That's his theory in a nutshell."

I squeezed my eyes shut and gave my brain a shake, as if trying to banish a maelstrom of conflicting ideas from my head—which, incidentally, was exactly what I was trying to do.

"So, let me see if I understand what you're saying," I said, squinting in thought. "It's not about dedication, perseverance, commitment, practice, practice, practice, it's just naturally using the gift of a body perfectly suited for a particular sport? It has nothing to do with the person, just the body."

"Correct, but that applies only to those rare specimens whose Gunnarsson scores are above the ninety-fifth percentile. He figures below that score, practice can help," she said. "Now, you're probably wondering just how many athletes there are walking around with scores above ninety-five in various sports?"

I wasn't wondering about that at all. I was more concerned about being late for my date with Allison tonight. But . . .

"Right," I replied. "I was just going to ask."

"Ahh, therein lies the rub. That's what I meant earlier about his optimal numbers being an extrapolation into the unknown. Dr. Gunnarsson has never encountered an athlete, let alone a civilian, with a score higher than eighty-nine, and he's worked with Olympic gold medallists and world champions. That's why this is still just theory, conjecture, informed speculation, and why it hasn't ever been embraced by other researchers. Dr. Gunnarsson is a bit of a rogue. I like rogues."

"And the Gunnarsson scores of the other guys in my class were only okay?" I asked.

She flipped back to the page where she'd recorded the scores for Eric, Scott, and Ahmed.

"They just barely entered the scale for football and hockey. Ahmed had the highest Gunnarsson score, at 71.4 in hockey. Nothing special. Average at best. According to the PIPP theory, none of them will ever earn a living playing sports."

"And from your earlier question, I'm assuming my Gunnarsson score for golf, a game I've never played, or even wanted to try, is quite high."

She glanced back at her pad of figures and then looked at me, nodding. Her voice dropped to a whisper.

"Yes, it is, son."

"Well, how high?"

"99.2."

WHEN I GOT home, I made myself a sandwich and read a photocopy of the journal article. Chock full of scientific jargon and obscure references that meant nothing to me, it was tough slogging and very dry—parched, even. I actually didn't think the writing was very good. Then I remembered that Professor Gunnarsson wasn't writing in his native language. But I did add a few new words to my vocabulary, so it wasn't a complete loss. I skipped over some sections, but I read most of the article. I didn't glean much more than I had already learned from Ms. Davenport's briefing, except perhaps that Dr. Gunnarsson must have had a lot of time on his hands to plunge quite so far down this rabbit hole. What I was really left with was the idea that if you truly are perfectly and innately designed for a certain sport—with a Gunnarsson score of ninety-five or higher —practice will actually hurt your performance, not help it. It just seemed so counterintuitive, yet I could kind of see a sliver of sense in it all, too.

Dad arrived home as usual, about 5:15. We were cooking dinner for the family that night. Actually, we cooked together most nights. Mom usually got home a little later.

"Hey, Dad. How was your first day back?" I asked when I joined him in the kitchen.

"Well, it could have been worse, I guess, but not much. I've got a group of tough guys and delinquents. They disrupted the class for a good part of the day, mainly the young men, but a couple of the young women had mouths on them, too. I can already tell it's going to be a tough and tiring year."

"Dad, they can't be that bad, they're only in grade four," I replied. "What are they, eight years old?"

"Adam, you have no idea what can happen when eight-year-olds organize. It's like when primates learn about tools. It's a game changer."

"You can handle it, Dad. You always do. Just remember, you know more than they do."

"Maybe, but I'm still vastly outnumbered," he said as he pulled the chicken thighs from the meat drawer.

We worked away in the kitchen, cooking dinner and emptying the dishwasher. We were getting close by the time Mom walked through the door and kicked off her shoes. She collapsed into a chair at the kitchen table. She was an engineer at PrimeHydro, the provincial power provider.

"Hi, guys. Something smells great," she said while rubbing first one foot and then the other. "And have I mentioned that my shoes are killing me a little more each day?"

"I'm not surprised," I replied. "They look like medieval torture devices."

"That's exactly what they are," she agreed. "It's all part of the patriarchal conspiracy to oppress women in the workplace. And I wouldn't be surprised if an engineer—obviously a man —designed them. I tell you, the best part of my day is when I'm on the site and have to don my steel-toed boots. They're like walking on pillows."

"Any meltdowns today?" I asked.

"None of the reactor variety, but a few of our project management staff who are a little too focused on task completion dates briefly lost their, um, minds, and needed to visit the quiet room for a bit. Other than that, just another day in nuclear paradise."

Mom was part of a team of engineers refurbishing one of the nuclear reactors at the Pickering station, just outside of Toronto. I thought she and her job were very cool. I still do.

"I've got the table," she said, standing up and limping to the drawer for the placemats.

"Just two, Mom," I said. "Alli and I are going to the Irving reading at Harbourfront."

"Right."

After filling in my folks about Ms. Davenport and my boundless potential as a professional golfer, I booked it over to Alli's house. Allison and I both lived in Leaside, a well-established, upper-middle-class residential neighbourhood in midtown Toronto with house prices that, according to my parents, were now strictly upper class. It was a very warm night—not unusual for Toronto in September. I only had about ten minutes to make the thirteen-minute journey and still be on time. I ran the first stretch but walked the last little bit so I wouldn't be swimming in sweat by the time I got there. I made it at exactly 6:15, my face shimmering with perspiration.

"Did you sprint all the way over, or are you just glowing because you're thrilled to see me?" Alli asked when she came to the door.

"Well, because we promised to be honest with one another, I confess that it's strictly the glowing-because-I'm-thrilled-to-see-you thing," I replied. "Any running I did contributed nothing to my glow, and was solely in service of seeing you sooner."

"There you go with that alliteration again. Are you a writer?"

"Why yes, I am. And one day I'll be rich and famous."

"As a writer?"

"Check that," I replied. "And one day I'll be famous."

"As a writer?"

"Check that. And one day I'll be impoverished and obscure, but I'll be happy."

"As a wri . . ."

"Yes, as a writer."

"Me too," she said, giving my arm a squeeze.

We were headed to a reading by John Irving, one of our favourite writers. We caught the bus to the Davisville subway station and headed down to the platform. We boarded the southbound subway and found two seats together. In the tunnel between Summerhill and Rosedale stations, I reached for her hand.

"Hey!" she snapped, jerking her hand away as if I'd just electrocuted her. I flinched as if she'd just electrocuted me, and banged my elbow on the wall of the subway car. It, or I, made quite a loud noise. I'm not sure which. Only nine other startled passengers looked our way.

"Sorry, I thought . . ."

"Gotcha," she said with a look that approached triumph.

She then took my hand and held it tight.

"I'm just trying to keep you on your toes," she explained.

"Or in the hospital," I said, patting my heart.

She laughed and rested her head on my shoulder.

"Making me laugh is no small thing, mister," she said.

I looked down at our interlaced fingers. Both our thumbs and five of our eight fingers were ink-stained.

"Did you like Ms. Davenport?" I asked.

She lifted her head to look at me.

"I really liked her, a lot," she replied. "The mobile library story was inspiring and I loved how she spoke about writing."

"I had to meet with her after school for a little phys ed experiment." I gave her a very condensed account of my afterschool session with Ms. Davenport, because after having given my parents the play-by-play, I was already kind of tired of the story. I downplayed my Gunnarsson score, largely because I simply did not believe I would ever be any good at golf. I was okay at sports and was never the last guy selected when teams were being picked. But in general, I'd rather watch sports than play sports. And in general, I'd rather read, cook, write, or fold laundry than watch sports. I figured as soon as I tried to swing a club, Professor Gunnarsson's vaunted theory would crumble under the weight of my golfing ineptitude.

"Anyway, Ms. Davenport showed me her two Edisons, the Pearl and Pearlette, both in Aztec Flake. She let me write with the Pearlette, and man, was it smooth," I said.

"I've never met a teacher who uses fountain pens," Alli said. "And I love that Aztec Flake finish."

The Irving reading was wonderful and exceeded all our expectations. It was quite late by the time I escorted Alli up her front walk towards the door. She stopped us short and pulled me into the shadow cast by the wall of the garage. After careful thought, I decided not to resist. We kissed for what seemed like a very long time, just not nearly long enough. Then, holding me tight, she whispered in my ear.

"That was fantastic."

"Just to clarify, are you referring to the reading or the making out?" I inquired.

"The reading," she said. "I was getting to the making out part. It was amazing."

"As much as I love John Irving, I'd trade his reading for more making out, every time."

She moved in for one more long kiss.

We finally came up for air a few minutes later, and Alli looked at her phone. "Okay, I've got to get inside before my parents start to wonder what all that moaning is outside. And you have to get home to read my new chapter because I want to see yours ASAP."

"Or as Ms. Davenport says, hot-foot-tattyo," I replied.

"What?"

"Never mind."

I walked her to the door, where I deposited a chaste cheek kiss and then headed home.

It was ten-thirty when I made it upstairs to my room. I did some easy history homework, and then pulled out the thick spiral notebook and opened it up to Alli's latest chapter. She had quite lovely handwriting that was only enhanced by the use of a good everyday-carry pen like her TWSBI Eco and the nice shading of the Kon-Peki ink. My handwriting was not quite as legible. Alli occasionally asked me to confirm that I was in fact writing in English. But for someone who only wrote on his laptop, I thought my penmanship was getting better with practice. Writing in longhand made me a more thoughtful and measured writer. Plus, my mentor—you know, John Irving— wrote by hand, too. So Alli and I decided we'd kick it old school for our joint manuscript and handwrite it in fountain pen.

Our antiphonal novel was about a relationship between a young man and woman. It was set in the early 1960s in the Northern Ontario town of Temagami, about an hour's drive north of North Bay. The young man works on the family farm, one of the few farms in the area, while she is the daughter of the town doctor. The couple falls in love while in school. The story captured small-town life in a different time. That was the fun part, writing characters who lived in a different place and time—no YouTube, no cellphones, no Xbox or PS4, no Netflix. They dreamed of getting out of the small town and heading to Toronto—"the Big Smoke," as it was known—to attend the University of Toronto. The boy's marks were not likely high enough to get into U of T, but he was something of a hockey phenom, patrolling the blue line for the minor-league Temagami Tamaracks.

Neither Alli nor I had any real insight into where the story was going. We were literally taking it page by page, building on what the other had written. I figured there was little sense in thinking too far ahead when someone else was writing the next chapter.

I was more than a little excited when I read Alli's latest chapter, which featured the couple enjoying a classic—if chaste— romp in the hay in the young man's barn. How risqué. I can report with some regret that the scene wasn't explicit. There was no partial disrobing or venturing near "first base." There was certainly not even the most oblique hint at sex. But the scene was at least on the spectrum.

The rest of the chapter had them stressing about whether they'd be together in Toronto in the fall. It was well written and reflected her spare and clean prose. Our different handwriting styles aside, anyone reading this novel would easily realize that there were two authors. I'm not so adept at the spare and clean prose thing. Nor did I really want to be. I love the English language too much to want to pare it down too much.

I closed our notebook as my wheels spun, unable to find traction on what would happen next in the story. I wanted them to be together in Toronto, but I also knew they needed to confront some hardship along the way. A car accident? A competing suitor? One gets into U of T but not the other? I was just lying in my bed wrestling with these ideas when I heard my mother's footsteps outside my door. She knocked. Both Mom and Dad were very good about respecting their seventeen-year-old son's privacy. They always knocked and waited for the all-clear before entering. That was a good thing.

"Come in, Mom."

"How was the reading?"

"Better than I dreamed," I replied. "It was a great night."

"I'm glad. And you and Allison are, you know, doing well?"

"Smooth sailing so far, Mom. I really like her. When she laughs at something I've said, I'm not going to lie, it feels almost magical."

"That's great, Adam. I'm really happy for you. I like her a lot, too. I think you're great together," she said. "By the way, while you were out, we had a call from your Ms. Davenport."

"Really?"

"Yeah. We talked for about ten minutes," Mom explained. "She seems very cool and no-nonsense. I quite liked her and the way she spoke."

"She's new to the school. But I like her, too," I replied. "She's also a fountain pen aficionado. What's not to like?"

"We didn't talk about fountain pens."

"No, I guess you probably wouldn't. What did you talk about?"

"She was just calling to ask permission to take you to a driving range after school on Thursday for a little experiment."

"Did she brief you on the whole Gunnarsson theory?"

"She filled in some of the gaps in that condensed version you gave us earlier. Fascinating. It makes me wonder in what sport I could have dominated. Skeet shooting? Sailing? Table tennis? Maybe I should try golf."

"It's just a wild and unproven theory, Mom," I said. "So what did you tell her?"

"I just said you're old enough to make your own decisions and that we'll support whatever you decide."

"Thanks, Mom. I'll think about it and let her know."

"Aren't you just the least bit curious?"

"I guess, but it all seems so far-fetched. I don't even know how to hold a golf club. I think there's some special grip that's important. I don't think Professor Gunnarsson's theory is fully baked."

"You know, Adam, every theory that now holds true and that we now see as self-evident passed through that stage when it was seen as half-baked. That's the nature of progress and discovery."

"Thanks for the teachable moment, Mom," I said. "And I'm with you on that, but we're not talking about Einstein's theory of relativity here. This is about knocking a little white ball into a hole. It's not going to save the world. Even if the theory is right, it just means we might end up with a few more overpaid professional athletes. I'm not sure that's what society really needs."

"Sometimes—most of the time—you don't sound much like a seventeen-year-old," she said. "You might be right. But this family could certainly use a new car, preferably a Tesla Model S, just in case the next overpaid athlete turns out to be you."

I laughed and then she laughed. My mom liked cars, and if they did their part to solve global warming, all the better.

"Good night, son."

"Good night, Mom."

She closed the door behind her. I lay there in the dark trying to corral the stray thoughts in my head and conjure up others that should have been there. I had no bright ideas about where to take our antiphonal novel next—and I was feeling the pressure to deliver my chapter. I didn't even know how to hold a golf club, let alone successfully swing it with enough competence to play the game. Oh, and I knew none of golf's rules and etiquette. At that precise moment—and I actually remember this quite vividly—I was focused on three other things that weren't golf-related in the least. I wanted a vintage 1950 Conway Stewart model 60 fountain pen in the grey-hatched colour with a fourteen-karat-gold medium nib. I wanted to write like John Irving. And I wanted Alli Clarkson. Not necessarily in that order.

Chapter 3

"SHOULDN'T IT BE called the Women's Golf Club of Toronto, not the Ladies' Golf Club of Toronto?" I asked as we turned into the course off Yonge Street, just north of the city. "My mom is not a fan of the term *ladies*."

"I'm with your mom on that one, Mr. Coryell. But tradition is a powerful thing," Ms. Davenport replied. "The club was founded in 1924 with that name. It was a different time."

She drove along the winding driveway, past first the beautiful old clubhouse and then what Ms. D. called the pro shop, before parking. I'd never been on a golf course. It was lovely, lush and green. I could see some older women playing on the course. Some were walking and pushing their clubs on wheeled carts. Others were riding in motorized golf carts. Now, that looked like fun—I mean driving the golf cart, not madly swinging at the ball.

Ms. Davenport led me back to the smaller building that housed the pro shop and we stepped inside. Several women and a few older men warmly greeted Ms. Davenport as Bobbie, and as if she were a big deal around the club. It turned out there was a simple explanation for this. Apparently Ms. Davenport was a big deal around the club. As we walked down the corridor, I looked at the photographs lining the walls. I stopped. Ms. Davenport did not.

"Hey, you were club champion in 1989," I said, pointing to the framed photo on the wall.

"Yes, I was," she replied.

I started walking again but kept my eyes on the photos.

"And again in '91. And '94, '95, '96, '98, and '99. And again in 2002, 2003, and 2004!"

When I looked down the hall again, she had already disappeared through the door to the pro shop. I looked back at the many different photos of "Bobbie Davenport, Club Champion." She looked pretty much the same, perhaps a tad slimmer but not much. A woman walked towards me. She saw me staring at the action shot of Ms. Davenport commemorating the 2004 club championship and stopped next to me.

"Lovely woman, and such an amazing golfer," she said,

looking at the photo. "We thought she was going to dominate the LPGA. Too bad."

I just stood there, too surprised to say anything. The woman then carried on down the hall and out the door towards the parking lot. *Dominate the LPGA?*

I found Ms. Davenport in the pro shop. We were the only customers.

"So what happened after 2004?"

She sighed and looked out the window to the first tee. "My back happened," she finally said. "My particular swing over time seemed to have some rather painful consequences for my lower back. It had been a problem for years, but I just played through it. But eventually, I was left with two choices. Reinvent my swing, or play a lot less golf."

Just then, a man emerged from a doorway behind the counter.

"Hello, Duke," Ms. Davenport said.

"Bobbie, so great to see you!" he said, beaming. "Do you want to squeeze in nine? I can get you out right away."

"Not today, Duke, but thanks. We're on a different mission. This is Mr. Coryell, one of my students. Mr. Coryell, meet Duke Worthy, who always lives up to his name. He runs the show around here."

We smiled and nodded at one another.

"We're going to hit a bucket on the range," Ms. Davenport continued. "And if you don't mind, Duke, I'd like to borrow a men's right-handed nine-iron and a five from the best rental set you have sequestered back there."

Duke disappeared into the back room and came back a moment later with two clubs in his hand. He passed them over the counter to her. "Callaway Diablo forged irons. Big sweet spot. Very forgiving."

"Just the ticket. Thank you, Duke."

"No worries, Bobbie. I'd love to see you back out on the course a little more often. We miss you around here."

"Well, I might just take you up on that. I'm feeling okay these days and I do love playing this time of year. The light is wonderful."

"That it is. Just let me know when you want to come out and I'll make it happen."

"Thanks, Duke," she said before turning to me. "Well, we'd better get out there, Mr. Coryell."

Duke pointed out the window towards a row of golf carts.

"Take any one in the front row. Keys are in them. And the ball bin is full at the range."

The carts were lined up on an angle to the asphalt path, not unlike the start of the 24 Hours of Le Mans. I liked auto racing. She pointed to the first one and I got in on the passenger side.

"Wrong seat," she said. "You drive."

"Really? Awesome, thanks," I replied and slid over behind the wheel.

"But keep it on the path. I don't want you to flip the cart and break your leg before we get a chance to test Professor Gunnarsson's theory."

"Of course. I'll leave the rollover until we're done and on the way back."

I was very happy about the long drive to the range at the other end of the course. I had just recently earned my licence but didn't get much opportunity to drive. The cart was electric, very quiet, and it cornered like it was on rails. And man, did it have great acceleration. I loved it. If golf included driving these carts, I was in.

"Mr. Coryell, it is not necessary to fully depress the accelerator pedal or to take each corner on two wheels. This is not the Monaco Grand Prix."

"Sorry, just getting used to it," I said, easing back on our speed and sticking for the most part to the path. "So what did you choose?"

"You have to give me a bit more context if you want me to answer that rather broad and open question," she replied.

"I mean, did you reinvent your swing or play a lot less golf?"

"Oh, right. Well, I tried both. I worked hard at altering my swing so that it placed less strain on my vertebral column. And it worked. I could finally play golf without back pain. But unfortunately, I just wasn't nearly as good with my new swing. My handicap increased, my scores increased, my tournament losses increased. The only thing that decreased was my interest in the game. Seems winning was my weakness."

"So, and . . . ?"

"So I reverted to my original swing. My game, my scores, and my back pain all returned to their previous levels. So it meant I just played a lot less golf."

"So it was more satisfying for you to shoot a good score and win, but play less."

"Precisely, Mr. Coryell. Precisely. I'm not always proud of my desire to win, but we all have our crosses to bear."

"Just how good were you?" I asked. "I mean, was it ever going to be more than just a fun thing to do on weekends?"

She was silent for long enough that I briefly took my eyes off the path to glance her way. She was looking off into the distance, at least until our front wheel slipped from the path onto the gravel shoulder and violently shunted us both sideways along the bench seat. That seemed to bring her back.

"Sorry," I said as I quickly regained control and returned the cart to the path where it belonged. "And we're back!"

"Mr. Coryell, I certainly hope you're able to keep your eye on the ball more assiduously than you keep your eye on the road."

Ten minutes later we finally arrived at the practice range. We got some balls and made our way over to the practice tee. We were the only ones there.

"All right, Mr. Coryell, if you're game, let's get started."

"Ready."

She reached for one of the clubs.

"This is a nine-iron, arguably the easiest club to hit."

"Why is it the easiest club to hit?"

"Bravo, Mr. Coryell. I like a curious mind," she said. "Two reasons. The length of the shaft from the grip to the club head is quite short, making it easier to control. And, there's considerable loft on the club head, and that makes it easier to make contact with the ball and lift it into the air."

"Makes sense," I replied.

"Now, this is the interlocking grip, the most common and easily taught golf grip. The game really cannot be played well without a sound grip."

She showed me how to position my hands with the index finger of my upper hand interlacing with the pinky of my lower hand to form a solid two-handed hold on the club.

"How does that feel?" she asked.

"To be honest, it feels weird," I replied. "I think it would feel more comfortable and secure if I grabbed it like I do a baseball bat."

"Bite your tongue, Mr. Coryell. There'll be no baseball grip on my watch," she said. "Fear not. The interlocking grip always feels strange at first, but it gives you infinitely more control over the club during the swing. The more you use it, the more comfortable it will become. In time, you won't be able to hold a club any other way. Trust me on that."

She looked closely at my newly minted interlocking grip and turned the club slightly in my hands so that when the club head rested on the ground in front of me, its face was straight.

"That looks good. Now, don't try to strangle the club. Your left hand should have a reasonably solid hold on the club, with your right hand snug but really just along for the ride. Understand?"

I nodded and relaxed my grip so my knuckles changed colour from white to a light pink.

"Feet just a little wider than shoulder width apart, knees slightly bent, back straight, and just hold the club so that it rests on the ground. The club is designed so your hands are positioned a little forward of the ball."

I did as she instructed. I didn't feel very comfortable in that position.

"All right. Now we just need to summon the spirit of Professor Gunnarsson, because I'd like you to empty your mind and close your eyes."

"Okay, I'm not sure my mind is completely empty, but my eyes are closed."

"Try not to think about anything except how your body feels, how your arms and legs feel. Relax your limbs but still keep that grip on the club secure but not strangulating."

"Okay."

"We're not quite ready to involve the golf ball yet. So don't worry about that," she said. "But right now, without thinking, I want you to let your body draw the club up and back over your head, and then let it swing back down, following through so that it's back up high around your head at the end. In other words, I want you to attempt a rudimentary golf swing without hitting the ground, yourself, or me with the club."

"Okay."

"But don't plan it. Don't think about it. Think about your next fountain pen acquisition if you have to, or the story you're composing in Writer's Craft. While you're doing that, just let your body tell you how to swing the club."

I took a breath, kept my eyes closed, and swung the club up and back around.

When I finished, Ms. Davenport was silent. I waited with my eyes still closed and the club up around my head where I'd finished my swing. I took a chance and opened one eye just slightly. Ms. Davenport stood there bug-eyed but her mouth was closed.

"What's wrong?" I said. "You looked, um, startled. Was it that bad?"

A few beats later, she seemed to regain her faculties.

"Mr. Coryell, I must insist that you be truthful with me, and I'm now uncertain that you have been."

"What do you mean? I've been completely honest with you," I protested.

"Let's go over it again. You told me you'd never swung a club in your life."

"No, I said I'd never even held a club in my hand, let alone swung one."

"And you stand by that statement. You're telling me to my face that never in your days on this earth have you done what you just did with that nine-iron."

"Of course! Why would I lie about something like that? What's in it for me to be anything but honest? I hate people who lie."

"Okay, okay, calm yourself. I'm just trying to understand what I'm seeing. Your very first swing looks a lot like Rickie Fowler's."

"Who's he? And is that good?"

"He's a star on the PGA Tour who has spent nearly his entire life perfecting his beautiful and efficient golf swing. You just achieved a reasonable facsimile thereof on your inaugural attempt."

"Beginner's luck, maybe?"

"Too early to tell. But please swing the club in the same way again, without thought, without planning. Just feel the swing."

I swung the club a second time.

"Again."

I did it again, and then four more times after that.

"Extraordinary," she said to herself. "Does it feel natural when you swing the club?"

"No, not at all. How could it feel natural? I've never done this before. So it feels like a new experience, each time."

"One more time, please, eyes closed, but wait when you get into position, and then I'll tell you when to swing."

I placed the club head back on the ground so it was straight. Then I shut my eyes, lightly gripped the club, and bent my knees a bit until it felt right—not necessarily natural, but right.

A few seconds later, Ms. Davenport spoke.

"Now."

I swung again but felt my club hit something about halfway through the swing. I hoped it wasn't Ms. Davenport.

I opened my eyes to see her watching a golf ball flying off to our right.

"Hey, did I hit that ball?" I asked.

"Well, let's say you shanked it."

"That doesn't sound good."

"It just means you mis-hit the ball and it spun off to the right. A very common occurrence."

"Let me try it again with my eyes open. Isn't that the way most golfers shoot?"

"Actually, I think the shank was my fault. I didn't place the ball in quite the right position."

She helped me line up again and checked my grip. Then she put another ball on the grass in front of me.

"Okay, you can keep your eyes open this time, but remember, do not—I repeat, do not—think about anything. Don't worry about the ball. Just make your swing the way your body tells you to. Let it do the work. Wipe your mind clean. And don't be trying to knock the cover off the ball. You can swing hard, but don't try to kill it or your swing will probably go off the rails."

"Wow, there's so much to remember."

"Ah, ah, ah," she scolded. "My mistake. Don't try to remember anything. Just swing."

I closed my eyes to try to relax. When I opened them, I looked at the little white dimpled ball on the turf. A big black stripe and the word *Range* stared back at me. Then I swung. When the club hit the ball, the impact was much softer than I expected. The ball left the clubface in a very big hurry and flew straight and high. I didn't wait for it to land before I looked at Ms. Davenport. Her wide eyes followed the ball. Her mouth was agape. That's a writerly word I'd recently discovered meaning "wide open." I liked words.

"Um, Ms. Davenport? Your mouth is open but there's no sound coming out. Is everything okay?"

She closed her mouth but kept her eyes on the ball.

"Was that good?" I asked. I had no idea what had just happened and I couldn't tell from looking at Ms. D.

She held up her hand for me to wait. She watched until the ball rolled to a stop. She reached into her pocket and pulled out a notepad and what I instantly recognized as a blue Kaweco Sport fountain pen. She took a note and then grabbed the club from my hands and stared at the number nine etched along the bottom.

"Extraordinary!"

"Yes, I love the Kaweco Sport, too. Very nice for a pocket pen."

"While I do love this pen, it is not what triggered my exclamation."

"Oh."

"Mr. Coryell, if my eyes do not deceive me, you just hit a nine-iron, dead straight and very high, more than 195 yards."

"Is that good? Because it didn't really feel like I'd hit anything at all. I think if I swung a little harder, I could knock it much further."

"First of all, you know you've hit the ball perfectly when it feels like you haven't hit anything at all. Remember that feeling. And secondly, the top PGA Tour pros hit a nine-iron 165 yards, 175 tops, on a very good day. You just beat that by twenty yards on your first swing with your eyes open."

"Oh. So I guess that's pretty good then."

I didn't feel any real satisfaction from making what was apparently a very good shot. It was as if someone else had made the shot. No, not really someone else. Just my body. I wasn't responsible. My body was. I just happened to be there, too.

I hit twenty more nine-iron shots under Ms. Davenport's close supervision. Before each attempt she'd remind me to empty my brain and just swing. Each shot landed within a few feet of the previous one, just shy of the two-hundred-yard marker. They were all straight. Finally, I decided to swing as hard as I could to see if I could hit the ball even further. I clenched the club in a death grip and swung really hard. Once again it felt like I hadn't hit anything at all. I scanned the horizon for my supersonic ball on its suborbital flight path, but couldn't find it. Then I noticed it was still sitting on the turf below me. I'd missed it completely.

"Oh, well, that explains why it felt like I hadn't hit anything at all."

"Okay, this is important. What happened on that swing? What did you do differently that time? What changed?" she asked.

"My fault. I was thinking too much about the shot. I consciously wanted to hit it harder and further, so I focused on swinging as fast as I could and holding the club as tightly as I could. I wanted to knock the crap out of that ball. I swung so hard, I think I almost came out of my shoes."

"And let that be a lesson to us both. It seems Professor Gunnarsson was right. Don't consciously do anything. Don't think. Don't plan. Don't adjust. Just let your body swing the club naturally at the speed it wants to. Do not let your mind have any control, or any influence, over the shot. That is Gunnarsson's critical principle, and you just proved it by abrogating it."

"*Abrogating*. A nice, shiny new word for me."

My next ten empty-headed, natural swings produced ten more apparently stunning nine-iron shots that behaved more like a Tour pro's seven-iron shots.

We then spent about half an hour on the five-iron as the twilight descended. The shaft on a five-iron is quite a bit longer than on the nine-iron, but that just meant I stood slightly further away from the ball. Ms. Davenport positioned the ball a little further up in my stance, more towards the level of my front foot. Then she set me up properly and stepped aside.

I relaxed, thought about absolutely nothing, and swung.

I hit it, but the ball didn't go nearly as high. I thought I'd messed up. But Ms. Davenport's long, low whistle as she followed the ball suggested otherwise.

"You just overshot the range," she said. "That carried just over 260 yards."

"It seemed kind of low," I said. "Am I supposed to be hitting it 260 yards with a five-iron?"

"No, son, you are not. Your first ever five-iron shot would be considered a perfect three-wood shot for most professional players. Your performance simply beggars belief."

"I don't know what a three-wood is and I have no idea what 'beggars belief' means, but I assume it's positive."

"It's positive all right, Mr. Coryell," she replied. "I think there might just be a Nobel Prize in Professor Gunnarsson's future, and a Masters championship in yours."

I hit fifteen more five-iron shots that were more or less identical. After a while, I was kind of bored with it all. Finally, while there was barely still enough light, Ms. Davenport stood behind me and used her iPhone to shoot video of one good shot with the nine-iron, and another with the five-iron.

"I'm not going to see those videos on YouTube later tonight, am I?" I asked.

"Tempting, but no. These are strictly for educational purposes."

On the drive back to the clubhouse, she only told me to slow the golf cart down seven times and felt compelled to grab the wheel once. But we made it. At her direction, I dropped her off in the parking lot by her car, then drove the cart back to the shop to return the clubs and keys.

I parked perfectly in the front row of carts, on my fourth attempt. I handed over the clubs and cart key to Duke.

"Thanks, son. Did you hit 'em straight and long?"

"Yes, I think I did," I replied. Since there was no one else in the pro shop, I couldn't pass up the opportunity. "Um, can I ask you a question, Mr. Worthy?"

"Fire when ready."

"How good of a golfer was Ms. Davenport?"

"Just between us, she was one of the best I've ever seen. Full-ride scholarship to Stanford. Plenty of NCAA victories. Two Canadian Women's Amateur Championships and two Canadian University Championships when she came back here for teacher's college."

"But her back just couldn't take it?"

"She played right through her back until it was too late. A real shame she never made the Tour. But you didn't hear any of that from me."

I nodded as I thought through what he'd said. "Got it. Thanks."

She picked me up out front, and we drove along the driveway to Yonge Street and headed back into the city.

"So you were obviously a great golfer when you were younger," I opened.

She sighed. "So we're back on this topic, are we? Well, I guess you could say I had a certain flair for the game. I loved it. Gadzooks, did I love it. The problem was, I loved it so much I ignored my body, specifically my back. I didn't want to stop playing and winning, so I just pretended I didn't see the warning signs."

"Until it was too late," I offered.

"Right," she said, almost in a whisper. She shook her head before continuing. "So my back and my game just got worse and worse until I was no longer competitive. Even now, all these years later, I'm lucky to be able to string eighteen holes together without my lower back protesting and making me pay."

"That's so sad. I'm sorry," I said. "I heard somewhere that you could have played on the Tour."

"Duke is a great guy, but he sometimes talks a little too much," she said wryly as she pulled up in front of my house. She turned to look at me. "Well, Mr. Coryell, if you're at all interested, you appear to have boundless potential as a golfer, and I don't just mean a weekend recreational player. I've been around the game a long time, and I've never seen anything like what you showed me today."

"You mean what my body showed you. I was barely there."

"There or not, there's no need to make any important life decisions based on an hour at the driving range. But I hope we can keep exploring just how good you can be. Remember, Professor Gunnarsson has never heard of anyone with a score like yours. So I think we owe it to him, to science, and to you to see where this might go."

"Sure, Ms. Davenport. I guess I'm up for that."

"You don't exactly sound like you've found your new calling," she said.

"Well, this is all kind of sudden. And playing golf wasn't really part of my plan for my final year at high school. I'm more focused on my writing and getting into university," I explained.

"I see," Ms. Davenport replied. "And I understand, even commend, your sensible priorities." Despite her words, she sounded a little disappointed.

"On the other hand," I said, "I figure we should explore this golf thing a little more, just in case it's real." I didn't want to let her down, but I was also curious about this little experiment.

"Marvellous. Can you come by my office after school tomorrow, say around four o'clock? I think I know what we should do next."

"Sure. And thanks for taking me to the course. That was kind of fun. Especially driving the golf cart."

"Well, you certainly drive the ball much better than you drive the cart, but we can work on that."

I said hi to my folks and headed up to my room. I hadn't told them what had gone down at the driving range. I was still processing it and wasn't really sure what any of it really meant. Had I fully understood the implications, I might have thought more about it all.

THE NEXT DAY, Ms. Davenport was waiting for me in her tiny office just off the gym when I arrived there after my last class. She pulled a chair around from in front of her desk and positioned it right next to hers.

She must have noticed my puzzled look, because she explained, "This seating arrangement may seem odd but there's a method to my madness."

Skype was open on her laptop screen. Suddenly, it all made sense.

"We're calling Professor Gunnarsson, aren't we?" I asked, though I already knew the answer.

"You're a bright boy," she replied. "I think he deserves to know, don't you?"

"Well, it's a little premature, isn't it? I mean, I only hit some balls. I've never even played on a course," I said. "Shouldn't we do some more, I don't know, testing, more swinging of clubs, before we bother him?"

"Mr. Coryell, as a first-time golfer, you are not really in a position to understand and appreciate what you did on the driving range yesterday. And I think that might even help you. But please trust my knowledge of the game when I say that I don't believe any golfer in recorded history has ever hit his or her first forty golf shots as consistently straight, long, and true as you did. I would never have believed it had I not been standing right there next to you."

She was clearly taking this more seriously than I was. "But it's not exactly a useful skill to have, is it?"

"You mean compared to drywalling or cake-baking? Look,

let's not worry about that just yet. We have to see how far we can take this before the future even becomes a consideration. Have a seat, Mr. Coryell." She looked at her watch. "Adelaide is fifteen and a half hours ahead of us, so it's almost seven-thirty in the morning for the professor."

"Is he expecting our call or are we hitting him out of the blue?"

"Perhaps a little of both," she replied. "I emailed him with a short synopsis of your Gunnarsson score and our experiences yesterday, and asked if we could call him today. He didn't respond, other than accepting my Skype contact info."

She looked at her watch again. "Oh, and it's time."

We sat side by side behind her desk, facing the screen. She clicked *Gunnarsson85* on her Skype contact list.

"Maybe he's not going to pick up?" I said after three or four rings.

But just then, as if on cue, an older, bald man with a full grey beard materialized on the screen before us.

"Professor Gunnarsson, I presume?" Ms. Davenport said.

"Yes, that is I. Who else would be answering on my Skype number?" he replied in very good English with just a hint of what I assumed was a Swedish accent. "And I assume by the same principle that you are Bobbie Davenport."

"Indeed I am."

He leaned in to train his very focused gaze on the screen.

"From your name, your appearance on my screen, and your voice, I cannot discern if you are a man or a woman. Could you clarify?"

I was mortified. Bobbie turned quite slowly and looked at me, her brow furrowed, before returning to Professor Gunnarsson on the screen.

"I'm sorry, professor, but I thought I heard you ask whether I am a man or a woman. And since that would be extraordinarily inappropriate at any time, let alone a first encounter, I realize now I must have misheard you," she replied. "Could you clarify?"

"No, no. You heard me correctly. I'm certain I was speaking clearly. I always try to because of my slight accent. And I can only assume that your hearing is sound. But I suppose I should probably explain something," he said slowly and loudly, as though he were teaching English as a second language to the hearing impaired. "You see, I am afflicted with an often troubling combination of severe impatience, unbridled curiosity, absolute honesty, and a congenital indifference to what others might think or feel. My direct approach often makes people uncomfortable, but it certainly saves time. I meant no offence and apologize if my intention was unclear. I simply want to know whether I'm addressing a man or a woman."

"I see. You are very, as you say, direct, professor. So just to get this out of the way, I am a woman. Bobbie is short for Roberta," she said. "At first, I could not tell if you were socially stunted, utterly oblivious, brutally direct, or simply deficient in English. So I appreciate your clear if unusual explanation."

"Oh, I assure you, my English is more than adequate. No, I have simply decided to remove the standard filter that exists between what I think and what I say. I admit this has caused me a lot of problems. And when I say a lot of problems, I assure you, I mean a great many problems. But I'm not search-ing for new friends, just the truth."

"Well, I understand how your particular, shall we say, social style could lead to trouble," Ms. Davenport responded.

"If I am being honest—and to be honest, I am always being honest—this little self-inflicted personal quirk at least partially explains why it is I am now in Adelaide and no longer in my beloved Stockholm. So there is sometimes a price to be paid for disabling one's filter." Professor Gunnarsson paused and then seemed to lean forward a little.

"Now, may I assume this is your so-called golfing prodigy beside you?"

Bobbie nudged me in the ribs with her elbow.

"Um, yes. Hi, professor. I'm Adam Coryell. I'm not sure prodigy is the right word." I wasn't yet sure how I felt about Professor Gunnarsson and his strange manner. But it was somehow easier to talk to him knowing he was on the other side of the globe.

"I suspect it is not," Professor Gunnarsson replied. "I was employing sarcasm, exaggeration, and maybe a little irony. It seems I'm not very good at it."

"Oh, I see," was all I could muster.

"It is very unlikely your Gunnarsson score is as high as your teacher says. Incompetence in measurement and arithmetic calculation are almost always to blame," he replied.

"Because you have removed your filter, professor, I'll overlook the charge of incompetence, but I can assure you I followed your measuring instructions to the letter and triple-checked our numbers," Ms. Davenport explained with an edge to her voice.

"We shall see." He sighed. "I have been doing this for five years now and measured hundreds of subjects. I have never seen a number like the one you claim for—sorry, the name again?"

"It's Adam, Adam Coryell," I said.

"Yes, Adam," the professor replied. "Anyway, back to my point. A ninety-nine score seems nearly impossible. You probably made a mechanical error."

"Professor, did you have a look at the two videos I sent yesterday?" Ms. Davenport asked. "The links were in my email and I consider them corroborating evidence of my more-than-adequate math skills."

"I saw the links but I have not watched the videos yet,

because there's something we need to do before we go any further."

Ms. Davenport sighed. "Okay, professor, what do you have in mind?" she asked, exasperated.

"I'd like to watch you take Mr. Coryell's measurements on camera. If the numbers and ratios are legitimate, then we can talk further. But as I am saying, I've never seen any subject come close to the ninety-ninth percentile."

"I can assure you, professor, the numbers are sound," she replied with just the slightest edge, though I doubt the professor noticed.

"Pray, indulge me," he said. "If your numbers really do add up, you will have my undivided attention."

Ms. Davenport pulled the tape measure from her drawer, and I moved the two chairs out from behind the desk so I could stand there with arms outstretched and legs slightly spread in front of the laptop camera.

"Back up a bit so I can see his full extension and then call out the numbers as you measure him," Professor Gunnarsson instructed. "And turn the tape measure so I can visually confirm each number and the correct positioning of the tape measure on his body. I'll record the figures myself and run the algorithm."

"I'm actually quite adept with the tape measure, professor, but have it your way," Ms. Davenport said.

"And Adam will need to take his shirt off so I can see exactly where the tape measure is placed, I guess you could say anatomically. I think we can handle measuring his lower extremities without removing his trousers."

"I'm sure we're both relieved to hear that," Ms. Davenport replied.

As weird as this all was, I did as I was told and pulled off my shirt.

There were more than a dozen separate measurements, so it took a few minutes. Ms. Davenport stretched out the tape, marked the right spot, turned it so Professor Gunnarsson could see it, and called out the numbers. Both the professor and Ms. Davenport jotted them down. Once he asked that the end of the tape measure be placed a millimetre or two from where Ms. Davenport had originally positioned it. The professor seemed to have a very serious commitment to precision. Finally, after calling out the last measurement, Ms. Davenport faced the screen again. "As I expected, these are almost precisely the same numbers I obtained the other four times I measured him."

"Be that as it may, I must satisfy myself that the data are accurate, or there is no point to all of this," Professor Gunnarsson said. "Okay, stand by if you will, while I run my algorithm."

I put my shirt back on. Then we resumed our side-by-side seats in front of the laptop and watched as the professor typed in the figures on his keyboard. A moment or two later, even across Skype and all the miles that separated us, we could see the expression on his face change, though he said nothing.

We watched him re-enter the data and run it again. He nodded slightly and looked back at us.

Finally, he spoke. "Ms. Davenport, I owe you an apology. Those measurements do in fact yield a Gunnarsson score of more than ninety-nine. I've never seen anyone above about eighty-nine, and they were top-notch, elite athletes, some with world championships and a few with Olympic gold medals. So ninety-nine is simply unheard of."

"Well, interestingly, golf is the only sport where Mr. Coryell seems to possess such wondrous natural talent, so this may shatter any aspirations he had of superstardom in soccer, baseball, or Greco-Roman wrestling."

"And I really had my heart set on a wrestling career," I said.

"Really? Why?" Professor Gunnarsson replied, perplexed. "Golf is so much more remunerative and much easier on the body."

"Oh, um, I was kidding, professor."

"Ahhh, thank you," he replied. "I cannot always tell. That inability also has caused some friction with my colleagues. I have never really understood humour, though I do try from time to time to employ it, almost always with less than stellar outcomes."

"Professor, maybe I can bring us back to our little situation. Perhaps now you might take a look at the two videos I sent," Ms. Davenport said. "They show you Mr. Coryell's twenty-second shot ever with a nine-iron and his sixteenth shot ever with a five-iron."

We waited while Professor Gunnarsson downloaded and played the videos.

"Quite amazing," he said at the end. "Even with the substandard lighting, his swing looks beautiful and the shots themselves looked straight and long. I'm not a very good golfer, but I know enough to understand that those yardage numbers you sent are quite striking."

"They're off the charts," she replied. "So we have your attention?"

"Yes, and as I promised, it is undivided."

I had to remind myself that they were talking about me. I felt a little strange. I mean, so what if my arms and legs and torso were a certain length, and I could hit a golf ball? What was the big deal?

"I'm delighted and maybe a little shocked to think the wholly theoretical part of my theory might actually hold water," he continued. "What an odd expression that is—*hold water*. Where and how could that phrase possibly have originated?"

"I'm afraid I don't know," Ms. Davenport replied. "But returning to the matter at hand, professor, what would you suggest we do to explore this phenomenon further? And to be clear, I'm referring to Adam's golfing prowess and not the roots of esoteric expressions involving water."

"Yes, of course. I have a few observations and recommendations," he started. "First of all, we're operating here in the rarefied air of the ninety-ninth percentile. So, Adam, forget about any practising. If my theory holds, it will simply make you a worse golfer. Your arms, your legs, your midsection, your ankles, your feet, your shoulders, your neck, and every other body part will naturally guide your swing. It should be completely unconscious, unthinking, and above all, unpractised."

Ms. Davenport and I both nodded.

"Also, you'll have to be content with hitting the ball straight. You won't be able to learn to fade or draw your shots, or shape them in any way. That would take too much practice and too many subtle swing adjustments. Your natural unthinking swing would be profoundly compromised. In your situation, practice will end your promising golf career. You'll just have to hit the ball straight and manage the courses effectively within that limitation."

I really didn't know what he meant, but Ms. Davenport seemed to.

"Absolutely," she replied.

"Now, there are a couple of aspects of the game that you will have to practise. First of all, there's putting. You see, your physical makeup and innate golf strengths, well, none of that has much of a bearing on putting. So you will need to learn how to putt—that means learning to read the greens, and judging the ball's path, distance, and speed to the hole," Professor Gunnarsson said.

"We'll spend lots of time practising on the putting green," Ms. Davenport replied.

I'd played miniature golf once or twice, and had done quite well. I figured I could learn to putt.

"And that brings us to sand shots. I don't imagine your ball will land in the bunker very often, but it will happen. You'll need to learn how to override your natural swing when in the sand trap so you can actually employ the right technique to get the ball out."

What's a bunker? That was something I didn't know. Ms. Davenport noticed my furrowed brow. "Mr. Coryell, *bunker* is another name for *sand trap*. They're the same thing."

"Finally," Gunnarsson continued, "I think it's important to enjoy yourself. The positive feelings will actually help you with shots."

Ms. Davenport had been taking notes and nodding throughout Professor Gunnarsson's commentary, and she looked up. "Understood, professor, that all makes sense. But what do we actually do now to help this young man take the next step?" she asked, pointing to me sitting beside her.

Gunnarsson nodded slowly with a thoughtful look. "Well, I'd suggest a bit more time on the driving range to make sure the natural swing technique works with all clubs in the bag and not just the nine- and five-irons. But not too much swinging at any one session. Not too much repetition. That would be dangerously close to practising. If my PIPP theory is valid, practice is, you could say, the nemesis of your natural swing. I quite like that. *Nemesis of your natural swing.* Yes. I do like that. *Nemesis* or *enemy?* No, *nemesis* is the superior choice. I'm just going to write that one down."

And he did, while we waited. Ms. Davenport and I just looked at one another. Professor Gunnarsson was one strange dude.

"Okay, I am back," he said after putting down his pen. "And then, you have to get out on a course and just see what happens. I expect putting will be the weak link in Mr. Coryell's game, or those shots that require anything less than a full swing. And so the moratorium on practice should be lifted when it comes to putting. He will need to practise that, along with his bunker shots. But that's about it. For just about every other shot, you must tune out the game completely. Choose the right club for the distance to be covered. Think of anything but golf, and swing away, naturally."

"Thank you, professor. Filter or not, I hope we get a chance to meet in person sometime," Ms. Davenport said.

"If all continues in a positive way, you will not be able to keep me away. Please keep me updated on the progress. There may be a groundbreaking paper in Mr. Coryell's golf exploits, and if I am very lucky, a triumphant return to Stockholm."

I walked home in a bit of a daze. Sure, I guess I was curious to explore my golf abilities, but none of it yet felt real. It still seemed like a long shot—but maybe a very straight, very long shot.

WITH MY PARENTS' blessing, Ms. Davenport and I spent Saturday afternoon together, this time at a different driving range that was longer than the one at the Ladies' Golf Club of Toronto. She was skeptical that I'd be able to hit the driver with as much mastery as I had the irons. It took a while to get used to the length of the driver, but twenty minutes after we started, I was hitting the Callaway Big Bertha Diablo driver straight and far, every swing. And when I say far, Ms. Davenport and her binoculars reported that I routinely drove the ball between 360 and 375 yards. Those are estimates, because the markers at the driving range stopped at 325 yards. I was, again, hitting the ball right through the driving range.

After the driver, we worked our way through the other clubs. My shots were straight and far, almost every time. It seemed that Professor Gunnarsson's theory was holding up for every club in the bag, except, as he had predicted, the putter. Later in the afternoon, we drove back to Toronto Ladies' to begin my putting instruction. Man, putting is boring. I started by spending over an hour putting ball after ball from various distances on the practice green. Ms. D. had me use the same grip but told me to lock my wrists and shoulders and bring the putter head back and then through the ball in one easy, smooth motion.

"Since you're still a vestal virgin in golf terms, I'd like you to try this newfangled heads-up putting technique that's all the rage these days," suggested Ms. Davenport. "Jordan Spieth has had considerable success with it from shorter distances."

"You're not going to make me look up into the sky while putting, are you?" I asked, half seriously.

"No. I don't think that would be particularly effective," she replied. "It means reading the green and lining up your putt as one always does, but when you're standing over the putt, instead of focusing on the ball below you, train your eyes on the hole. It's all about concentrating on the ball's destination, not its starting point. Studies suggest golfers find it easier to make it all the way to the hole when they're looking at it and not at the ball."

I worked on this for quite a while. And she was right. I was definitely a better putter when I fixed my eyes on the hole when making the shot. As a complete rookie, it helped that I didn't have to unlearn the traditional putting style before embracing the heads-up method.

We hit bunker shots after that for a good forty-five minutes. I was learning the technique, even though I couldn't always execute it and the wind routinely showered me with sand when I hit the shots. On a positive note, the sand showers made the endless swinging marginally less boring.

"I feel like Lawrence of Arabia, without the cool robes," I said.

"Come on, now, one more," she pushed. "Remember, hit your sand wedge behind the ball."

"As soon as you said 'sand wedge,' I was suddenly hungry."

"Everyone's a comedian." She sighed. "Okay, why don't we call it a night?"

To my relief, we didn't talk at all about golf on the ride home. Instead, we discussed books, writing, and fountain pens —three of my favourite subjects—at least until we pulled into my driveway.

"Okay, Mr. Coryell, I think it's time to take the next step," she said.

"Will it be more fun than on the range, or on the putting green, or in the practice bunker?"

"I promise it will be. After all, there'll be lovely views, the flora and fauna of a natural setting, good conversation about anything but golf, and the ever-present threat of an errant ball beaning you from a distant fairway."

"Well, when you put it that way."

"I'll speak with your parents. We'll aim for Sunday if that works for you."

Chapter 4

MS. DAVENPORT PICKED me up at two-thirty on Sunday afternoon. She was wearing another Ladies' Golf Club of Toronto shirt, this time in green, and dark pants. I was wearing a short-sleeved blue collared shirt and what she called black dress shorts. We pulled in to the club and found an empty spot in the parking lot. She popped the trunk, reached in, and handed me a pair of golf shoes.

"I think we're about the same size. Try these on. They're mine, but white really isn't my colour."

"Can't I just play in my running shoes?" I pleaded. "What if someone sees me in those, those very white women's shoes. I'd never live it down."

"Mr. Coryell, these are actually men's shoes. They fit me better," she began. "More importantly, golf shoes are essential. They help you keep a stable and solid setup for each shot. You'd be slipping around in those Nikes, and I really want to get a clear sense of how you play this game."

"Do you have a different colour? I'm not sure I should be wearing white shoes after Labour Day." When she just kept looking at me, I kicked off my runners and put on her golf shoes. I was surprised that they fit.

"For once in my life, my water-walker feet have come in handy," Ms. Davenport said, giving me a thumbs-up.

"I don't think I've ever heard anyone refer to their feet as handy."

"Very nice." She sighed. "I see your sparkling wit is in full plumage this afternoon."

"Sorry, I can't help it."

When we reached the pro shop, she disappeared into the women's locker room and I went to see Duke to pick up the rental clubs Ms. Davenport had arranged for our game. Duke produced a full bag of clubs from the back room and handed them over to me.

"That's the full set of the Callaway Diablos you used on the range," Duke said. "Bobbie tells me you hit them pretty well for a stone-cold rookie."

"Beginner's luck," I replied, but I felt good anyway.

"Well, playing on the course ain't the same as hitting balls on the range."

"Ms. Davenport said you would say that," I replied.

"We've been pals for a long time so I guess she knows me pretty well," Duke said. "By the way, I shoved some balls and tees into the bag so you don't have to buy any. And here's a golf glove someone returned because it was too small. I can't really put it back on the rack, so you might as well use it. I think it should fit."

"Thanks so much," I said, pulling the glove on. "It feels a little snug."

"It's supposed to be snug," he said, looking at my gloved hand. "It wouldn't work if it were any looser."

"Got it. Thanks again."

"I put Bobbie's bag on that end cart. You might as well put your bag on, too."

I thanked Duke again and lugged my golf bag out the door. It seemed to weigh slightly more than a subcompact car. I hoisted the bag onto the back of the cart next to Ms. Davenport's, then climbed into the driver's seat, excited. Truthfully, I was more excited about driving the cart than I was about playing my first official round of golf. A minute later, Ms. Davenport sat down next to me.

"Ready?"

"I guess so," I replied. "I really like driving the cart."

"This is all about how you drive the ball, not the cart," she said. "If Professor Gunnarsson is right, this could be a very important day."

I sighed. She was so serious about it all.

"But, we're doing all of this for the privilege of hitting a little white ball into a hole in the fewest strokes possible," I declared. "It's not exactly saving the world, is it?"

"You're right, Mr. Coryell. It is a game. But do you know how much money Jordan Spieth earned at the tender age of nineteen when he won the John Deere Classic PGA tournament last July?"

I shook my head.

"Eight hundred and forty-six thousand dollars."

"U.S. dollars?"

"Yes."

"For one tournament?"

"Yes."

"Which way to the first tee?"

"Right. That's more like it. Just drive up and park next to that ball-washer," she said, pointing up the path.

I pulled up as instructed but wondered about the big noise I heard behind us.

"Uh oh," I said to no one in particular.

It sounded like a big golf bag falling off the back of the cart. I stopped and looked behind us. My big golf bag had fallen off the back of the cart.

I was horrified and hoped I'd done no damage. As I hopped out, Ms. Davenport was massaging her forehead as if in the throes of a migraine.

"Mr. Coryell, it's customary to secure your bag to the cart using the strap provided," she deadpanned. "See how my bag is held in place?"

"So sorry about that. I hope I didn't break any of the clubs," I said, dragging the bag back to the cart.

Ms. Davenport got out to take a peek.

"They look fine. Don't worry about it," she said. "Here's how it works."

She passed the strap through the handle on the golf bag and then secured it in the plastic clampy thingy. It was so simple, a two-year-old could have figured it out.

"Okay, Mr. Coryell, with that calamity behind us, here's where we really put Professor Gunnarsson's theory to the test. Grab your driver, a ball, and a tee, and step this way, please."

"That's the biggest club, right?"

"Yep, it sure is."

I did as I was told as she grabbed her own driver and led the way to what I now know is referred to as the first tee.

"What ball are you using?" she asked.

"My ball," I replied.

"I'm well aware that it's your ball. But what kind is it?"

"Oh, it says TaylorMade on it, and a number three," I replied, holding it up for her to see.

"Fine. I'm using a Titleist Velocity, number four," she said. "Okay, have a look here at the scorecard. It tells us that this first hole is 354 yards and it's a par four, which means you're trying to put the ball into the hole in four shots. Got it?"

"Got it."

"You can see the flag out there. So, for that distance, you're going to hit your driver. Almost every golfer would hit their driver on this hole."

She took my ball, rested it on a tee, and holding both in her hand, pushed the tee into the ground so the ball sat a couple of inches above the grass.

"So go through your pre-shot routine like we did on the range."

I lined myself up, gripped the club as she'd taught me, and relaxed my body. She adjusted my alignment ever so slightly.

"The pin is on the right side of the green, so you want to aim for the left side of the fairway to give yourself a better angle coming in on your next shot," she said.

"Fairway?"

"Sorry, that strip of closely cut grass that leads directly from here to the green where the pin and the hole are. You always want to be on the fairway."

"Okay," I replied. "So you're worried about what side of the fairway I should aim for, while I'm worried about making contact with the ball."

"Shush, now. Don't think so much," she scolded. "Just empty your mind and listen to your body."

"My body is feeling a little peckish right now," I replied as my stomach growled.

"Mr. Coryell, you are a seventeen-year-old boy. You're always hungry. But I confess I've never met one who can use the word *peckish* correctly in a sentence."

"I love that word. I think I read it in a *New Yorker* short story."

"You may also be among the few seventeen-year-olds who has read a short story in the *New Yorker*, though I might be selling a whole generation short."

"I'm not the only one, Ms. Davenport. If you hang around with Allison long enough, you'll learn lots of new words, and she'll lend you her *New Yorker* magazines when she's read them."

"Yes, you're right, son. That does sound like Ms. Clarkson. She's a fine wordsmith. I can see why you two are close," she said. "How about this: try thinking about Ms. Clarkson and swing the club."

So I did. I swung and heard that distinctive thwack I remembered from the range.

I lost sight of the shot almost immediately, so instead, I watched Ms. Davenport as she watched the ball. After what seemed like a long time, she shook her head.

"Good night, nurse!" she said.

"Pardon?"

"Let me offer a more contemporary idiomatic translation to assist your comprehension," she said. "'Holy shite, but you just hit that a mile!' Forgive my colourful language."

Until she told me, I had no idea my shot was solid. I guess I was pleased with myself.

"To be precise, Mr. Coryell, your ball finally landed on the left-hand side of the fairway just short of the green, or about 340 yards from where we now stand. All I can say is, all hail Professor Gunnarsson."

Ms. Davenport then teed up her ball and hit it straight down the fairway about 220 yards.

"Was that as far as you can hit the ball?" I asked.

"Yep, that's about my limit, and I hit a pretty long ball for my heavyset, older, strong-like-bull, women's demographic."

I drove us up the fairway to where her ball had come to rest. Her second shot landed on the green and rolled about ten feet past the hole. She was clearly pleased, so out of respect, I clapped and she bowed.

I had a little trouble with my second shot. My ball was only about thirty yards from the hole, so with Ms. Davenport's guidance, I used my pitching wedge but didn't give it a full swing. But I swung a little harder than I should have and the ball rolled well past the hole.

Ms. Davenport handed me my putter. Her ball was blocking my line to the cup, so she marked it and picked it up so I could make my putt. I lined up the shot, taking note of the slight slope as I'd been taught to, and putted the ball. It rolled towards the hole but stopped six inches short.

"Blast!" I said.

"No need to beat yourself up. That was a nice lag, as we say," Ms. Davenport said.

"Thanks. I've always been very good with the lag. I've worked tirelessly to perfect my lag. Lag Coryell is what they often call me," I replied. ". . . I have no idea what a lag is."

"Clearly," she said. "On long putts, where sinking it is highly unlikely, a good lag putt brings the ball up close enough for a simple tap-in on your next shot."

"Like this?" I asked as I walked up and tapped the ball towards the hole. It hit the pin and dropped into the cup.

"Yes and no," she replied. "The lag putt was solid, but you just violated at least three all-important rules of golf etiquette."

"What do you mean?" I asked as I pulled my ball from the hole.

"Number one. My ball was further from the hole than was yours, so you should have marked your ball and let me putt first. Whoever is further from the hole shoots next. It's called 'being away,'" she explained. "Number two. When you tapped in, you were standing directly on my putting line, and that's a big no-no. And number three, when all balls are safely on the green, the pin must be pulled out and set down on the green so that it doesn't affect the putt." She smiled at me. "Golf is a game of etiquette, tradition, and rules. Lots of rules."

I lifted the pin out of the hole as she put her ball down on the green just ahead of her ball marker, which she then picked up. She missed her putt, but not by much, and then tapped in.

"Well done. We each put the ball in the hole in four strokes. We shot par on that hole, so we mark a four on the scorecard for us both."

"And we have to do that another seventeen times to complete the round?"

"You're a quick study, young Adam."

Other than when we were putting on the greens, we talked about everything but golf. On each shot, Ms. Davenport would suggest the right club based on her detailed records of how far I could hit each one. She also helped to ensure I was properly lined up for each shot, although with each completed hole I was getting better at that part of the game.

My biggest problem remained putting, but I could feel myself improving as the game wore on. I liked the discipline of focusing on the hole when I putted the ball. I guess I was enjoying myself. It was kind of hard to tell, as I was also bored for a good part of the round. Even to my inexperienced eye, Ms. Davenport really looked like she belonged on the golf course, and she hit some awesome shots very close to the hole. But her back flared up around the seventh hole, and by the tenth she'd picked up her ball and focused all of her attention on my game.

"Okay, you're about 175 yards from the pin. What club should you hit?" she asked.

"As I recall, I was hitting the nine-iron 175 on the range, right?"

Ms. Davenport handed me my nine.

"So what are your grail pens?" she asked as I approached my ball in the centre of the fairway.

"Grail pens? I don't know what that means," I replied.

"It's a reference to the search for the holy grail," she said. "What fountain pens do you covet, even if their cost puts them out of reach? Those are your grail pens."

"Hmmm. How long do we have? This could take a while."

"Make sure you're lined up with the pin."

"I'm all about pins and pens," I said.

I checked my positioning and made a small adjustment in my stance.

"I'd really like an Aurora Optima in the blue Auroloide finish," I responded.

Thwack!

"Nice ball," she said, watching my shot. "You're dancing."

I looked at my legs. "Dancing?"

"It means you're on the dance floor, or your ball has landed
on the green."

"Oh."

"I don't have the Optima but I do have the Aurora 88, which
is essentially the same pen but with rounded ends. It's really
lovely, though the nib has a touch more feedback than I would
like," Ms. Davenport said.

"I love the 88, too. Maybe I could see yours sometime."

"Sure. What else?" she prodded as I drove up the fairway.

"Okay, one day I'd love to have a Conway Stewart Wellington
in their Classic Brown acrylic, but that's like saying one day I'd
like to own a Lamborghini Aventador. It's not going to happen."

"I'm afraid I don't have a Conway Stewart—or a Lambo, for
that matter—but you clearly know your fountain pens. That
particular CS might just make my grail list, too. The material is
stunning."

By this time we'd pulled up to the green.

"Mr. Coryell, just so you know, you've parked a little too
close to the green and that bunker. The cart should stay on the
asphalt path when we're up here near the green. Okay?"

"Right. Thanks."

Golf is full of little rules of etiquette. I swung the cart around and parked it back on the path before grabbing my putter. Much to my surprise, I actually sunk the eight-footer for a three on a par four. There's a name for that, but it slipped my mind. On to the next tee, though I don't remember what number.

"Now, clear your head. Think about fountain pens, or Allison, or anything else you want. Just let your body do the work and don't think about your swing."

"Right."

Thwack!

My drive was long and straight but not exactly where I wanted to go. It landed just off the fairway in what Ms. Davenport called the first cut of rough.

"Good swing and nice ball flight, but you weren't quite lined up right. You hit the ball exactly where it was supposed to go, given your setup," she said. "You really have to check each time to make sure your body and club head are aligned to send the ball where you want it to go."

"Okay."

"Do you like broads?" she asked when we were back in the cart and heading for my ball.

"To some, that might seem a rather personal question," I replied.

She just stared at me, shaking her head.

"You're right, that was lame," I admitted. "But to answer your question, I swing both ways. If it's a Japanese nib, I prefer broads. But on European pens, particularly German, I'm more likely to go with medium. I'm just not a fine or extra-fine kind of guy."

"Mr. Coryell, we have a lot in common. I feel the same way. There's too much feedback on finer nibs. I like it nice and smooth."

We carried on. I shot. We talked. I drove. She shouted. I slowed down. We talked and I shot. Playing a round of golf sure eats up a lot of time. It took hours, maybe three or four.

I thought I was doing quite well—at golf, I mean, not at cart driving—but I really didn't know enough about the game to be certain. Ms. Davenport was encouraging and very helpful, but other than on my opening shot, she wasn't exactly doing handsprings and hurling superlatives whenever I finished a hole. Maybe she was a little jittery from my driving. But honestly, there were only a couple of close calls, and she wasn't even in the cart for one of them. We finished the eighteenth hole and after handing the rental clubs back to Duke, we had a drink on the patio. Ms. Davenport looked a little shaky, even stunned. I was a little concerned. She downed her Arnold Palmer—iced tea and lemonade—in two big gulps.

"Are you okay, Ms. Davenport?"

"No. No, I can't say I am," she replied, shaking her head. "This is absolutely shocking, and I suspect it has never happened in the long and rich history of the game."

"I already apologized," I protested. "I swear I thought I had steered clear of that garbage can. And how was I to know the pond was right behind? My view was completely blocked. It was an accident."

"Mr. Coryell, I am not referring to your sudden and unauthorized immersion in the water hazard. The golf cart will dry out, eventually. I'm talking about your golf game."

"Oh. Okay, then," I replied. "But I do feel kind of bad about the whole driving-the-cart-into-the-pond thing."

She consulted the scorecard. "Well, you finished with a seventy-four, which for men is four over par on this course."

"Well, that's a little disappointing. Aren't you supposed to make it around in par?"

"Mr. Coryell, only a microscopic slice of recreational golfers ever, *ever*, shoot par, and even those who do have played the game for years. It's quite possible you are the one and only first-time golfer ever to have shot four over par on an eighteen-hole championship course. Heck, most golfers in their early rounds shoot four over par on every blessed one of those eighteen holes!"

"Oh. So I did okay?" I asked hopefully.

"*Okay?* Adam, if I may call you by your given name, if *Sports Illustrated* happened to have had a reporter on the course today, you'd be in next month's magazine, possibly on the cover."

"Cool. I guess I'd be one of the few non-athletes to appear in those pages, I mean except for the swimsuit issue."

She ignored me and studied the scorecard, which featured not just numbers but notes as well. Finally, she spoke. "So listen up. That was a great first round. In fact, it was astounding. What is even more impressive, however, is that you achieved that seventy-four with nine three-putt greens. If you could turn each of those nine three-putt greens into two-putt greens, you would have shot a sixty-three and would be a PGA-calibre player!" she marvelled. "Holy shuddering shite, that makes my mind a maelstrom. Pardon my language."

"I got a few of those birdie thingamajigs, too, didn't I?" I asked.

"You surely did. Six of them, in fact."

"I guess that's pretty good."

"Listen, Mr. Coryell," she said, leaning forward. "I'd really like you to play on the high school golf team. I only had one player show up, and he promptly sprained his wrist at football practice and is out. If I can get you registered for the tournament next week, will you play?"

She seemed very excited. I'd forgotten there was a golf team.

"Will you be there so I know what I'm doing?"

"I'll be there, but I can't coach you during the tournament. It's not allowed. So you'll have to memorize the distances you hit with each club so you know which one to choose based on the yardage markers in each fairway. Just like we did today. So what do you say?"

I felt a slight twinge of panic. This was getting a little out of hand. What about my writing? What about Alli? I already had a lot on my plate. "I'm not sure, Ms. Davenport. Can I think about it?"

"You get the whole day off school, Adam."

"Okay, I thought about it. I'm in," I replied after deep deliberation. "So I get to take a cart all by myself?"

She smiled. "Ah, no. You walk and carry your own bag in tournaments."

"Wait, I have to walk the whole course, carrying that heavy bag?"

"I'm afraid so. That's how tournaments work," she replied. "And did I mention the day off?"

"Okay. I'll walk."

"Splendid. I'll try to make the arrangements."

EVERYTHING MOVED QUICKLY after that. One minute I was just a regular student with a girlfriend, stressing about my grades as I navigated my last year of high school. The next, I apparently had boundless potential as a golfer and was wearing my school colours in a tournament. I was having a hard time keeping up. It was like being swept along on the crest of a massive wave. If I windmilled my arms, I could just keep my head above the foamy, swirling water.

The tournament the following Friday was held at a public golf course just a little north of the city. On the drive up, with the clubs borrowed from Duke in the back, Ms. Davenport grilled me on the distances I could hit each of the clubs. She also tried to school me on golf etiquette. But there was so much to remember.

By the time we arrived, most of the other players were practising on the driving range. Ms. Davenport and I went directly to the putting green so I could try to get used to the speed and behaviour of the greens. I got the hang of them quite easily, and within a few minutes I was getting the balls quite close to the hole from various directions. I noticed I was one of the few players using the heads-up putting technique.

Finally it was time.

"Now listen, Mr. Coryell. The wind is picking up. At its current strength, if you're shooting against the wind, you need to club down one. What I mean is, if you were going to hit a six-iron with no wind, take a five-iron against the wind. If you're hitting with the wind, club up one. Hit the seven, not the six, when the wind is with you."

I nodded. I could remember that.

"Here's your scorecard and a couple of pencils. Carry them in the your back pocket. You must remember to mark down your own score after each hole. Just record your own score and don't worry about the other guys' scores. They'll keep their own."

I nodded again.

"I'll be walking along the edge of the fairway to cheer you on, but I really can't be seen to be giving you any counsel. But feel free to look my way if you get into trouble. I'll see what I can do. Finally, take this book. I want you to read it whenever you're not actually shooting."

I took the slim paperback volume. It was *The Adventures of Sherlock Holmes*. I wasn't expecting that.

"Have you read any of the Holmes stories?" she asked.

"No, but Allison is a huge fan, so I've been meaning to dip into them."

"They're wonderful and, best of all, very distracting. I want you to get wrapped up in those stories while you're on the course. Think about the mystery Holmes is solving, not your golf swing," she said with a smile. "You might start with 'The Adventure of the Blue Carbuncle.' It's one of my favourites. Now get up there, and good luck."

I played in a foursome with three other students from other schools in our district. I shook their hands before we teed off. I wasn't sure I was supposed to do that, but it seemed appropriate.

"Hey, who are you?" one of my opponents asked me when I offered my hand. He was wearing an ugly neon-green ball cap with his high school logo on it.

"Adam Coryell, from Leaside."

"I didn't see you on the range earlier. And I haven't seen you at any of the other tourneys either. Did you just move here?"

"Um, no, I grew up in Leaside," I replied. "But I just started playing golf a couple weeks ago. This is my first tournament and only my third time playing on a real course. And I'm not supposed to go to the range. Practice hurts my game."

"Yeah, right. So it's like that, is it?" the guy snarled. "You're already playing head games, eh? Just like a Leasider."

"What? Sorry?" I had no idea what he meant by his Leasider crack.

"Ladies and gentlemen, this is the 9:40 tee time and our fifth of ten foursomes. First on the tee, Adam Coryell, Leaside High School," crackled the starter over a very bad PA system.

I looked at Ms. Davenport and she nodded towards the tee. I pulled my driver out of the bag and set my ball on the tee at just the right height. I lined myself up so I was aiming for the middle of the fairway. Then I thought about Allison and how I really needed to get moving on the next chapter in our antiphonal novel. There was so much going on, I hadn't yet written a word.

Thwack!

I looked up just in time to follow the ball on its trajectory. It seemed like a pretty good shot, dead straight and about the height my driver shots usually reached.

"Holy shit!" said neon-green ball cap as he followed my ball. "Your third time playing, eh? As if! Looks like you must be on the 'roids, too."

I also had no idea what he meant by that.

Using the distance for each hole in the scorecard and the yardage markings on the sprinkler-head covers in the fairway, I could generally determine how far I'd driven the ball and how far away the hole still was.

When all four of us had shot, I hoisted my bag onto my shoulders and started walking and reading 'The Adventure of the Blue Carbuncle.' I was soon so absorbed in the story that I walked right by my ball.

Two of my three opponents hit it about 275 yards, while my new friend in the retina-threatening green lid hit it deep into the woods. My first drive flew and rolled about 325 yards. The wind was in my face and I estimated it was about 125 yards to the hole. I remembered I could hit my sand wedge about 145 yards. So against this wind, I figured that was the right club. I pulled it out when it was finally my turn to hit and glanced at Ms. Davenport, who was standing on the cart path about thirty feet to my right. She gave me a subtle nod.

I lined myself up, thought about Sherlock Holmes, and swung.

Thwack!

"Nice ball, Mr. Coryell," Ms. Davenport said. "Nice ball."

It landed short of the hole but then rolled forward a bit and ended up about three feet from the cup.

I carried my bag up to the green and set it down before grabbing my putter.

"Hey, you can't put your bag on the green," said the tournament official following our foursome. "What is this, your first time on a course? Come on!"

"Sorry, sorry!" I said and snatched my bag off the green. "I'm still learning the rules. My mistake."

"Next time, that'll cost you a stroke!" he snapped.

He was really steamed. I worried he might not only take a stroke from me, but have one himself.

About ten minutes later I sunk the putt to birdie my first tournament hole.

The rest of the day unfolded in much the same way. I made some etiquette and club selection mistakes that others were certainly happy to point out. But in the end, I thought I played reasonably well, not that I had much to compare it to. I managed to read four of the Sherlock Holmes stories while walking the course. I loved them and just wanted to talk to Ms. Davenport about them, but she was so excited at my performance she had some difficulty focusing after we finished up on the eighteenth hole.

I had just recorded my scores for each hole but hadn't added them up at the end. Turned out I'd scored a seventy-one, or one under par. I guessed I was satisfied with that, though Ms. Davenport's reaction, and the effusive comments made at the awards presentation, clearly suggested I was entitled to feel something more than merely satisfied.

I won the tournament by three strokes, and the next two tourneys as well. That's when the trouble started.

Courtesy of media coverage that included a look at Professor Gunnarsson's theory, news of my special gift spread quickly, and aroused more than curiosity. A group of parents of competing golfers from other high schools complained to the Toronto District School Board that it was unfair for me to compete, that I had an unearned advantage. Ms. Davenport was appalled but kept me out of the official proceedings.

I probably would have been fine with a decision to exclude me from the Toronto District School Board City Championships coming up in a few weeks. I didn't love the game, and it took so much time. But Ms. Davenport considered the idea to be a grave injustice, and became my advocate. The protest culminated in a public meeting of the school board, where both sides could argue their case before a decision was rendered.

The meeting was to be convened in the auditorium in a

neutral school nearby that had no golf team. More than a hundred people showed up, along with reporters and videographers from three different Toronto television stations. My parents and Ms. Davenport came for moral support. My mother gave an impassioned plea from a parent's perspective that seemed genuinely free of anger, though I knew she was very angry. A few others spoke in my favour, but the vast majority of presenters were not fans of my newfound golfing prowess. The final speaker, who wanted me banned from playing in the city championships, summed up the argument quite nicely, I thought.

"Madame Chair, my son played his first golf game eleven years ago, at the age of six. Since then he has lived and breathed golf almost every waking hour. He's a good kid and a good student. He practises hard and long and has become a very good golfer. He embodies the principle his mother and I, and his teachers, have always tried to communicate—that there is a relationship between hard work and success. That nothing comes easily in this life. That perseverance, dedication, and commitment are important."

By the time he was halfway through his remarks, I found myself nodding in support.

"Madame Chair, Adam Coryell's rapid rise to the top of high school golf in this city flies in the face of that principle. We have nothing against Adam and I'm sure he's a good kid. But his success has not been earned. His ability as a golfer is not rooted in hard work, practice, and a passion for the game. His apparently perfectly proportioned fluke of a body is what is winning golf tournaments. For crying out loud, he's only played on a course a handful of times in his life. He hadn't held a golf club in his hands until a month ago. It is unfair to all the other golfers who have dedicated themselves for years to get here to make them play against a freak of nature."

After he finished, I was ready to cross the floor and join their side. I thought he made a lot of sense.

Then Ms. Davenport spoke.

"Madame Chair, on the surface, the argument my friend makes seems to have some merit. I can understand his position, and I feel for the high school golfers who have worked very hard to make it to this annual championship tournament. So let me take a different approach. I have always believed that one of my principal responsibilities as a teacher is to help students find what they're good at. We help reveal students' strengths, sometimes when we have more confidence in them than they do. Adam Coryell is also a good student. And he's a very nice young man who is kind to those around him. He is funny. And he has passions, too. He wants to be a writer. Several weeks ago, I had the opportunity to help Adam Coryell discover something else about himself that neither he nor his parents knew. He has a rare gift for golf."

Ms. Davenport was very good on her feet, though I knew this already. It was very quiet in the room as she continued.

"I have played a lot of golf in my years. I know something about the game. And I have never seen a more natural talent than Adam Coryell. It is true he knew nothing of his physical affinity for the game until I put a club in his hands in September. But that does not diminish his gift. In fact, it makes it more impressive, more exciting, more profound. Does he have the same passion for the game that some of his competitors out on the course do? Not yet, and who knows, perhaps he never will. But in the end, Adam Coryell is a seventeen-year-old boy, just like the other golfers. He'll be swinging a regulation club and hitting a regulation ball, just like all the other golfers. There is nothing separating him from the other players on the course except, it seems, that his body is very well suited to this special game."

I have to confess, it was very strange hearing her talk about me in those terms. It was kind of like watching a movie.

"Should he be penalized for something that is completely beyond his control? Of course not. Would it contravene natural justice to ban him from playing in the championship? Absolutely. Would it violate his rights to exclude him? Yes, I believe it would. This is a matter that should be decided on the golf course and not at a board meeting. Let this extraordinary young man play."

I switched my allegiance back to my own cause in the middle of Ms. Davenport's address. In the end, the board ruled in our favour, and I was cleared to play.

Two days later, Professor Gunnarsson arrived from Australia to see me, and my game, for himself.

Chapter 5

"IT WAS NICE to learn that the theoretical part of my theory —the flight of speculation, if you will—seems to be true. That there should be a few individuals whose bodies are so perfectly and naturally designed for a particular sport that practice, which inevitably alters the natural perfection of their bodies, will actually make them worse. Adam Coryell is such a specimen. He is the first evidence, the early and so far only, proof that this portion of my theory is sound," Professor Gunnarsson said. "Also, it is very hot and bright in here."

Even on television, I could see the sheen of perspiration on his face as he shifted in his chair. He wiped his brow and squinted under the extreme illumination.

"It's just the lights. That's television for you," the host said with a chuckle.

The media seemed fascinated by the movement to ban me from the city championships. When word somehow leaked that Professor Gunnarsson was arriving, the issue became even hotter. Ms. Davenport and I were in the pro shop at the Ladies' Golf Club of Toronto watching Professor Gunnarsson's interview live on TSN, Canada's sports network. I wasn't much of a sports fan, but it was kind of cool to hear a guest on a talk show mention my name.

"So, professor, have you seen Adam play since you arrived from Australia?"

"Yes. Yesterday I watched him on the driving range and then followed him for nine holes with his high school coach."

"And?"

"And what?"

"And how did he do?"

"As expected. He hit the ball very long and very straight. He shot it right through the far end of the driving range sometimes. And his swing looks like the product of years of practice when in fact he is new to the game, and it is just his arms, legs, torso, hands, and feet all working naturally and perfectly together."

"Do you think Adam could become a professional golfer? Does he have a future on the PGA Tour? Is he the next Tiger Woods?"

"You just posed three queries. Do you have difficulty choosing which question to ask?"

"Let me simplify it," the host said. "Is Adam Coryell the next Tiger Woods?"

I was startled. I hadn't been expecting that question. Me, the next Tiger Woods? No, I didn't think so. It made no sense. This wasn't a movie.

"I cannot say at this time. But if he keeps playing golf naturally, improves his putting, and is not unduly distracted by temptations like drugs, alcohol, sex, cars, music, food, films, and other sports, he could do well. He could do very well," Professor Gunnarsson said. "I do not know if he will be as good as Tiger Woods, but it is within reason to contemplate the possibility. It may well be within reach. But it is entirely in Adam's hands, and in the rest of his special physical being." He paused and squirmed in his seat. "Now, are we almost done? I am wilting here in this heat, and my eyes are starting to hurt from all the lumens your lights are firing at me."

"I see. Yes, we're close to wrapping up," the host said. "Um, changing gears a bit, I understand there are a few players on the Toronto Raptors and the Toronto Maple Leafs who, having heard about your Predictive Innate Pinnacle Proficiency in Major Sports theory, actually took their own measurements and sent them to you."

"Yes, that's true. I ran their measurements through the algorithm as they requested, and sent them back the results."

"And?"

"And what?"

"Well, what were the results?" the host said, doing little to hide his exasperation.

"Oh, I see. All five of the players are reasonable athletes, but each has pursued a sport for which he is not ideally suited."

"Wait, what? What do you mean?"

"I thought I was being clear. Let me try again. I mean that one of the basketball players had quite an impressive Gunnarsson score for volleyball, much higher than he rated in basketball. And another would likely be a better football player. And I must say, one of the Maple Leaves was interesting."

"Actually, we say Maple Leafs," the host corrected.

"Why would you say that?" Professor Gunnarsson asked. "English is not my first language, but I am quite certain *leafs* is not a legitimate word."

"Yes, well, be that as it may, it's a long tradition," the host said. "Anyway, what was interesting about the Leafs player?"

"Well, his score is so low, it is a miracle he can compete in hockey at this level at all," the professor explained. "It is almost certain that he cannot get any better than he is right now."

"Can you share the names of these players?"

"I don't recall the names. But in view of their Gunnarsson

scores, I don't think I'll be the only person to forget their names."

"Ouch! Now, that was a burn," the host chuckled, shaking his head.

"Burn? I do not know what that means," the professor said. "I'm not aware of any burning, except the skin on my face from your infernal lights."

· The interview ended shortly thereafter. Probably a good thing.

"Well, that ought to send the Toronto sports media into a tizzy," Ms. Davenport said to me. "I told him not to mention the Raptor and Leaf players. It was a no-win situation."

"It was a bit awkward," I replied. "If there were a Gunnarsson score to predict proficiency in television interviews, I think the professor's number would be quite low."

"Agreed. Another consequence of his missing filter."

Ms. Davenport was right. The sports media went crazy the next day. The professor had to change hotels to escape the reporters trying to track him down to reveal the identities of the Raptors and Leafs who submitted their measurements. If he'd remembered their names during the TSN interview, I think he would have gladly provided them.

The following week, after the professor had returned to Adelaide, I won the Toronto District School Board City Championships at St. Andrew's Golf Club in Toronto's west end. My nearest rival was four strokes behind.

It had been just about a month since Ms. Davenport had measured my extremities and lent legitimacy to Professor Ingemar Gunnarsson's wild theory—and turned my life upside down. Going to school felt almost normal, except for my automatic ascension to the cool kids' clique. I didn't ask for it, or even want it. It just happened. If I'm being completely truthful, I liked all the attention, though I tried very hard not to show it. I promised myself I would stay grounded in who and what I was, regardless of all the publicity swirling around me. Alli, on the other hand, found all the hoopla amusing, for which I was grateful. I was worried things might change with her if the spotlight on my golf burned too bright. So I tried to pretend it wasn't happening and just focused on being myself. I never missed a class (except for when I had tournaments). I always did my homework. I still read my favourite writers, and tried to keep writing. I still dreamed about my grail pens. And Alli and I were still together and still committed to writing our antiphonal novel, though I was having trouble getting to it.

Beyond quietly enjoying the attention, I also liked winning. It felt good to win the city championships, even if I was somewhat disconnected from the feat. After all, my body won the tournament, but I guess I was there, too, along for the ride. My victory was written up in all the local papers, and I'd done several television interviews. By this stage, my parents had bought me the rental set of Callaway Diablos from the Ladies' Golf Club of Toronto.

A week after the city championships, I won the provincials by six strokes and set a new Ontario scoring record. It was much bigger news than my city championship victory. There were long reports on the nightly sportscasts, a hastily produced video profile ran on TSN, and they had a special assembly in the school auditorium to celebrate my unexpected achievement. The general view of the media, the local golf world, my fellow players, and my classmates was that I was truly a special, amazing, perhaps even generational golfer. I was more interested in becoming a special, amazing, perhaps even generational writer, like Robertson Davies, Alice Munro, or John Irving. But in the last four weeks, it felt like I'd moved a long way from that world, drifting even further away with each tournament victory.

My problem was, I just didn't like golf that much, and it didn't feel like I was suddenly going to fall in love with it anytime soon. It took a very long time to play and didn't seem to accomplish anything particularly redeeming or constructive. When you stripped everything away, I didn't really care that I was a high school prodigy at shooting that stupid little white ball into that stupid little hole. The world wouldn't be a better place if I could shoot lower scores than other golfers. But I believed the world just might be better if I could write a story or a novel that moved people, that made them think, that made them laugh, that empowered them. And my writing had certainly suffered since I had picked up the game of golf. I had less time to think and less time to write. Our antiphonal novel wasn't going to write itself. I had to find the bandwidth to get back to it. But it seemed my ability to hit a golf ball interfered with my ability to write, or at least my opportunity to write. I simply had less room in my life for writing. That didn't feel good, and it didn't feel right.

But was I truly unhappy? No, not yet. Annoyed? Occasionally. Fulfilled? Not really. Bored? Often. Chuffed with my modest level of fame? Sometimes, but I just wished I'd earned the enhanced public profile as a writer, and not as a golf savant. Eventually, these private thoughts busted out of my head and into the open.

"I don't deserve any of this!" I complained to Ms. Davenport one day. "I'm not responsible. I'm not doing anything. My arms and legs are to be congratulated. But I'm just the sentient being attached, with no influence, no agency over my golf success. I'm not even trying."

"That's the paradox, Mr. Coryell," she replied with a look of concern. "If you were trying, you'd never win. You have a gift, a natural gift. It's like Darwin decided to evolve only your body because your survival as a human being depended on golf."

"I don't want my whole world to be defined by golf. I have other plans that don't involve hitting a ball into a hole."

"There's room and time for both," she replied patiently. "The reality is, you are one in a billion, Mr. Coryell. You are three royal flushes in three consecutive hands. I believe there is no limit to what you can achieve in the golf world if you decide to stick with it. It can give you, in a relatively short time, the kind of personal and financial freedom that the rest of us mere mortals work our entire lives to secure. And you can use that freedom to pursue your dreams—like being a writer."

I sighed. Silence hung between us for a few moments. "Did you read my short story yet?" I finally asked.

"I did, and I think it's quite good. I'm handing them back in class tomorrow. I think you can make it better. It needs a bit more tension. The stakes aren't quite high enough. And I'm wondering if it might have more urgency and immediacy if you tried the present tense."

"Hmmm. The present tense. Never thought of that," I said, playing with the idea in my mind. "I think I see what you mean. I'll give it a shot and see how it reads."

"One more thing for you to consider. It's just a matter of time before U.S. colleges catch wind of your unusual talent. I have no doubt you'll be offered full-ride scholarships to the best schools. So be ready for that."

"Well, I think my short story is good and all that, but I'm not sure U.S. schools will have seen it yet."

Ms. Davenport laughed. "Nice one. But they will call."

That night I finally wrote, in one long stint, the next chapter in our antiphonal novel. In the story, the young hockey player from the northern town down on its luck is suddenly drafted by the Boston Bruins. He can't pass up the opportunity a shot at the NHL represents, so he tells his girlfriend he won't be going to Toronto for university. He hopes she can understand. He wants to try the long-distance relationship thing, but all she can say is that it's a very long way from Toronto to Boston.

A couple of nights later, the phone rang just after dinner. I picked it up.

"Hello, could I speak with Adam Coryell, please," drawled a man's voice.

"This is he," I replied.

"Hello, Adam. I'm Scott Fitzgerald, and I run the golf program at Vanderbilt University in Nashville."

"You have a very literary name, Mr. Fitzgerald."

"Oh, really, you think so?" he replied, sounding perplexed. "Now, why do you say that?"

MAY 2014

It was a very long drive from Toronto to Lake Temagami on the Friday night. Alli and I held hands in the back seat for most of the way. I was ready for a break from all the attention on my golf exploits. You see, by this stage, there'd been a ton of media coverage, and I'd become quite well known locally as "that young golf star" (or "freak," as some put it). Professor Gunnarsson's theory had become much more than informed academic speculation. I added real, evidence-based experience to the mix. To me and a growing number of others, Predictive Innate Pinnacle Proficiency in Major Sports was by then a rock-solid fact. Around the world, amateur athletes and couch potatoes alike were breaking out measuring tapes and calculators, hoping for a ninety-plus Gunnarsson score in a sport that paid well. But so far, I was still the only one.

Of course, there was a price to be paid for all the accolades, attention, and opportunities. And the price was that I had to play golf—a lot of golf. And on my personal list of things I enjoyed, golf ranked about even with snow shovelling and only slightly higher than the flu.

So, by the time the Victoria Day long weekend rolled around, I was *really* looking forward to spending it with Alli and her family at their cottage on Lake Temagami, far away from golf. When we had started seeing each other, I'd been bowled over to learn that her family had a cabin on an island about half a day's paddle from the camp I'd attended eight summers in a row. I'd loved it there.

But there was a problem. There was something I hadn't yet told Allison, and I knew I'd have to while we were away.

Ms. Davenport knew. My parents knew. Hell, there were several people in the United States who knew. I couldn't wait any longer to tell Alli. I figured the pristine wilderness setting might make it easier. Yeah right, that's it. Good thinking.

During the long drive, our antiphonal novel sat next to her. It had been eight months since I'd written the chapter where the young man is drafted by the Boston Bruins. Alli apologized every week or so for not writing her chapter, but promised she would soon. I told myself she was busy with school.

It was nearly ten-thirty when we finally arrived at the small marina on the shores of Lake Temagami. We unloaded the car and loaded the boat. It was dark, but the running lights on the boat and Alli's mother's back-of-her-hand knowledge of the lake delivered us safely to their dock in about twenty-five minutes.

Later that night, after her parents had gone to bed, Alli and I sat on the dock, looked at the ceiling of stars, and listened for the periodic splash of a fish jumping. A cool breeze washed over us and we could hear small waves colliding with the boat moored beside us. It was idyllic. I almost didn't tell her. It took every ounce of resolve I had.

"Um, Alli, I have to tell you something," I opened with breathtaking originality.

"You're sleeping with four other women?"

"What? No!"

"Guys?"

"No."

"You won the lottery?"

"Well, you could say that, but not really."

"I have spinach in my teeth?"

"No. Alli, please. I'm serious."

"Sorry. You're hardly ever serious. That's part of your charm."
She sighed. "I haven't eaten spinach for weeks, anyway."

"Okay. I have good news and bad news. What do you want
first?" I asked.

"Let's get the bad news out of the way."

"Right. Okay, here goes. This has been a really hard decision,
even though it kind of feels like I have no choice. That it would
be foolish not to do this. It could change my life."

"Adam, don't you think you should actually tell me what this
mystery decision is before you give me all the reasons you've
made it?" She was smiling when she said it, but there was
some tension in her voice.

"Sorry. Yes, of course," I said. "I'm an idiot."

Suddenly, she swung around to face me with a serious look.
Her eyebrows were all scrunched.

"You're not going to U of T with me next year, are you?" she
asked, making it sound more like a statement than a question.

That hit me hard and spilled what little wind was in my sails. I just looked up at the stars for a while. Then I drew and released what seemed like the deepest breath of my life.

"I've accepted a full-ride athletic scholarship to play golf and study creative writing at Stanford. It's near San Francisco." I looked at her sadly. "I'm sorry, Alli."

Even in the dim light offered by the stars, I could see her just staring at me, nodding her head almost imperceptibly. I let it sink in a bit. Then she lowered her head and seemed to be staring straight through the dock to the water hidden beneath.

"But you don't even like golf," she almost whispered.

"Alli, I have this bizarre gift—a lightning strike—that could set me up for life. I'm too good at this game not to pursue it. And Stanford is a great school where the academics come first, even for scholarship athletes. Their creative writing program is well known and respected."

"But California. There was nothing closer, like maybe Boston?" she asked.

"The golf program at Stanford is always strong in the NCAA, and if I can stay on track it will give me a shot at playing professionally, on the PGA Tour. But I think we can make it work. We're not the first couple to deal with a long-distance relationship."

She was quiet for a few moments. Finally, she spoke. "So what's the good news—I mean, besides that you're not sleeping with four other women or guys and there's nothing caught in my teeth?"

"The good news is of a slightly different magnitude, but it is good news," I started. "I have to play a tournament in upstate New York next weekend, so I wanted to give you your birthday present here and now."

I pulled out a gift-wrapped package from my backpack. She didn't look like she was in the mood for a gift, but she took the box when I handed it to her. It was kind of dark to be opening a present under the stars, so I opened the flashlight app on my phone.

She ripped the paper away, and then looked at me with wide eyes when she saw the Parker name on the box. She lifted the lid and gasped. "You did not just do this," she said, holding it in her hands, stunned. "You didn't."

"I've been saving for a while."

Then she began crying. I didn't know what to do, so I let her cry for a moment or two. Finally, she gathered herself.

"A Parker Duofold," she said, shaking her head and staring at it. "Given the orangey-red colour, I bet it's an early one."

"The first year they were made—1921," I replied.

"And a bottle of Parker Quink Blue. Perfect," she said, sniffling and holding it up in the small pool of light. "The pen is in pristine condition. And look at this beautiful gold nib. It's just gorgeous."

"And you do know why I chose this particular pen and model, right?" I asked.

She looked at me, smiled, and nodded her head. "Conan Doyle wrote some of the Sherlock Holmes stories with a pen of this very make, model, and vintage. It's perfect." Then she began crying again. I thought it was because she was so happy.

Early Monday morning, Alli stole into the bedroom I was staying in and slipped her hand in mine, gently easing me out of the bed. We tiptoed through the cottage, put our jackets on over our pajamas, and walked down onto the dock. The sun was just starting to rise and there was a mist clinging to the glassy surface of the lake. A few of the brighter stars were still visible in the darker western sky. We sat cross-legged, facing one another. Finally, she handed me the notebook we were writing our novel in. There was an expression on her face I'd never seen before. The closest adjective I can come up with, and it's still not quite right, is melancholy—a word that sounds kind of like what it means.

I opened the notebook and turned to where I'd finished off the preceding chapter back in September. I immediately recognized the Parker Quink Blue. She must have been up half the night thinking and writing.

It only took me half an hour to read the chapter. Alli sat still and watched me the whole time. I didn't cry—but I could have, and man, I wanted to. Finally, I looked up at her. "So you don't think they could somehow make it work with her in Toronto and him in Boston?"

She reached for my hand. "No, Adam. I don't. It wouldn't be fair to either of them," she said sadly.

"But they're meant for each other. You said it yourself."

"It's just not realistic. They're so young. And if they are truly meant for each other, a few years apart won't change that. They'll get back together if it's meant to be."

"What about having her go to university in Boston so they could be together?"

She just looked at me with the same furrowed eyebrows she'd shown me Friday night.

"That came out wrong," I backpedalled. "She needs to keep focused on her dream, not his. I know. I know. I get it."

"I'm sorry," she said, squeezing my hand.

"I am, too." My heart was pounding and breaking at the same time.

It was a very, very long drive back to Toronto. Really, really long. When Allison's parents dropped me at my house, she handed me the box holding the vintage Parker Duofold and the bottle of ink. "I don't think I should keep this. It's lovely but it's too much, especially, you know, now."

I'll spare you the details, but she kept the pen and ink at my insistence. I think she acquiesced because she just didn't want to make a scene in front of her parents. That was why I didn't get out of the car until the box was back in her hands.

No matter what happened in the years ahead, it gave me some comfort to know that she'd be writing with the pen I'd given her. It felt like there was still hope for us as long as she was holding the pen; that a piece of me would always be with her even if we weren't together. Now, that's some heavy romance novel stuff right there, don't you think? But I sure wasn't looking at it that way as I slid out of the car that night.

Chapter 6

WITH MY PARENTS' BLESSING, Ms. Davenport escorted me down to Stanford in late August. She was very helpful in easing me into the golf program. Thanks to her, the coaching staff all understood and accepted my completely unorthodox approach to golf. It also didn't hurt that she had delivered me to her alma mater. Top golf schools remember their star athletes from the past, and Bobbie Davenport was no exception. By then, they'd all read Professor Gunnarsson's theory and measured the extremities of every student athlete they could corral in the hopes of finding another prodigy, in golf or any other varsity sport. Nobody they measured scored higher than seventy-eight for any sport.

While the coaches certainly appreciated that practice would not help my game—in fact, it could ruin it—my fellow student athletes weren't quite as accepting. A few of them had trouble understanding why I was somehow exempt from the hours of driving-range practice while they had to hit bucket after bucket of balls, day in and day out. While they toiled to move from good golfers to somewhat better golfers, I was able to maintain my status as the best player on the team simply by enjoying my classes, staying on top of my courses, eating whatever I wanted thanks to my unlimited meal plan, and practising putts and bunker shots a couple of times a week. I could see why I wasn't warmly embraced.

I lived in one of the on-campus residences, in a large and lovely private room that even featured a small putting green in one corner. Until classes started in September, I just tried to work on my putting, my bunker shots, and learning the rules and etiquette of golf. Studying the rule book was a colossal bore, even though I understood why it was important. Ms. Davenport gave me a couple of very old books on golf and etiquette that were more interesting just because the writing was from a bygone era.

"Call me anytime you want to talk about anything," Ms. Davenport said, standing next to the cab that would whisk her to the airport for her flight back to Toronto. "Do not think about golf when you're out on the course, or you know what will happen. Keep up with your schoolwork. A degree from Stanford is respected, even revered. Don't discount it by phoning in your classwork. Keep reading and keep writing. And try to have some fun along the way." Then she leaned in and gave me a hug.

After she'd left, it felt different. I was lonely. I kept thinking of Alli, imagining her walking through the campus of the University of Toronto while I was three time zones away. I wished I were with her, experiencing university life together, studying together, finishing our novel together. It was what we'd talked about for so long. I'd botched that plan, and that was on me. But then I remembered all the reasons Stanford made so much sense. Yes, on paper, I was in the right place. But in my heart, I was a long way from where I wanted to be. The world should have my problems, right?

The first NCAA tournament I played for Stanford didn't start off in the right way. I wasn't used to walking the course on my own, without Ms. Davenport to talk to and keep my mind off of golf, and as a result I messed up the first round. I found myself thinking about my shots more than I should have been, and finished the round at two over par. For me, it was a very mediocre score. Before the next day's resumption of play, I cooked up a list of interesting topics to occupy my mind, and wrote them on a Post-it note that I stuck onto my scorecard. Then, during the second round, I studiously tackled each item on the list. It wasn't just so I'd play better; I needed to combat the tedium of eighteen holes of golf. Sure, watching paint dry is boring. But if golf were the only other option, it wouldn't necessarily be an easy call.

The only golf-related brainwork I was permitted was calculating yardages, selecting clubs, and reading putts. Over time, I became more adept at fleetingly turning my mind to choosing the right club and lining up my shot, before refocusing my brain back on whatever non-golf topic I'd been wrestling with before my game so rudely interrupted me. It seemed to work quite well. Occasionally I'd make minor club selection errors by not properly accounting for the wind or elevation changes on the hole, but for the most part, I did just fine.

I shot sixty-six on day two and took a three-stroke lead into the weekend that I never relinquished. But maintaining the lead wasn't my biggest challenge. What I struggled with was thinking up enough interesting topics to occupy my mind for two entire rounds of golf. I worked my way through the benefits of piston fillers over cartridge/converter fountain pens, the great gold-versus-steel nib debate, and which writers, dead or alive, I'd most like to have dinner with. Finally, in an act of desperation with three holes to go in the final round, I mentally drafted a letter to my parents, assembling sentences as I walked and shot, and then memorized it. I thought it was an awesome letter, and I wrote it all down later that night and mailed it the next day. The team toasted me after my victory, but I could tell I still wasn't one of them.

Missives to my parents weren't the only letters I penned. Every week or so I'd write Allison a letter, seal it in an envelope, address it, stamp it, and file it in my bottom desk drawer. We'd agreed not to communicate with one another, to make the break cleaner and more painful (okay, I added the "more painful" part), but I couldn't stop myself from writing to her. Sometimes I'd just recount what was happening in my life. Other times I'd tell her how much I missed her, how much I still loved her. I would ask her what she was writing, and what pen she was using. But I never mailed them. Yes, I wrote letters that were never sent.

I knew, intellectually, that I should have been elated at winning an NCAA golf tournament. By all rational and reasonable measures, it was quite an achievement. And it did feel good holding the trophy for the photographers and speaking to reporters. But the good feeling was muted, because I knew that I hadn't really won that golf tournament—my ideally proportioned body had. Professor Gunnarsson had won a piece of it, too. And even Ms. Davenport had a stake in my place at the top of the leaderboard. Victory just isn't as sweet when your role in the win seems so passive, so minor, so incidental, even accidental. And by the way, despite my success, I wasn't finding golf any more enjoyable, fulfilling, fun, inspiring, exciting, etc.

I found it as time-consuming as it was boring—and it was a boatload of both. And really, what was it accomplishing? What was it contributing to the greater good?

All that golf would have been the end of me were it not for my courses. I was majoring in English and creative writing, with a minor in NCAA golf, in a way. I studied Fitzgerald, Hemingway, Dos Passos, and others, and found my course work the exact opposite of golf—time flew, and it was fascinating and fulfilling. I took the only course with Canadian content I could find, called Looking North: Canadian Literature. It was actually taught by a Canadian professor. In the course, she covered the heavyweights, like Alice Munro, Margaret Atwood, Robertson Davies, Mordecai Richler, and Michael Ondaatje, along with several other lesser-known writers. It was fascinating to read these writers closely, analyzing and assessing their styles and techniques. It was reading and thinking about novels at an entirely new level for me. And I loved it. All of it.

My creative writing classes forced me to broaden my writing horizons. We covered short stories, novels, playwriting, screenwriting, essays, creative non-fiction, memoir, and poetry. We had to write from various perspectives and in many different styles and voices. And while a lot of the writing I was doing was for class, some of it was just for me. I even started writing some poetry outside of class, just to push myself beyond the kind of writing I typically pursued. As it turned out, I'd learned just enough about poetry to know I wrote really bad poetry.

My social life at Stanford wasn't exactly flourishing. I made some friends in my classes, but I didn't seem to be connecting with any of my golf teammates. It made some sense when I thought about it. Most of them had golfed with, or against, one another all through their high school years as they rose to the top of the collegiate heap. I was a Canadian they'd never heard of with an innate gift for golf. I never spent any time on the range with them, because I wasn't allowed to practise. And to make matters worse, I was winning. I was a threat to their success. I could take their spot on the PGA Tour and push them onto the second-tier professional tour. So I wasn't surprised that I was shunned, even though I thought of myself as a nice guy. I guess the stakes were too high to make being a nice guy a relevant factor.

One afternoon, I walked across campus to the library to do some research for a paper on expat writers in Paris in the 1920s. Just as I approached the front door, four of my golf teammates came out of the library. Given the time, I was sure they were heading to the range for daily practice under the close scrutiny of our coaches.

"Hi, guys," I said.

"Well, if it isn't the golf freak," said Tom McCann, the de facto leader of the foursome. His tone was not warm and friendly.

"At your service." I said it casually, but my guard was up.

"Well, it looks like you're going the wrong way. That's the library, the range is at the other end of campus," he sneered. "Oh, but wait, I forgot. You're the chosen one from the frozen North who's not allowed to practise because it might hurt your God-given golf magic. Yeah, well, I think that's a load of crap. You're just a lazy-ass who's somehow gamed the system."

"Sounds like you've got it all figured out," I said, my rhetorical arsenal apparently offline.

"Listen, Captain Canuck, when I win a tournament—and I've won plenty—it's because I've worked hard, studied the game, respected golf traditions, and focused on nothing else," Tom said, pointing to himself. Then he pointed at me. "When you win, it's because your mother and father's DNA combined to create a golf freak with no control over his own ability. I'd much rather win because of what I've *done* and not because of what I *am*."

I paused for a moment to let my anger flare just a bit. "Two things. First of all, to be honest, I'd rather win your way, too. And second, just in case you're unclear about what *you* are, I can tell you. You're an asshole."

"You're the asshole," was all Tom could muster, giving me his fiercest look. I've always considered the old *I know you are but what am I* gambit to be quite lame. So I told him so.

I would like to say that I caught the punch out of the corner of my eye and ducked just in time. Instead, I caught the punch full on the side of my head. I hadn't been in many fights growing up. Okay, I hadn't been in any fights growing up. But I knew enough to at least be able to give the impression that I was in a fight. On instinct, I adopted the "go crazy" fighting strategy reminiscent of the berserker warriors in the Icelandic sagas I'd studied. They fought with fire and fury, almost as if they were in a trance. I could feel Tom on top of me, raining down blows on my torso and head—somehow, I was kneeling on the ground by this time. So I went all berserker on him. I just started throwing elbows into his midsection to get him off me. Then I jumped to my feet and rushed him, my shoulders, arms, and fists windmilling in front of me like the giant rotating brush on a street-cleaning machine. I was in my own little bubble. I seemed to lose contact with time and space. But on a positive note, I somehow made contact with Tom's face, not to mention his head, chest, shoulders, stomach, and several other body parts for which I wasn't aiming but struck all the same.

I may be making it sound like the brawl was a little one-sided after I summoned my inner Icelander, but Tom was landing a few punches of his own. I can report with firsthand knowledge that nothing quite grabs your attention like a direct blow to your nose. That was a pain with which I'd previously been unfamiliar. We alternated between boxing on our feet and, when we had tired one another out, wrestling on the ground. And I know what you're thinking. As the Canadian in the bout, I was probably a great fighter, right? But despite the stereotype, I'd never actually played organized hockey, so my fighting skills were, shall we say, underdeveloped for my age.

To me, it felt like an epic battle worthy of stage and screen. But I was informed afterwards by several unbiased witnesses that neither Tom nor I was a particularly adept combatant. Our combined Gunnarsson score for any of the martial arts probably wouldn't break fifty.

The incident ended when Stanford security arrived—and not a moment too soon. We were both exhausted. Upon learning we were both on the golf team, security hauled us straight to the office of our coach, who'd been just about to leave for the team's daily practice on the range. It's fair to say he was not very happy. He proceeded to yell at us for several minutes, tearing both Tom and me additional bodily orifices that we apparently deserved.

"You guys are idiots! You're both key members of the varsity golf team and you decide to start beating your fists against each other's very hard skulls. You're lucky no one broke a knuckle. You need your goddamn hands to play goddamn golf! And you're both here on full-ride deals. Don't you dare fu . . . mess that up." He turned to me. "And you, Coryell, it's your job to fit the hell in and be a member of this team. I don't care if you have some divine frickin' gift for golf and can't screw around with it by practising, you're still a goddamn member of this goddamn team! Okay?"

I just nodded, the Kleenex I had plugging both nostrils failing to stanch the blood dripping all over my shirt. It was not a good look.

"And McCann, you jackass! Why do you have to be such a prick all the time? Tone it down, be a team player, and pull your head out of your ass. Coryell may be our best shot at the championship in years. Don't you ever lay a hand on him again! You got it?"

"Got it. Sorry, Coach."

Then, in a scene right out of a Family Channel movie of the week, Coach made us shake hands before sending me to my residence room and taking Tom to the range. My nose looked like someone else's for the next couple of weeks, before the swelling eventually subsided. It hurt every time my club hit the ball.

BEYOND AVOIDING SCANDAL, arrest, and incarceration, not to mention on-campus brawling, there was really only one rule I had to honour to keep my very generous four-year scholarship. I had to play golf. It helped if I won—which, I say without conceit, I usually did—but I really only had to show up, play, and acquit myself reasonably well.

In September alone, I won all three tournaments Stanford entered. A coach would walk around the course with me, offering advice on yardage, and course and wind conditions. It was helpful and I came to trust what the coaches said. Once in a while, I'd make the wrong club selection, usually when the required yardage fell neatly between two clubs. The coaches also took lots of video of me on the course to try to see if they could identify anything in my swing to explain how and why I could hit any club a good twenty to forty yards further than the pros. No one could figure out anything beyond a lovely and fluid swing. It was just what Professor Gunnarsson's theory had predicted. My perfectly proportioned body and natural swing somehow led to a higher club-head speed, which, when my ball striking was true, inevitably led to greater distances and a dead-straight ball flight. Simple but rare.

But I didn't win every tournament. I'm not sure I could have handled the publicity had I swept the NCAA. So in a few tourneys I purposely thought about my shots, with predictable results. I guess it was self-sabotage, but it took some of the pressure off if the world around me periodically viewed me as mortal. Don't worry, I never fell off the front page of the leaderboard and usually came second. The other way to lose was to putt badly. Since it was the only part of the game—along with bunker shots—that was truly in my own hands, it was easier to mess up without it looking too obvious.

My teammates eventually came around to me, even Tom. I apologized for calling him an asshole, though in truth I was just sorry he *was* an asshole. Tom offered his own weak-assed apology and even thanked me for putting Stanford on top of the NCAA golf rankings. Other players on the team had played well, but I was the only one to win.

Given the distance from Stanford to Toronto, I only made it home once in the fall term, for Christmas. It was really great to be back with Mom and Dad. They seemed to be the only ones, other than Ms. Davenport, who understood what was happening to me—you know, the paradox of the unexpected campus celebrity who everyone seemed to know and the low-level loneliness that came with never quite fitting in. And even though I had a strong desire to see Allison, I honoured our agreement and didn't reach out to her.

"You're not loving it, are you?" my mother asked on Christmas Eve. "The whole golf thing at Stanford."

"I love my classes, and I've got lots of time to write," I carefully responded. "And it's not costing me—or more accurately, you and Dad—anything."

"But if you're miserable, you can always just bail and come back here, you know," she said, sitting down next to me. "You can go to school here."

"I know. But I'm not ready to do that. Golf is more of a minor distraction. It helps that I'm pretty good at it and don't have to think too much about it, or practise much. So I'm okay. I'll ride it out for the writing. But thanks for asking."

"That's what parents do, among other things."

JUNE 2015

As expected by then, Stanford won the NCAA golf championships with yours truly, or at least my special golfing machine of a body, leading the way and breaking collegiate records right and left. The following week, I had my first national cover shot, on *Sports Illustrated*. Ms. Davenport coached me through the media frenzy that followed. I had dinner with the president of the university, and was the star attraction at a campus-wide pep rally to celebrate our NCAA victory. As my coaches and Ms. Davenport had predicted, along with anyone else with two synapses to rub together, I was named NCAA player of the year. It was all very gratifying. Check that. Actually, it wasn't. *Gratifying* is the wrong adjective. But it did make me feel special, even if I had nothing to do with it.

"COACH, THIS IS Professor Ingemar Gunnarsson," I said as the professor and I entered his office.

Coach stood up from behind his desk and offered his hand. The professor looked at Coach's outstretched hand and eventually, after what seemed like an hour-long pause, shook it.

"How do you do," Professor Gunnarsson said. "It is a very odd ritual, is it not? Two people who have never even laid eyes on one another begin by a most intimate gesture. We hold hands and lift them up and down briefly. I cannot fathom why we do that."

"Yeah, well, good to meet you, too, Professor Gunnarsson," Coach said before resuming his seat.

At Ms. Davenport's suggestion, I'd briefed everybody I thought we might encounter during the professor's Stanford visit. So Coach already knew about the famous Ingemar Gunnarsson's notorious social graces.

"I'm really glad we could arrange to have you visit the campus. Thanks for making the trip and for checking out our golf team," Coach said.

"It was good of you to fly me here," Professor Gunnarsson replied.

"I hope you've been enjoying your tour of Stanford."

"I wouldn't say I'm enjoying it, but I am finding it fascinating and enlightening, which is more important than finding it enjoyable," the professor replied. "The sports facilities are extraordinary and much better than at the universities with which I have been affiliated. If the money spent on athletics was redirected to the sciences and other more worthy intellectual pursuits, I can only imagine the strides that could be taken here on many important fronts."

"Well, professor, Stanford has a great reputation as a leading academic institution, as well as a strong contender in the NCAA," Coach replied with a defensive tone he utterly failed to mask, if he tried at all. I grimaced.

"Yes, yes, yes, I'm well aware that Stanford is a fine and respected university. But it could be so much better with fewer weight rooms, gymnasia, and practice fields, and more labs and lecture halls."

"Well, be that as it may," I interjected. "Professor, perhaps you can report back to Coach here on what you found when you ran the numbers for the team. We're both eager to hear."

"Yes, good idea, Adam," Coach jumped in. "How did we do?"

"I can summarize if you wish," began Professor Gunnarsson, pulling a sheet of paper from his very old-school leather briefcase.

He flattened the briefcase on his thighs and placed the paper on top so he could see the results. It was like a lectern on his lap. In my mind, I christened it a "laptern." But I digress.

"Of the eight women and twelve men on your vaunted NCAA golf team, no one, other than Adam of course, even breaks into the eighty-first percentile," Gunnarsson said, reading from his paper. "Two of the men and three of the women would likely be much stronger swimmers than golfers. Four of the men and two of the women might wish to give track a try, particularly middle-distance running. Finally, the two weakest men and the worst performer on the women's team should probably just give up the game, for they have already reached their maximum potential in golf and are unlikely ever to get any better."

I don't think Coach was very happy with his report. I could tell by the hue of his neck and the way his chin vibrated. He clenched his jaw so tightly I feared it might shatter.

"Is there anything else?" Coach asked, confirming that certain short sentences can in fact be enunciated and understood through a locked jaw, if the lips are parted.

"Only that given the team's Gunnarsson scores, and the fact that most of them are already playing as well as they will ever play, any coaching they've had over the course of the year has likely been superfluous and ineffectual," the professor said with his eyes fixed on the paper.

Coach then stood up . . . rather quickly. His desk chair crashed into the wall behind him, generating a noise I'd not thought possible in such a confined space.

Professor Gunnarsson convulsed in his chair at the sound.

"Ahhhh, Coach, remember the filter thing we talked about," I said, also rising to my feet. "And your blood pressure."

Professor Gunnarsson ended his visit to Stanford a tad early, and I rode in the taxi with him back to the airport.

"Remember during our first Skype call, I said it would also be important for you to have fun when you're playing?" he asked.

"I remember," I replied. "If I have such a high Gunnarsson number, what does it matter whether or not I'm having fun?"

"Simply because it is easier to listen to your body, empty your head of all golf-related thoughts, and swing perfectly naturally for four hours at a time if you feel good, if you are happy," he explained.

"Well, I usually feel fine—physically, I mean—when I play. And sometimes I'm happy, because I have time to think about other things. I plot my stories. Map out my future. When I play alongside Bobbie, we talk about a vast array of different and interesting topics. So we have hours of great conversation, interrupted only when we reach my ball and I have to take another shot."

"But is the actual golf fun?" he persisted.

"Well, for me, fun is not a word I associate with golf."

"What words would you associate with golf?"

We were almost at the airport. To respond or not to respond? *Just tell him.*

"*Tedium. Boredom. Unimportant. Overvalued. Insignificant. Lucrative. Enervating* . . ." I stopped when the taxi stopped.

"It seems your filter may be malfunctioning," said Professor Gunnarsson as he stepped out of the taxi.

I hopped out and hauled his suitcase from the trunk before the driver even got out of the car.

"It was good of Stanford to bring me over, though it was likely motivated by something other than generosity," the professor said. "Thank you for showing me around, Adam. It was very illuminating."

With that, he pulled his small suitcase behind him into the terminal.

IF YOU ASKED me what was my best memory of my first year at Stanford, it wouldn't be winning the NCAA championship, or being named player of the year, or watching the half-hour documentary ESPN produced about my short but extraordinary golf career. Those were all nice, I guess, but what gave me my biggest high was having a poem of mine published in the *Stanford Daily*. It was tough to get published in the *Daily*. What made it all the more satisfying was that it had been submitted on my behalf by one of my professors, under the name Adam James—my middle name standing in for my surname—with an assurance to the editors that it was in fact written by an undergraduate student enrolled in the creative writing program. Had I sent it in myself, under my full name, they probably would have published it whether it was good or shite—I'd learned the word *shite* in a Roddy Doyle novel and loved its exotic sound. But as a campus celebrity, I'd never really know if I was being rewarded for writing a good poem or winning golf tournaments. Only my professor and I know who really wrote that poem. It was called "If At First You Succeed." A cryptic, meandering, and metaphorical piece, few knew what it was really about. But I knew.

Chapter 7

"YOU DON'T HAVE TO explain everything. Let the reader do the work," said Professor Edwards as I sat across from her. "Readers want to do some of the heavy lifting. So let them figure some stuff out for themselves. They'll be more engaged and invested in the story. Give them enough, but not too much. Easy to say, I know. Figuring out that balance may be difficult, but it's a big and important part of writing."

I really liked Professor Edwards. She said we could call her Amy, but I never felt right doing that. I was meeting with her during her office hours to discuss a short story I'd been working on in her creative writing class. She'd told us during our first session that she'd been born and raised in Texas and was still getting used to California. She had a Ph.D. and two collections of short stories published by a small and very literary press. I'd read both her books, but found that most of the stories flew right over my head. She was also working on a novel, but she taught because the royalties on her two short-story collections wouldn't even cover the brake job her 2007 Honda Accord needed. Such was the life of the working writer.

"So you're saying I should stop pounding my point into the ground? Stop giving readers a full, interactive, detailed map of the story? And just let them get there with a few chalk marks on the sidewalk once in a while?"

"That's all readers need. They know what two plus two is. You don't have to provide the equal sign and the four."

"Hmm. Makes sense," I said, nodding. "Okay, I'll take another run at it and leave a little more to the reader's imagination."

"You're Canadian, aren't you?" she asked as I slipped my unfinished story into my backpack.

"I am," I replied. "Wait, don't tell me. You could smell maple syrup on my breath. Or no, it was the plaid toque, wasn't it? I knew I shouldn't have worn the plaid toque."

She smiled. "Hey, I'm from Texas. I think I suffer more stereotyping than you Canadians ever will. Hell, I'm a progressive and a feminist from Abilene, and I've never even owned a pair of cowboy boots. I was lucky to be allowed back into my hometown at Christmas," she replied. "I just had a hunch you were from north of the border. It's in your writing. A different touch. A different tone. A different sense of humour. It just feels like it comes from a different place—that you come from a different place."

"Thank you, I think," I said. "And now I'm trying to decide if that's a good thing for my writing."

"Oh, it's a good thing as far as I'm concerned," she replied. "You've clearly worked very hard in this course, particularly for a student athlete. In fact, you're the only athletic-scholarship student I've ever taught who seems in any way interested in my course, let alone dedicated to his writing."

"Well, that's why I came to Stanford, for its English lit and creative writing reputation."

"I thought you came for golf."

"An understandable misconception," I said. "My golf is paying my tuition, but I'm really here for my writing. I had offers from thirteen other big schools, some of them higher in the NCAA golf rankings, but none had Stanford's creative writing rep. That's why I'm here."

"How refreshing and utterly unprecedented, at least in my experience," she said. "I just don't know how you find the time to keep up with the terms of your scholarship *and* put in the hours academically to succeed."

"Well, it helps if your extremities are precisely the right length and you stumbled upon an obscure Swedish kinesiologist peddling what sounds like a ludicrous theory that actually turns out to be true."

"Oh, if I had a dime for every student athlete who spun me that story, well, I'd have exactly ten cents," she said, shaking her head.

I learned a lot from Professor Edwards. She made me want to write more.

APRIL 2017

I was invited to play in the Masters on a special amateur exemption, courtesy of my meteoric rise in the NCAA. If that weren't enough, I was to play a practice round at Augusta with Phil Mickelson, Dustin Johnson, and Jordan Spieth on the Tuesday, two days before the start of the 2017 Masters. If I'd grown up obsessed with golf, playing with those three legends certainly would have been a much bigger deal. I mean, I am an informed citizen of the planet, so all three names were familiar to me, even though I could only have picked Phil out of a police lineup.

Then there was the course itself. Augusta National was unlike any golf course I'd ever played. Then again, I hadn't actually played on that many courses. I had no idea there were so many different shades of green on Earth until I walked onto that fabled chunk of Georgia real estate. It was such stunning natural beauty. Well, as natural as you can get with inlaid sprinklers, surgically manicured flowerbeds, and discreet colour-coded TV towers everywhere.

I was fine until I met them on the tee. For a practice round two days before the real show, the crowd was huge. I kept reciting the mantra *It's only a practice round. It's only a practice round.* I hoped I was only reciting to myself and not out loud, but I can't be certain. They were all really good guys and seemed pretty down to earth for the fame each shouldered. What blew my mind was that they knew about me, and my unorthodox journey to the top ranks of college golf. Even though they'd reached superstar status on the PGA the old-fashioned way, by working their bodies to the bone for years, they were genuinely curious to hear that there was another route. As we walked the course, they acted like there weren't hundreds of spectators and about fifty sports reporters and cameras following us around. They just kept asking questions about my game.

I didn't play very well, but the rest of my foursome could not have been more patient and encouraging. The caddie I was assigned clearly didn't understand my unique approach on the course. He kept urging me to shape my shots and try a little cut here and big draw there. After a while I just kind of tuned him out and tried to fly solo. It helped that I had some great shots along the way. They were particularly impressed with how long and how straight I consistently shot the ball using at least one club higher than they were using from the same position. The game actually passed quite quickly. I shot even par while my fellow players were all in the red and dialled in for the start of the tournament on Thursday. I survived.

So in my junior year at Stanford, my first official PGA tournament turned out to be the Masters. Nothing like starting at the top. I didn't really want to participate in the media circus that is the Masters. I wasn't sure I was ready. I wasn't sure I could handle it. But a few months earlier, when I'd gingerly broached the idea of declining the invitation, I had endured so much vehement pushback from, well, from every single person I approached and many I didn't, I felt I didn't really have much of a choice in the end. So I accepted. The practice round made me feel a little better, but not much. So I called her from my hotel room in Augusta that evening.

"Mr. Coryell, you've been given a gift from the golfing gods. Playing in the Masters when you don't bear the pressure that most of the other players face is an opportunity too good to miss," said Ms. Davenport after we'd chatted for a few minutes. "There'll be no expectations on you. You can just go out there, enjoy the pristine beauty of Augusta, think about anything but golf, and play your game. I fear you'll regret it later if you don't step up to the tee."

"But there's so much I don't know. If you hadn't told me I

had to wear long pants on the course, I would have shown up in shorts. I don't think I've ever played golf in long pants," I replied. "It felt a little weird for the first few holes."

"Your wardrobe is not exactly a justifiable reason to withdraw from golf's premier marquee event. I can see the headlines now. 'NCAA Champion Only Plays in Shorts, Pulls Out of Masters,'" she chided. "What's really going on, son?"

"I just feel so out there on my own. I know they're trying, but even my coaches don't really get me. I'm an aberration, an anomaly, an outlier."

"And a master of synonyms," she interrupted.

"I guess I do like my synonyms," I concurred. "Anyway, Ms. Davenport, I called because I think you can help me. But it's a big favour to ask, so don't feel any pressure."

"Ask away, Mr. Coryell."

"I'd be so much more comfortable out there on the course if you were on the bag. The caddie with me today was not helpful. But you know just what to say and what not to say. You understand what I need to do to play my best. You understand me," I said. I paused before continuing. "Would you come down and be my caddie for the Masters? I think I could just make it through if you were there alongside me."

Nothing. Nothing but the sound of her breathing, and it sounded more like a force-nine gale.

"Um, Ms. Davenport, are you there? Are you all right?"

"I'm here, son. Just collecting myself and ensuring control over various bodily functions that just threatened to go rogue on me," she replied. "Are you seriously asking me to caddie for you at Augusta?"

"I don't think I could make it through with the guy who nattered at me all through my round today."

There was another long silence. I just let it hang there.

"Let me be clear, Mr. Coryell. To a lover of the grand game, you are not asking a big favour. You are bestowing an extraordinary honour," she said in a soft tone I'd never heard her use. "But I see two flies in the ointment. I'm not sure the powers that be at Augusta National would permit my participation as your caddie. It might not be within the rules."

"I picked that fly out of the ointment before I left the course this afternoon. Your name was pumped into Google and your various golfing exploits were revealed. And, on my coach's recommendation, I cited your NCAA success while at Stanford. Anyway, we've been given permission to bring you in. And Stanford will pay the expenses."

"Merciful heavens and hell's furnace, you are a resourceful young man."

"What's the other fly?" I asked.

"It's the bigger, nastier fly with a painful bite," she replied. "My back."

"I've got your back. I promise," I said.

"No, I mean my wonky, blasted, lamented, cranky, cruel, and malevolent vertebral column. I can't carry those gargantuan professional tour bags around eighteen holes. I'd be on morphine and a backboard by the fifth hole."

"I meant it when I said I've got your back," I assured her. "You won't believe this, but when Bobby Jones—he's a big-name golfer from the past who was around when the Masters started, and . . ."

"Mr. Coryell, I'm quite familiar with Bobby Jones and his founding connection to the Masters. Do carry on," she said.

"Right. Anyway, when he would play the course on his own just because he loved it so much, he'd carry his own clubs in this very small and light fabric bag. It weighs next to nothing. They still have it in the pro shop at Augusta. Anyway, they're going to let me use the bag in the Masters."

"Wait just one blessed moment. They've agreed to let you use Bobby Jones's personal golf bag that he once carried around the course?"

"Exactly, and it's nowhere near as heavy as my Stanford bag."

"But son, even so, I don't think I could even carry a light bag around the course." She sighed. "I think we're scuppered."

"No, no. You don't understand. I'll be carrying the bag. You just have to wear those funny-looking white caddie coveralls and walk the course beside me."

"But that's never been done before," she persisted.

"I checked the rule book. There's nothing in it that says players can't carry their own bags. We can't use a power cart, or a pull cart, or transport my golf bag on a donkey, but the rules do allow me to carry my own bag."

"By the beard of Odin and the winged feet of Hermes, you've got it all figured out, Mr. Coryell. I commend you," she said. "But I have one condition. If you agree, I'll be there for all four rounds with scads of conversational gambits to keep your mind far away from the game you'll be playing."

"Okay. Shoot."

"I carry the bag onto the first tee and perhaps partway through number one. And I carry the bag up the eighteenth fairway to the green. You'll probably have to carry it the rest of the way. But I'll be snookered in sunshine if I'm not hoisting the bag for one and eighteen. Deal?"

"Deal," I replied. "And I wish I knew what 'snookered in sunshine' means."

THE WEATHER WAS nasty on Thursday for the opening round, just not quite nasty enough to suspend play. The temperature was low, the wind high, and the drizzle occasionally horizontal. The elements needed to be quite a bit harsher to call off the round. With lucrative TV deals in place and tickets sold, there had to be lightning, a monsoon, and a looming tsunami before they ever sounded the horn to call the players back into the clubhouse. So we soldiered on in the drizzle. I was playing with one other amateur and a veteran Tour player who was enjoying the denouement of his professional career. None of us was expected to be anywhere near the first page of the leaderboard. But they were very nice, and pretty well kept to themselves from tee to green. The crowds that followed us around in the rain were smaller and quieter, which was just how I liked it. The big swarms of spectators amassed around the stars of the PGA. Fine with me.

Ms. Davenport was the only woman sporting the white coveralls and the only caddie in the tournament who wore a perpetual smile on her face through an hour of putting practice, the rain, the formal first-tee introductions, and all eighteen holes. She was also the only caddie carrying to the first tee a comically small and spartan beige fabric golf bag that looked as out of place at Augusta as a Model T at the Indianapolis Speedway. I relieved her of her burden partway down the first fairway, as promised.

I didn't have much experience playing in the rain. I can't imagine why anyone would want to gain experience playing in the rain. It was not pleasant. It was, well, wet. We did have giant golf umbrellas, and they worked to keep us relatively dry. But I never figured out how to shoot and hold the umbrella above me at the same time. So I was plenty wet by the ninth hole. I could feel rivulets of water running down my backbone from my neck to my waist.

Ms. Davenport and I talked about home and what was going on at my old school. I quizzed her on her teams' performances that year. We talked about the new Visconti models that had just been released, and why the company seemed to have quality-control issues with their nibs. We talked about a lot of different things, as long as it wasn't golf, beyond brief exchanges about yardage, alignment, club selection, and putting. She even briefed me on Dr. Gunnarsson's growing fame. He seemed to be taking it all in stride. His ultra-direct approach to human relations still got him into trouble now and then. But as his notoriety grew, his odd responses became almost predictable, though still inappropriate. Despite the publicity for his theory, I was still the only human found to have a Gunnarsson score north of ninety.

For the entire round, a teenager walked along with us, carrying a sign that listed the scores in our threesome. He seemed confused by the range of topics Ms. Davenport and I tackled in our walk around Augusta National. At the end, he even asked me what starter fountain pen I'd recommend, as he'd been intrigued by what he'd overheard on the course. I suggested a TWSBI Eco or a Pilot Metropolitan, both good, smooth writers right out of the box.

We finished the first round in the middle of the pack. Despite the weather, with Ms. Davenport on the bag—or at least near the bag—I'd never been more at ease in a tournament. I'd have been even more comfortable if my clothes weren't so wet. But it was really nice to have Ms. Davenport with me again. I'd forgotten what it was like to walk a golf course with her. She kept me occupied and entertained. For the spectators, it was quite unusual to see a golfer and his caddie laughing their way up to the green.

"Are you at least enjoying the courses?" she asked at the hotel restaurant that night.

"I'm certainly enjoying my literature and writing courses. The golf courses, not so much."

"But your scholarship demands you deliver in both areas."

"That is true," I agreed. "My classes and profs are all wonderful, and the campus is lovely. But I do find the golf tougher to enjoy."

"But you're winning almost every tournament Stanford enters. You're the talk of the NCAA," she said. "You're a rock star."

"Yeah, but only because of my chart-topping Gunnarsson number. I wouldn't mind so much if I had even the slightest ability to influence my golfing prowess, but I don't. The only thing I can do is make my game worse."

"What about your teammates? Do they laugh and call you names and never let you join in any reindeer games?"

I smiled. "Well, yes, you could say that. But that doesn't really bother me anymore," I explained. "If I were in their shoes, I think I'd resent me, too—this guy who just showed up one day, never goes to the range, never goes to the weight room, never hits the running trails, never swims laps, and never needs to worry about junk food or beer. I'm living a charmed collegiate existence and it bugs them. It would likely bug me, too. Sometimes I feel like punching myself in the face to save them the trouble."

"But they must like it when you win for old Stanford?"

"I'm not sure about that. If I win, it means they don't. So school loyalty only stretches so far."

"You know, if you win this little tournament we call the Masters, you'll be under tremendous pressure to skip out on your last year at Stanford and join the Tour."

"Hmmm. I hadn't thought of that. What if I come second?"

"Well, it would still be pretty big news if an amateur came second at Augusta, but in the end, they only hand out one green jacket."

THREE DAYS LATER I was one stroke clear of the field as I lined up my birdie putt on eighteen, a 465-yard par four. I was on the green in two shots, though the wind took my second a little further from the hole than we'd expected. The undulations in the green made it a long and winding putt from about fifty feet. I abandoned my trusted heads-up technique and took four putts before my ball finally dropped into the cup. The crowd gasped at my collapse. Ms. Davenport gave me a funny but knowing look. A look that said, I'm onto you, Mr. Coryell. But we never talked about it. We didn't need to.

I came second in the 2017 Masters. The media play was that as an amateur, I'd cracked under the pressure and choked just as I was about to make history and slip on the coveted green jacket. The truth was that I never really coveted the green jacket or the media circus that came with it.

"Same time next year?" I asked as I dropped Ms. Davenport off at the airport.

"Same time next year, if you'll have me," she replied.

"Are you kidding? I couldn't do it without you."

"Well, I'm retiring in a couple of months," she said, taking her bag from me. "So I'll have some time on my hands."

She hugged me as the wheels in my head turned.

"I'm proud of you, Mr. Coryell," she said, releasing me. "Keep writing, get that degree, and let everything else unfold as it will."

DECEMBER 2017

I made it home again for Christmas. It was great to step out of the glare of the NCAA spotlight in the U.S. and just retreat into my family. They really did keep me grounded, although even they couldn't fully grasp the kind of media exposure and

hoopla that enveloped me in California. I had continued winning golf tournaments and was by then the top PGA prospect
in the collegiate ranks. All I really wanted to be was the top-
ranked writer at Stanford, but I thought plenty of my classmates were better candidates for that title than I. I knew my
writing still needed work. That just made me want it all the
more. But at home, if only for a couple weeks, everything
returned to normal. Sure, the local TV and radio sports shows
all wanted a piece of me, but I got that over with early, so for
most of my stay in Toronto I was just who I'd always been.

"So what's next? You've got one more term before graduation. What happens then?" my mother asked as the three of us
lounged in our family room.

"Well, unless I sign a lucrative publishing deal for my block-
buster debut short-story collection, I suspect I'll see about the
PGA Tour. I'm told by my coaches that my performance on
the golf course these last three years pretty well assures me a
spot, if I keep playing the way I have been."

"Is that what you want to do?" my dad asked.

"I think of it more as, it's what I'm built to do," I replied.
"And it seems almost unforgivable to turn my back on golf
and squander the gift you two passed along to me."

"Well, let us know if you plan to give it all up, because we
might just try for another golfing prodigy who can keep us in

the lifestyle to which we'd like to become accustomed in our retirement years."

"I'll keep you posted," I deadpanned.

On Christmas Eve, an uncontrollable force seemed to propel me over to Allison's house. I'd kept my promise for nearly three and half years and figured the statute of limitations on contacting her had passed by then. Of course, I wasn't counting that time a couple of years earlier when I happened to see her at the mall while I was doing some last-minute Christmas shopping. She hadn't seen me, so I admit I just watched her for a bit from a distance before heading to the subway. My heart felt funny afterwards.

I could hear music coming from inside her house and noticed several cars parked in her driveway and on the street in front. Arriving during a Christmas party may not have been my best idea, but I rang the bell before I lost my nerve. As luck would have it, Allison opened the door, as Christmas carols spilled out around her. She was wearing a long-sleeved white blouse and a short black skirt.

"Adam!" she said with a shocked smile. "Look at you. The famous golfer returns to his roots."

"Hi. I'm sorry. I know we agreed not to see each other, but it was so long ago I thought it would be okay. I mean, it's Christmas and all."

She closed the door and stepped out to join me on the porch.

"It's good to see you," she said as she leaned in to give me a very delicate hug that felt reserved for an aging relative rather than a romantic interest. *Okay. Got it.*

"You must be freezing," I said. "Would you like my pants?"

She had the manners to laugh. "I'm fine. It's so hot and crowded in there. It's my mother's office party. I'm supposed to be bartending."

"Are you writing?" I asked.

"All the time—mainly short stories. Some for school and some for me."

"So at least one of us is doing just what we dreamed about."

"Hey, you're living a dream, too."

"Yeah, well, I'm not sure it's my dream," I replied. "Hey, will you send me a few of your stories? I'd love to read them."

"Um, yeah, sure, I guess so. But you're still writing, aren't you?"

"As often as I can. And I love my writing classes. My profs are awesome and they're really pushing me. I'm learning a lot."

"Submitting anything?" she asked.

"I had a poem published in the *Stanford Daily* under a pseudonym."

"A poem? That's new for you. Fantastic," she said. "Why didn't you use your own name?"

"I never really liked my name," I quipped.

"Ha. No, really, why?"

"I just wanted to be sure I was being published on my own merits as a writer, and not as that guy who is miraculously topping the NCAA golf rankings. You know?"

She smiled and nodded.

"I like that. Will you send me your poem?"

"Sure," I said. "So what do you have inked?"

"Well, of course, your amazing Duofold is always inked. But right now I'm also loving my new Kaweco Elite, with a big, fat, smooth, and wet broad nib. It's like butter on hot glass. It was an early Christmas present from . . . It was an early Christmas present."

"I love the shiny piano-black finish on those," I replied.

Just then we both noticed a rather good-looking young guy eyeing us through the bay window before disappearing from view. My spidey senses were tingling, and not in a good way.

"I guess I'd better head back in," Alli said.

I could feel it all slipping away. "Really? And here I thought things were going so well." Then the door opened and the handsome dude was standing there.

"There you are," he said to Alli. "I wondered where you'd gone."

In a move I will never forget, he sidled close to her and put his hand on the small of her back. I was gutted. But I don't know why I thought she'd still be single.

"Sorry, just catching up with an old friend," Alli said in a voice that sounded a little tight. She turned back to me. "Adam Coryell, this is, um, my friend Robert Usher."

"Adam Coryell the golfer?" he asked, shaking my hand.

"Guilty. Nice to meet you, Robert." I looked at my watch. "Well, hey, look at the time. Allison, I really should be going. Great to see you, and um, you too, Robert."

I resisted the temptation to sprint and affected a casual stroll down her front walk and back to the street. It took me a very long time to "stroll" back home. I should never have even gone over to Allison's house. Of course she'd have a boyfriend. Why wouldn't she? They could have been together for years by now. I hoped I hadn't seemed desperate. I just needed to see her. I felt a little sick by the time I let myself in the front door. It had started off so well. It had briefly felt like it had when we were together all those years ago. And then *he* interrupted us and it suddenly felt quite different.

JANUARY 2018

It happened at a Stanford golf team pub night. I hadn't exactly been a social butterfly in my time at university, particularly on the golf side of my collegiate experience. I felt a little closer to some of my English and creative writing classmates, but still was never really fully immersed in the social life of the campus. But I made sure I'd been seen at the pub night by at least some of the coaches and players so I could bail a little early with a clear conscience. When it was time to pull the ripcord, I carried my jacket and sauntered for the door. I'd almost made my escape when I felt a tap on my shoulder.

"And just where do you think you're going, hotshot?"

I turned to see Wendy, her left hand now resting on my shoulder. Wendy was on the women's golf team, so we'd bumped into one another on the practice putting green, at team meetings, and on the bus to tournaments. I wasn't much of a drinker and clearly neither was she—she was swaying ever so slightly, but enough to confirm that the very large plastic beer cup cradled in her right hand was likely not her first of the night.

"Oh, Wendy, hi," I stammered. "Um, I actually have a paper due tomorrow so I'm cutting out a little early to finish it up."

"Walk me home?" she asked. "I'm on your way. I think I need to get out of here, too."

She put her beer down on a table and led me by the hand through the door, down the stairs, and out into the darkness. I wanted to pull my hand away from hers, but then I didn't. It felt nice. Now that she was walking, it was even easier to tell she was a little tipsy, though you'd never know from her talking. She just seemed wholly unfamiliar with that old *the shortest distance between two points is a straight line* thing.

"You are an odd one, Adam Coryell," she said.

"Really? Why do you say that?"

"Well, first, you're all Canadian and everything, and that's kind of cool. I don't know many Canadians. Second, you're some kind of golfing machine, which makes you different from the other guys on the team. And third, it's like golf isn't the most important thing in your life. And that's sure different from the rest of us, too. And you keep to yourself. Why?"

She was leaning against me now, holding my upper arm.

"Hmmmm. Well, I guess I'm kind of shy, and I'm still learning what it means to be a competitive golfer. You've played for most of your life. But I'm still relatively new to the game."

"But I like you anyway," she said, pulling herself closer.

We walked and chatted for another three minutes before her residence loomed on our right.

"Well, we're here," she said.

"Are you okay to make it up to your room?" I asked without thinking.

"No, I am absolutely not okay to make it upstairs. I desperately need you to see me there safely," she replied, grabbing my hand and leading me through the double doors into the lobby.

I could see where this might be headed and felt conflicted. This kind of thing hadn't happened very often to me and I wasn't sure what to think, feel, or do. But my heart was suddenly banging out a heavy metal backbeat.

The sleepy security guard avoided eye contact with us as Wendy dragged me past the front desk and into the stairwell. Before we climbed the first flight, she pressed me against the wall and kissed me. I'd had a couple beers but I was in full command of my awareness. My head might have been a little heavy but it was clear. Yet I did not resist.

I'd avoided relationships since I'd arrived at Stanford. I just didn't want to go down that path. I didn't really know why, but I guess the fact that Alli kept popping into my head should have been a pretty significant clue. I'd had a few opportunities but never pursued them. It felt like a complicating factor in my life I didn't really need. I had a lot going on, between my golf and my course work, so I'd stayed to myself. But I guess I'd forgotten how great this felt.

She broke the clench and pulled me up the stairs to the second floor and into her large, single, full-ride-athletic-scholarship residence room. My heart was still pounding and, well, other things were happening. Her room was dark, but the lamps lighting the path outside her window cast a surreal glow on the proceedings inside.

We were kissing again. She made it very obvious by words, moans, what she was doing with her hands, and where she was trying to put my hands, that kissing was only the preliminary event.

Then I heard someone say, "I can't."

"Sure you can," Wendy said.

"No, I really can't. I'm so sorry. This is really nice, but it wouldn't be right. Sorry."

I slipped out of her grip and out her door, and walked uncomfortably back to my own residence. It took Wendy to show me what I probably should have already known. I don't know why it hadn't been clearer to me before. I guess with school, golf, life, and everything else, I hadn't really noticed the torch I'd still been carrying around with me.

FEBRUARY 2018

"I think you're almost there with these two," Professor Edwards said. "Think about word choice. I've underlined a few that might be replaced with less common words to add clarity and interest. And also look to tighten it up. Think about the *less is often more* rule. There are two paragraphs in particular towards the end that seem like they're slowing me down when I want to be going faster. I think that idea of pacing came up when the class workshopped it as well. Do you know what I mean?"

I nodded and took the two stories she was handing me.

"You know, Adam, you're very good at taking in your colleagues' critiques and then actually making your stories better. You should be pleased about that. Lots of writers, perhaps even most writers, don't take criticism well, let alone assimilate it to improve their writing."

"Well, it just seems like the right way to go," I replied. "They usually give great feedback that almost always makes sense to me. It's like they see deeper into my writing than I do. Plus, some of them are really good wordsmiths, and that makes me listen to their advice even more."

"Yeah, well, our egos often get in the way. Just keep doing what you're doing," she said. "So including these two, how many stories do you have now that are close?"

"I think maybe nine," I replied, knowing the number was exactly nine, along with the precise word count for each.

"You should submit what you think are your best three for the departmental anthology. You might just snare a spot."

"*Snare*," I said, nodding. "Good word."

"Thanks," she replied, with a quizzical look.

"It's simple, clear, yet most people would probably have used a different, more common word in that sentence," I said. "Is that what you meant when you said I should think about word choice?"

She nodded. Then I nodded. There was a whole lot of nodding going on as I stood to leave her office.

Chapter 8

I DIDN'T KNOW why the president of Stanford was standing there watching me. I was in a small seminar room that had been specially arranged for me to write my very final university undergraduate exam, for my American literature seminar course. I was the only student in the room. My professor and a rather dour examination invigilator sat at the front along with the president, who had just arrived in the room. I doubted it was coincidental that she had made her entrance when there were only four minutes remaining in the time allotted for the exam. So now there were three university officials in the room, all staring only at me, their solitary focus, while I wrote and thought and wrote some more. Had I ever harboured even the remotest notion of cheating on the exam, the odds were certainly not in my favour. Fortunately, I loved this course and had happily studied long and hard, unlike so many athletic-scholarship students before me. It was a refreshing change from my golfing success. In my courses, there was real work involved in achieving my academic goals, and real satisfaction came along with it.

I lowered my eyes back to my paper. I scanned the essay-question answers I'd written on Melville, Hemingway, and Wolfe. I had three fountain pens lined up on my desk and a fourth warm in my hand. I hadn't needed any of the three spares, as I'd relied on my TWSBI Vac700 and its huge ink capacity. But I didn't want to take any chances, so my Diplomat Aero, Platinum 3776, and Pelikan M400 were inked and ready should the TWSBI fail me.

"Time's up," the invigilator finally said, looking at his stop-watch. "Pens—or more accurately, pen—down, please."

I slid all four pens into a small leather case, gathered my papers together, and slipped them into the envelope provided. I handed it to my professor.

"Good luck," she said.

"Thanks. I think I did reasonably well on it, but you'll be the judge of that," I replied. "Unless you'd like me to mark my exam for you."

"No, no. I'm sure you did fine on the exam. I meant good luck tomorrow."

"Oh, right," I replied. "And again, I appreciate your efforts in accommodating my schedule. I swear I won't breathe a word about the exam to any classmates."

"I know you won't. But I don't imagine you'll have the chance anyway, given what lies in your immediate future."

The president then stepped forward and extended her hand.

"Congratulations. I understand that with this exam, you are now officially finished your undergraduate academic program," she said.

"I am, and it's been wonderful," I replied. "Again, thank you for everything."

"And I also have been told one of your short stories will soon be appearing in the departmental anthology. That's quite an achievement. Is it true you submitted it under a pseudonym?"

"Yes. Professor Edwards helped me out. We just went with my first and middle names, as opposed to a full-blown pseudonym."

"I guess I understand why. Good for you," she replied. "And, thank you for everything you've accomplished here, in the classroom, on the page, and on the golf course. All are important in your collegiate experience."

I just nodded. I couldn't think of anything to say. It was a little disorienting knowing that this stage of academic life was now over. I wasn't even thinking about the next few days.

"Okay, enough of this. I know you're on a tight schedule. Good luck, and now get the hell out of here," she said with a laugh. "I do not wish to be the one who makes you late. It might affect my reappointment."

I laughed with her. My backpack and small rolling suitcase were at the front of the room. I slung the pack over my shoulder, wheeled the suitcase out of the building, and bumped it down the concrete steps—or at least started to. I probably should have just lifted it down. The bouncing suitcase wrenched itself from my grasp about halfway down. It lurched the rest of the way down the stairs all on its own before rolling across the sidewalk and into a telephone pole. Two students took cover. With a casual *I meant to do that* look and quiet apology, I retrieved my bag and started to hoist it into the already open trunk of the black Lincoln Town Car at the curb.

"Hey, I've got that," the driver said, leaping out of the front seat and intercepting my suitcase. "We don't want you pulling an oblique muscle. Hop in the back. There's juice and fruit there for you, and the new *Golf Digest*."

"Thanks."

I wasn't really in the mood to read about golf, particularly the latest issue of *Golf Digest*. Without even a glance, I tucked the magazine into the pocket of the seat back in front of me. I knew who was on the cover. I'd seen the shot. In fact, I'd been there when it was taken. It was my first international magazine cover, and I just didn't feel like looking at it anymore. The anonymous airbrush artist deserved some kind of an award, or at least an extra week's vacation—they'd made me look far better, happier, and more engaged than was actually the case that day. I buckled in for the ride and sipped on freshly squeezed grapefruit juice. By this time it was nearly two p.m. I pulled out the new edition of the *Paris Review* that had landed with perfect timing in my mailbox that very morning.

We drove right by the San Jose Airport departures exit and continued until the left turn for the private-aircraft terminal. The driver turned in and parked near the door. I thanked him and rolled my suitcase, without incident, into the small office.

"Mr. Coryell?" asked the young woman behind the counter.

"Yes," I replied, puzzled. "How did you know?"

"Well, your coach gave me this when he dropped off your clubs earlier this morning."

She waved the *Golf Digest* around like she was dispersing a swarm of locusts.

"Oh, right. I see."

"Anyway, your bird is all fuelled up and ready to go. Your clubs are already on board. I don't think I need to see any ID, unless you have an identical twin brother nobody knows about." She pushed a sheet of paper in front of me. "So just sign here, and here, initial here and here, and then you can make your way out to the tarmac. You'll see the jet. It's the one making the noise."

It was my first time on a private jet, and aside from the one flight attendant and two pilots, I was the only passenger. After the flight attendant welcomed me on board and got me settled into the amazingly comfortable leather seat that could have accommodated at least two of me, he walked to the front and knocked on the cockpit door. A few seconds later, a young woman with a pilot's gold-braided epaulettes came back to see me.

"Welcome aboard, Mr. Coryell. I'm Captain Jody Carpenter."

"Please, call me Adam, and thanks so much for flying me. It would have been a very long drive."

"Our pleasure. We'll be wheels up in a few minutes. We're going to head straight across the country pretty much as the crow flies, except we'll be travelling much faster than your garden variety crow. This is a Gulfstream G650 and it is a beauty," she said, stroking the arm of my seat with apparent reverence. "We'll be flying at about forty thousand feet, with a cruising speed of about 950 kilometres an hour. I know you're Canadian so I switched the numbers to metric."

"Very kind of you. Metric or imperial, that sounds very fast."

"Yes, we'll be travelling at a pretty good clip, but we'll need the speed. There's more than thirty-six hundred kilometres ahead of us. We'll do it in one hop but it's going to take about five hours, gate to gate. That puts us in Augusta around eleven o'clock tonight, including the time change."

"Well, if I can do anything to help, I have no plans for the next five hours," I replied.

"That's a kind offer, Mr. Coryell—I mean Adam—but we've got this one, thanks," she said. "Strap in and we'll get this bird in the air. Jeremy here can get you whatever you might need. But your coach wanted us to remind you that alcohol is probably not a good idea."

The flight was smooth, uneventful, and really quite lovely. The time seemed to pass quickly. It helped that I slept for about two hours, and then watched a mindless but well-executed action movie. I forget the name of the film, but I think the word *blast* was part of it—or should have been. I drank a Coke and chewed on the fresh fruit they'd laid on at my coach's suggestion. Unfortunately, there were no chips, pretzels, or honey-roasted peanuts anywhere on board. After half a cantaloupe and a big bowl of strawberries, I figured I was safe from scurvy, but all I craved then was a bag of Cool Ranch Doritos. The world should have my private-jet snack problems.

SHE WAS WAITING for me at the Augusta Regional Airport with a car arranged by the Masters. She looked perhaps a touch thinner and a little more relaxed, but pretty much the same. "Mr. Coryell, you made it!" she exclaimed, reaching to hug me.

"So did you," I replied. "Great to see you, Ms. Davenport."

"All right. Now that you've finished your last exam, and I've retired, I think it's time you called me Bobbie like everyone else, don't you?"

"Well, that would be quite simple and convenient given that, as far as I know, Bobbie is in fact your real name," I replied. "Okay, if you call me Adam, I'll call you Bobbie. Then we're square."

"Done."

"Is Roberta ever appropriate, or is it completely off the table?" I asked.

"Not just off the table. It's buried forever," she replied.

"Understood. Bobbie it is." I didn't probe why, but I was curious.

One of the ground crew loaded my golf bag and suitcase into the car. Bobbie drove.

"I am just so happy to be back here in Augusta again," she said, pulling out of the airport parking lot. "You must be about ready to detonate from all the excitement."

"I'm not sure *detonate* is the right verb. More like *doze*. For me, it's just another golf tournament, except at the end the winner is forced to wear a jacket in a colour that should really only be appropriate on St. Patrick's Day, when people are inebriated enough not to care."

I could sense her shaking her head in the darkness of the car and issuing a long exhalation.

"You know, fate is a cruel mistress," she said. "For more than forty years, I've dreamed of playing and winning this tournament, I mean beyond the minor issue of my gender. The Masters is the very pinnacle of golf. I've never wanted anything more in my life. And I'm here at Augusta with someone who is not only playing, but could well be wearing the green jacket. And you're ambivalent at best, disdainful at worst. It's just so strange."

She was smiling when she said it, but I could feel the serious tone beneath. I felt bad. I sometimes forgot just what this tournament meant to people who loved golf.

"Sorry, I guess I was a little harsh," I said. "Believe me, Bobbie, if this were a Disney movie and we could switch places, I'd like nothing more. I know this is a special tournament, in a special place, with special traditions that carry a lot of weight in this world. But it's never really felt like my world. You know?"

"I know, son," she replied. "And therein lies the rub—the cruel, cruel rub."

She pulled in to the hotel parking lot a short time later. We were in adjoining rooms in the same hotel we'd stayed in the previous year. It was nice, if unspectacular. We were really just using it for sleep, and the beds were quite good. She made sure I got into my room and insisted on carrying my backpack and rolling bag while I lugged in my golf bag.

"I've brought you a graduation present and a Masters present."

"And I didn't get you anything for your retirement," I lamented. "I should have thought of that."

"Horse hockey! You just finished your finals and are about to play in the Masters," she said. "Your gift to me is inviting me here again to walk Augusta National with you. That, my dear boy, is the best retirement present I can imagine."

"Ms. Daven . . . um, Bobbie, I couldn't do this without you," I said. "I really couldn't." I meant what I said. I was never completely comfortable on the golf course, but I came close when she was alongside.

She slipped into her room next door and returned carrying something in a big plastic bag. She pulled out a slim, sleek, and by the way she was wielding it obviously very light golf bag. It was in Stanford's familiar cardinal-red and grey. My name had been embroidered on one of the backpack-style shoulder straps.

"First, a gift in honour of your second appearance at the Masters," she said. "This is my rather ham-handed way of telling you I'm afraid I still can't lug your bag and may never be able to. So this is actually a gift for both of us."

"It's so light," I said after she handed it to me.

"And it'll take a PGA regulation set of clubs and stand upright on its own, too."

"Thanks, it's perfect," I replied. "I kind of like carrying my own clubs. I think of it as the cross, or rather bag, I must bear for never having to practise."

Then she handed me a small gift-wrapped box.

"More importantly, this is for finishing your degree. Of course, I'm assuming you've passed all your exams and will be cleared to graduate in June."

I knew what it was. I just didn't know what kind. I opened it and immediately identified the brand by the ornate logo on top of the faux-leather box.

"A Conway Stewart? No, you didn't. You didn't. I can't believe it."

I lifted the lid and there it was, the CS Wellington in Classic Brown, a stunning acrylic in various shades of, you guessed it, brown.

"I can't believe you remembered after all these years," I said, beaming at her.

"I tend not to forget things like grail pen preferences," she replied.

"Oh my gosh, it's breathtaking," I said before unscrewing the cap on its lovely, smooth threads and examining the eighteen-karat gold nib. "A medium! You remembered my taste in nibs, too."

"I have always loved my Conway Stewarts. I've had three over the years, but only have one now. It's a lovely writer. I think you'll really enjoy this pen," she said.

I immediately inked it with the Diamine Espresso I had in my backpack and pulled out my Rhodia notebook. I was in heaven. It was such a smooth writer. It laid down a thick, wet line, but not too thick or too wet. Just right. Perfectly tuned.

"When I tested it in the store, there was just a bit more feedback than I knew you'd like. So I had a nibmeister smooth the nib. Now it's dreamy."

"It's perfect. Just as I like it," I said. "If you're trying to get my mind off the Masters, you've succeeded."

"I was, and I'm glad."

"This means so much to me. I've been pining for one for a very long time."

"I remember."

"I can't believe it. It's too much," I said. "Thank you, thank you. I'm not sure how I can repay you."

"Repay me? It's a gift, Adam. It is not to be repaid," she scolded. "Besides, you're giving me my second chance to walk the hallowed ground of Augusta National. A mere Conway Stewart doesn't even come close."

"Well, let's win this year and sweep out some of the cobwebs around this place," I said. "Hey, has an amateur ever won the Masters?"

"No. It's never been done. In 1961 a fella by the name of Deane Beman, I think, won the annual par-three competition on the Wednesday of tournament week—that would be today —but that's a very far cry from winning the Masters on Sunday."

"Maybe it's time."

"I like the steel in your eye, son, but for crying out loud, do not start thinking about the game. We've got four days to talk about whatever strikes your fancy, as long as it's not golf. Just let your body tell you what to do when you stand over the ball, and you'll be fine."

"That's my plan. Our plan."

WIKIPEDIA REPORTS THAT there have only ever been five golfers who have notched wire-to-wire victories at the Masters. Jordan Spieth, Raymond Floyd, Jack Nicklaus, Arnold Palmer, and, back in 1941, a guy named Craig Wood all finished each of the four rounds of the tourney at the top of the leaderboard. I wasn't thinking about this when rising PGA star Justin Thomas and I teed off Sunday afternoon as the final pairing. In fact, golf in general, and the Masters in particular, could not have been further from my mind. And that was why I was still clear of Thomas by four strokes with eighteen holes to go.

Bobbie never once complimented me on my shots. Not once. That was our agreement. That was our plan. We spent a good part of the Sunday round talking about Allison. I hadn't seen her, or spoken to her, since the painful episode on her front porch when I was home for Christmas.

"She can certainly write," Bobbie said as we made the turn for the back nine, including holes eleven, twelve, and thirteen, the daunting trio known as Amen Corner. Many a Masters has been lost around Amen Corner. But I wasn't thinking about that. For once, I was glad to have Alli as a distraction, if only in my head.

"I've taught precious few writing students, before or since, as talented as she," Bobbie continued. "Her sentences were beautiful and balanced yet seemed effortless. That is a rare combination."

I wondered if the TV commentators were discussing just how much Bobbie and I talked to one another on the course. It was certainly not the norm on the Tour.

"Countless writers have written countless beautiful sentences, but they so often feel like they've been painstakingly carved out of marble. Ms. Clarkson's prose is pristine, nearly perfect, yet also feels like it just flowed easily and naturally from the nib of that favourite Parker Duofold of hers."

We stopped at my ball and I set my bag down beside us.

"Okay, Adam, six-iron. Aim for the TV tower, not the pin. There's wind. Full swing. I really think Alli has a chance of breaking through as a writer if she wants to."

"Oh, I'm pretty sure she still wants to," I replied. "It's been her dream for a very long time."

Thwack! The ball started toward the TV tower and then arced with the wind back towards the pin. It landed softly on the green and ran towards the cup. It was still rolling when I stopped watching.

"You never speak in such glowing terms about my writing," I said, without thinking.

"Ah. Hmmm. Yes, well, Adam, you are also a fine writer. But there is a difference. You've gotten there through hard work, careful analysis, and a willingness not only to listen to comments and criticism but to sift through conflicting advice and act only on those points that will actually improve your writing. That is a different kind of gift, but a gift nevertheless," she said as we walked up the tenth fairway, considered the toughest hole at Augusta National. She paused before continuing.

"Think of it this way. Like some special fountain pens, Alli writes beautifully right out of the box. Now, I'll try not to stretch this analogy too far, but you, dear Adam, write quite well first time out but then work assiduously to improve, as it were, by optimizing your ink flow, aligning your tines, and smoothing your nib. You both end up with fine writing, but you've likely expended more time and effort to get there. I make no judgment on either approach."

"So you're saying Alli writes the way I play golf—that if

there were a Gunnarsson score for writing, hers might be up in the nineties," I said, pulling the putter from my bag when we reached the green. "And I write like most people golf, where improvement and success is a lengthy, iterative, and often frustrating process."

"Precisely, son. Nicely put, and a damn sight better than my fountain pen metaphor, not to mention your impressive use of the word *iterative*," Bobbie replied, eyeing my putt. "Okay, I've got outside edge with moderate speed, or two inches above the hole with slow speed. You?"

"That's what I see, too. Outside edge it is."

I lined up, locked down the triangle formed by my arms and shoulders, and sank the birdie putt to move five clear of Justin Thomas and six clear of Bubba Watson.

"I wish I wrote like I play golf."

"But consider the sense of satisfaction earned by working so hard to yield a jewel of a story that is as good as you can possibly make it. Imagine how it feels to get so deeply inside the prose as you polish it, knowing that you're making it better and better. That, to me, is the joy in writing."

I looked at her, smiled, and nodded. Of course, she was right. I knew what she was talking about. I'd felt it, too. I clearly needed to work on my patience.

We made it through Amen Corner—birdie, par, birdie—but most of my competition didn't fare quite as well. Bobbie and I were having such a great conversation, I don't really remember much about the rest of the back nine. But we were still talking about writing and Allison as we walked up the eighteenth.

"Okay, hold that thought," Bobbie said. "It would be rude not to acknowledge the gallery. They are doing this for you." Her voice was calm, but as she motioned to the crowd, I noticed that her hands were trembling.

She reached over and lifted my golf bag from my shoulders.

"I should be able to manage your clubs for this last wee bit. Now go."

I surfaced from our discussion and finally noticed the thunderous ovation from the massive crowd lining both sides of the fairway and surrounding the green. It was mayhem. The chant of 'Adam! Adam! Adam!' echoed across the course and was so deafening I suspect it spilled well beyond Augusta's precincts.

"Your hat, son," Bobbie said under her breath.

"Right."

I took off my Stanford ball cap and kind of waved it around a bit in appreciation of the ovation. I smiled, too. But strangely, I didn't really feel anything. No excitement, no sense of accomplishment, no understanding of the history of the moment. Nothing. I just wanted to putt out and escape. I looked back at Bobbie, who usually walked right beside me. Her eyes glistened, and I don't think it was hay fever.

Justin Thomas, who was still five strokes adrift of me, also fell back and let me approach the green on my own. I stopped and waved him up with me. I thought it was the magnanimous thing to do. The people roared.

The outcome was a foregone conclusion. It had been for most of the back nine, short of a major meltdown on my part. And now at the eighteenth, even if I tried, I couldn't reasonably take six putts to sink my ball. In the end, Justin Thomas bogeyed anyway. So I surrendered to the moment and two-putted for a six-stroke win. Thankfully, my margin of victory was nowhere near Tiger Woods's record-setting twelve strokes back in 1997. That would have only stoked the media fire higher.

As she watched my final putt drop, Bobbie's moist eyes gave way to full-on waterworks. She put the flagstick back in its place and then locked me in a bear hug that lifted me right off the ground. She squeezed me so tight I feared my sternum might fail. ("Caddie's Hug Sends Masters Champion to Hospital with Broken Ribs and Collapsed Lung.") I survived.

"Thank you for this, Mr. Coryell," she snuffled.

"No, thank you, and your measuring tape, too. You started all of this," I replied.

I beamed like a Masters winner would, and waved to the crowd. Justin Thomas even hugged me the way pro golfers do. I'm sure I looked like the winner of the Masters, but that was mostly acting—and mostly for Bobbie.

Then as the reporters who'd shadowed us all day out on the course moved in for the first of too many media interviews, I noticed Bobbie removing the eighteenth-hole flag from its stick and stuffing it into the pocket of her white Augusta coveralls. Tradition.

About half an hour after my final putt, I sat in Butler Cabin under the TV lights. Someone padded a bit of powder on my face seconds before we went live. When the 2017 Masters champion, Sergio Garcia, helped me slip into the famed green jacket, I was surprised to find that it fit almost perfectly and felt really nice. But it was still green. It would enjoy a prized position in the bowels of my closet—that is, once I had a closet of my own. Then another idea for the jacket loomed into view. But a moment later I heard my name and I remembered I was still being broadcast live on CBS. Jim Nantz was talking to me while Sergio and the new chair of Augusta National, Fred Ridley, looked on. Bobbie was off camera, on the other side of the room, with a smile that two root canals and a funeral could not have extinguished. Normally the winning caddie did not accompany the champion into Butler Cabin. But I knew she'd want to be there, and so I had asked Mr. Ridley. Turned out I had just acquired some influence about thirty minutes earlier.

"Adam, you punched your ticket to Augusta by winning the U.S. Amateur Championship last August, and now you're the very first amateur to win the Masters in the storied history of this very special tournament. You're only the sixth player in history to top the leaderboard in all four rounds of the Masters. You looked calm and collected out there all day, almost oblivious to the pressure. And you did it all, including carrying your own clubs and building a six-stroke cushion in the end, after only having played golf for about four and a half years. It's an extraordinary and unprecedented achievement in sport, let alone in golf. How did you do it?"

"Um, thanks, Jim," I started. "Well, we have a simple formula. We just focus on choosing the right club, and then hitting the ball straight and long. We don't shape my shots. I don't even know how to shape shots. I just swing, and the ball seems to fly straight and cover the distance we know I can hit it for each club."

"When you say *we*, you're of course referring to Bobbie Davenport, your caddie. Bobbie's back issues mean you have to carry your own bag—and that has never happened here at the Masters—so it must be important to you that she be by your side."

"It sure is. I mean, she was the one who discovered that I might be good at golf, and she was the one who first put a club in my hand. So I wouldn't be sitting here wearing this, um, very green jacket without her."

"Well, you both seemed very engaged in the round, talking your way around the course, never losing your concentration. How important was that?"

"Well, talking to Bobbie shot by shot, hole by hole, and keeping my mind, um, focused on the right things, is critical. So, I kind of wish we could both fit into this green jacket, because we did this together."

"Adam, this major victory gives you a lifetime exemption to play here every year at the Masters, and perhaps more importantly, this stunning win gives you a five-year exemption on the PGA Tour. Now that you're about to graduate from Stanford, I assume we'll see you as a regular PGA Tour player?"

"Oh, really? I didn't actually know about the five-year PGA Tour exemption. I guess Bobbie and I will talk it over in the coming days. But it's kind of nice to know I have options," I replied.

"You're the 2018 Masters champion, yet you've taken a different path to get here than every single one of your predecessors. I imagine that you've made a certain Swedish kinesiology professor in Adelaide, Australia, very happy tonight because you are the first living evidence of his Predictive Innate Pinnacle Proficiency theory."

"Bobbie and I spoke to Professor Gunnarsson last week and I can tell you he was very happy, even before the Masters."

"Will this be the most important achievement in your life?"

"Well, um, I kind of hope not. I mean, I'm only twenty-two," I replied. "But this is pretty special."

"Finally, Adam, how are you going to spend the next few days in the wake of this historic victory here at Augusta?"

That question caught me a little off guard, and I answered without thinking.

"Oh, um, well, I've been working on a short story for a writing contest that I have to finish soon or I'll miss the deadline."

"Remarkable," said Jim Nantz, laughing and shaking his head. "Live from Butler Cabin here at Augusta National, we've been speaking with the 2018 Masters champion, Adam Coryell, on the heels of an audacious, miraculous performance for an amateur still very new to the sport. Stay tuned for 60 Minutes, coming up next on most of these CBS stations. I'm Jim Nantz."

Fifteen minutes later, the presentation of the green jacket was repeated in a more private ceremony on the practice putting green beside the clubhouse. I insisted that Bobbie be up front with me. She chose to stand behind me, rather than beside me, but she was there. I pulled her forward when the trophy was presented. In fact, I didn't turn to face all the cameras until both Bobbie's and my hands were lifting the sterling-silver recreation of the Augusta clubhouse above our heads. That turned out to be the money shot.

Bobbie was doing her best not to blubber while the cameras were flashing all around us, but her best often wasn't good enough. I just kept smiling and stuck close to her. The next day, there were very few photos published around the world that did not feature us both. Just as I'd hoped.

While all I wanted to do was jump in our car and head back to the hotel, it took another couple of hours before we could make good our escape. There were many more interviews to do—it felt like I just repeated myself for about ninety minutes. Finally, with my voice failing me, Bobbie and I drove out of Augusta National.

Back at the hotel, I slipped off the green jacket and turned to Bobbie, who had just carried my clubs into my room.

"Bobbie, I really have no place to keep this, and I know it means a great deal to you. I'd like you to have it," I said, handing her the jacket. "I may need to borrow it each April, should I come back here, but other than that, I'd truly like you to have it. Green is really not my colour."

She just held the jacket, impersonating a deer in the head-lights.

"What! No. Adam. Um, no, I couldn't possibly accept this," she sputtered. "No, I couldn't."

"Yes, you can and you will," I said, looking her in the eye. "It's important to me that you have this."

WE HAD FINALLY made the key decision as we drove from Augusta National back to the hotel. We'd studiously avoided the topic while on the course.

"So? What's the plan, young Adam?"

"Despite some misgivings on my part, it feels inevitable to me," I replied. "This past weekend has made it perhaps even more inevitable, if there are gradations of inevitability."

"Have I ever told you that you don't talk like most twenty-two-year-olds I've encountered?"

"Frequently," I replied. "But a five-year exemption on the PGA Tour? No need for Qualifying School. No junior feeder tours. No daily practising. No camping, tournament to tournament. No scratching and scraping for local sponsors. None of that. Just playing with the big boys for the big money, every week."

"I see what you mean about it feeling inevitable," she conceded.

"Not to make the leap would almost be ungrateful, not to mention stupid when factoring in the financial potential of our situation."

"There's more to life than money," she countered.

"Yes, but having some money would make it so much easier to revisit this decision in the future."

"A thoughtful way to view it," Bobbie said. "So?"

"I'll do it, but only if . . ." I held my tongue and stared her down.

"Are you trying to say you'll join the PGA Tour only if you can carry your own bag while I walk beside you, dispensing pearls of golf wisdom and leading conversations on a multitude of obscure topics, none of which is golf?"

"I think we understand each other," I said. "If you're up for it, I'm up for it."

I was still registered as a student at Stanford during the Masters. Becoming the first amateur to win the green jacket merely added gasoline to the already raging inferno of publicity around my strange golf gift. Thousands of emails rolled in and I was all over social media. It was my first time trending on Twitter.

Winning the Masters as an amateur did mean that victory brought with it no money. But that was about to change. In the ensuing days, I appeared on every major television and radio talk show across North America, and several minor ones. I didn't feel I had much choice in the matter. But I declined to wear the green jacket the way previous winners had on their post-victory media tours. I just kept telling people it was out at the cleaner's. I made sure to do all the Canadian shows, too. Just talking to Canadian sports reporters made me feel more at home. Whenever possible, I made Bobbie appear with me.

My mother couriered me a card from Alli, knowing I'd be eager to see it. She'd addressed it to my Toronto home in what I was sure was Kaweco Ruby Red ink. The message in the card was written in a nice blue ink. It said:

Parker Duofold, Waterman Mysterious Blue.

Adam,

I'm thrilled and happy for you. What an amazing performance. It was surreal watching you and Ms. Davenport on television.

All the best,
Alli

All the best? All the best?! She might as well have written, *Yours in platonic perpetuity.* Where were the X's and O's? Still, I supposed it was nice to have at least something from Alli, even if her heart wasn't included.

Chapter 9

EVERYTHING CHANGED WITH the Masters. My parents floated me some money to get me started. Given what happened at Augusta and what it portended, they decided it was a good investment that would pay off quite quickly. Two weeks later, Bobbie and I were set up in San Francisco. We were both renting smallish furnished condos in the same building on a month-to-month basis. Many of the PGA Tour players settled in Florida, but I had come to love San Francisco while at Stanford. It's an amazing city oozing literary history. I particularly loved browsing in the City Lights bookstore on Columbus. It had been instrumental in bringing the Beat Generation of writers to global prominence. Bobbie and I liked to spend what little downtime we had at that special bookstore. Downtime? Yeah, right. We squeezed in two or three visits amongst the media mayhem and the growing demands on my time.

So much happened in Augusta's immediate aftermath. I often didn't know where I was, who I was, or what I was doing. Bobbie and I just hung on for the ride and tried to make sound, informed decisions on the fly. I likened it to being caught in churning whitewater, where turning back and paddling upstream was just not possible—particularly when it felt like we didn't have a paddle between us anyway. We just had to ride the rapids to the end and hope we made it to calmer waters without being sucked into a whirlpool. My parents were as helpful as they could be on the phone, but really, Bobbie and I just took it day by day and tried to do the right thing at the right time. It was a new world, but I just didn't think I was cut out to be an explorer. Despite my best intentions and efforts, I missed that short-story contest deadline courtesy of the Masters maelstrom. I resented that more than you can imagine.

Bobbie and I won the first PGA tournament I ever played as a professional when I officially joined the Tour, about five weeks after Augusta. Okay, we actually won the first three tournaments we played. We hadn't rushed right back to golf after the Masters, though there was considerable pressure from various quarters to do just that. No, we took our time, gathered ourselves, tried to set up my impending golf career on a solid footing, and prepared for the weekly grind on the Tour. We made our professional debut in May at the Players Championship at the famed TPC Sawgrass course in Ponte Vedra Beach, Florida. Bobbie was amazing the whole way through. She really had a knack for keeping me talking and thinking, and sometimes laughing. We won by three strokes and collected our first cheque. The winner's share of the purse was $1.9 million. I didn't hyperventilate on the course, but I did as soon as we made it back to the car.

The day after the Players victory, we flew to New York for a meeting. Lisa Griffiths was a former successful investment banker who had turned in mid-career to managing the personal fortunes of various high-profile athletes. Bobbie had done her due diligence in the search for just the right advisor and Lisa had risen to the top of the list.

It was a small operation in a nice office on Fifth Avenue. Lisa came out to greet us and then escorted us into her office, which had a great view of Manhattan. I put her in her early forties. Her auburn hair was short and I guess you would say stylish, though I'm not exactly an authority on the matter.

"Thanks for making the trip up, and congratulations on your Players win and of course your Masters victory a while back. You're certainly not wasting any time establishing yourself on the Tour. I'd like to make sure we're not wasting any time making your winnings work for you to maximize your future flexibility and security."

"Right. That sounds good to me," I replied.

She then talked at some length about her approach, tailored to the needs, wishes, and comfort levels of her clients.

"Some of my clients are single, with no responsibilities beyond themselves and their entourage. Many of them opt for a more aggressive asset mix, with more upside potential and more risk. Others, whose careers are just a knee injury away from over, or who have families to support, often adopt a more conservative route, where returns are lower but more secure. Given your long-term potential, we could probably do a little of both for you. Protect some of your holdings—safe and secure, and growing slowly—and then invest the rest more aggressively and opportunistically to yield higher and faster returns."

We talked for quite a long time. I liked her. And so did Bobbie. Lisa Griffiths became my personal financial advisor and investment manager. I was about to have investments. We agreed on a fairly conservative approach. It seemed the right way to go. After all, I honestly didn't know how long I'd be earning money on the PGA Tour.

"May I ask who your agent is for sponsorships, endorsements, promotions, and appearances?" she asked.

"Well, we've been inundated with overtures from sports marketing firms but have avoided doing anything on that front until we'd sorted out financial management," I replied.

"Probably wise. But given your earning potential, particularly right now in the wake of the Masters and the Players, it's likely time to sort that out. You can probably earn more off the course than on."

"The agents we've come across so far all seem a little slippery to me," Bobbie said.

"And whatever I know about sport agents I learned from a Tom Cruise movie," I added.

"Would you be prepared to share a few names?" Bobbie asked.

"I've only ever recommended one agent, and I haven't yet regretted it," Lisa said.

AFTER THE PLAYERS, I won the next week at the AT&T Byron Nelson in Dallas ($1.4 million), and the week after that at the Fort Worth Invitational ($1.3 million). As spectators and reporters kept telling me, no one in the history of the game had ever won their first three PGA tournaments—four, if you counted my Masters win as an amateur. It was golfing history. All I could think of was that no one had ever been quite so bored winning his first four PGA tournaments. That was also golfing history.

Bobbie was having the time of her life. She was a true professional on the course. Her great respect for the game made her popular with other players, caddies, and fans alike. She was in her element during tournaments, though her approach to the game was unlike any other caddie's on the Tour. The only time we ever spoke of the game was when we both arrived at our ball. Then our golf interactions were very brief and in a code we'd developed. She'd say something like "Five-iron, full, ten degrees high, don't think, feel." I knew exactly what that meant and I'd make the shot.

I wasn't exactly shunned by the other players, but neither was I warmly embraced. Perhaps I was overly sensitive, but I thought I could sense simmering, if not seething, resentment just below the surface. As in college, no one ever saw me on the range working out swing problems. No one ever saw me working closely with a coach. No one ever saw me shank a drive or smash my club into the side of a bunker in frustration. I just won. That got under some players' skin, and I understood why. Of course, I worked on my putting, sand shots, and even some light chipping when full swings weren't needed. But that was about it. I made a few friends among the other players, but not many. Instead, I spent my evenings during tournaments hanging out and having dinner with Bobbie, and then writing.

I was a little blocked creatively from everything else going on in my life. So Bobbie suggested I start journaling, just to try to wrestle with what was happening and how I felt about it all. So I did. I began filling these lovely notebooks I'd ordered from Amazon with Tomoe River paper. I just loved the feel of a fountain pen nib against that special paper. I didn't really record anything profound, but it did give me a way to process what was happening to me and my life. It also seemed to reinvigorate my creative juices. So I'd journal for a half hour or so, and then work on a short story. The important thing to me was, I was still writing. Finally, I still wrote letters to Alli. I just never sent them.

The next stop on the Tour was the Memorial in Dublin, Ohio. It had one of the larger purses. I was the odds-on favourite given my victories in the previous four tourneys. I was the clubhouse leader after the first three rounds. I could feel the pressure building for another win. It was getting to be a little much. I wanted more time for myself and my writing. Winning again just didn't feel like a good idea, I mean other than the $1.6 million victor's cheque.

Bobbie suspected but said nothing. I didn't have a meltdown on the course and start shooting balls into the woods, ponds, and gallery. No, I just started on Sunday's back nine to miss a putt here and there. No one suspected. I'd learned how to be discreet. I came second by a stroke. I could feel the pressure drop like a relief valve on a boiler that's too hot. It was just what I needed. Yet I still took home a cheque for more than $800,000.

She approached us in the clubhouse after the TV lights had been extinguished and most of the other players had already left. Bobbie and I were seated in the restaurant when she appeared. She was decked out in casual golf attire to blend in. Her shoulder-length dark hair bounced a bit as she walked. She wore glasses in tortoise shell that gave her a very studious mien.

"I thought I might find you here," she said. "I'm Susan Maddocks."

"You made it," Bobbie said, shaking Susan's hand and making room for her in the booth.

"Yes, it was touch and go for a bit, and the traffic is brutal out there, but at least it's going in the opposite direction," she replied. "Sorry about you coming second, but it does little to slow the interest in you, financial and otherwise, as a valuable asset. But nevertheless, we should strike while you're hot, if I'm not getting too far ahead of myself."

"Lisa Griffiths speaks very highly of you, and she suggested we meet," Bobbie said.

"I like Lisa a lot, and we tend to see eye to eye on most things," Susan said. "Why don't I just give you my philosophy around sponsorships and endorsements and we'll see where it takes us."

"That sounds grand," replied Bobbie.

"For me, unlike many player agents, it's seldom about the *show me the money* moment. You, Mr. Coryell, are a fully formed person with certain beliefs and interests and behaviours and ideas, all of which come together to create, whether you like it or not, your brand. And to be clear, you do not define your brand—others do, in how they perceive you. Sorry to go all Marketing 101 on you, but people are already beginning to discern your brand. You're the biggest thing to hit golf since Tiger Woods. So it's time to take active control of how you are perceived so that your brand becomes closer to, if not the same as, who you really are and want to be. We do that by how you conduct yourself in the public eye—ideally in the same way you would in private—and with what, and whom, you are associated."

"All of that makes sense to me," I replied. "I want to be seen as who I actually am, and not as a manufactured commodity. I don't want to be a boy band. I'm just a nice guy who happens to be able to hit a golf ball straight and far when I need to."

"Good. That's what I like to hear," Susan replied. "Right now I could sign you up for long-term endorsement deals starting at ten million dollars a year for companies in medicinal cannabis, liquor, beer, and the largest singles resort company. You'd be rich. I'd be doing okay out of it, too. But knowing a little about you, and having spoken to Lisa, I would not put those deals in front of you, and if you asked for them, I'd counsel against them. They will not shape your brand in the way you want."

"Right," I replied. "So we take a pass on the easy money, for all the right reasons. What do we go after?"

"Well, we will not need to 'go after' anything. We'll just

signal what we're interested in and then watch as the lineup forms at the door."

"So who is in the lineup?" Bobbie asked.

"It's a diverse group depending on your tastes, but I'd suggest a car company, an airline, a golf conglomerate, probably Nike, maybe an industrial interest if they're enlightened about global warming, a hotel chain, and perhaps a big tech company that's going to be around for a long time, like an Apple or a Samsung."

"And then we make a decision and sign some kind of a deal with one of those big companies?" I asked.

"No, Adam, we'd sign contracts with all of them, covering off all the major sectors," she replied. "And there's one other area we should consider. The luxury goods segment. Golf is seen as a luxury game. So companies like Rolex and Montblanc might also be in the queue."

"Did you say Montblanc?" Bobbie asked with elevated eyebrows.

She nodded.

"Cool," I said.

Twenty-four hours later, Susan Maddocks became my agent. Within a week, the line of suitors at the door was long and lucrative. It all unfolded just as she said it would. We signed one-year deals only. That was my idea. Susan recommended longer terms, but I didn't really want to be locked in for the next decade. We'd take it year to year. She balked a bit, but understood and made it happen.

We skipped the FedEx St. Jude Classic the next week. Then we waited until we won the following two tournaments before signing any deals. Incidentally, the first of those two victories was the U.S. Open at Shinnecock Hills in New York, the second major of the Tour. I didn't look at the cheque until we were in the car, pulling out of the parking lot. It was for $2.2 million. The following week, we won the Travelers Championship up in Connecticut, adding $1.3 million to the pot. Those two wins strengthened our bargaining position, raised the value of the endorsement contracts, and gave our new corporate partners comfort that I was the so-called "real deal." With six tournaments then under my belt as a professional, I amassed five victories and a second-place finish, taking home just under $9 million. Not bad for six weeks' work. It certainly made Susan's negotiations with corporate partners quite easy.

The Nike deal was for $10 million. BMW North America came in at $6 million. Those were the two anchor deals, with several smaller agreements with Air Canada, General Electric, and Breitling, the high-end watch manufacturer. And yes, Susan did broker a deal with Montblanc, which in addition to a very large chunk of change included pens and inks and other paraphernalia for Bobbie and me. I carried around some guilt that so much came to me so fast, but I confess it didn't stop me from writing my short stories with a Montblanc 149 Meisterstück in Oyster Grey ink. Oh, and I almost forgot to mention that shortly after we signed the BMW deal, both Bobbie and I were driving new Beemers. I opted for a dark blue X5 so we always had room for my clubs and luggage in case we decided to drive to some of the Tour stops. Bobbie chose a bright red 335i. She loved that car. It was a little unusual to cut the caddie into endorsement and sponsorship deals, but given my apparent status and potential on the Tour, Susan could dictate terms that weren't possible for most other elite athletes. That was the term often used to describe people like me—*elite athletes*. Hyperbole at its finest.

I never really thought about the money. I never really saw it, either. It went directly to Lisa Griffiths for safekeeping, or rather safe investing. But without a doubt, I was quite suddenly rich beyond any mortal's wildest dreams.

OCTOBER 2018

With Bobbie on the bag, we seemed to be almost unbeatable. On some holes, particularly sharp doglegs, my inability to shape the ball was sometimes a disadvantage. My competitors could often draw or fade their balls around the dogleg and be much further up the fairway than my ball. I would have to hit an iron straight out to the turn, and then make a very long second shot into the green. Still, I often birdied those holes anyway. We cooled off a bit in the summer. It just felt weird to keep winning, and you could feel the resentment building among some of the other players. So I happily took a few weeks off here and there, and "putted badly" at key points in other tournaments to ensure I wasn't always hoisting the trophy. This kindled a little flicker of hope in the hearts of the rest of the field and kept them coming back, week after week. But by the end of August, I'd notched another five tournament wins, and two seconds. I missed five tournaments, including the Open Championship at Carnoustie in Scotland. I could tell Bobbie was disappointed not to be there, but I just didn't want to deal with all the hype around the vaunted Grand Slam—winning all four majors in the same year. Skipping the Open Championship took the pressure off. It also made it a little easier when we won the PGA Championship in St. Louis, in August.

I probably missed a few more tournaments than I needed to, but given the choice of playing or not playing, I preferred quiet weekends that left me time to write. Many people think the life of a top-ranked professional golfer is pampered and privileged. And to a very great extent, I guess it is. But even for me, the great anomaly who didn't spend hours on the practice range each week, my days were still packed. Thursdays through Sundays were of course consumed with tournaments.

There were travel days, depending on the location of the next Tour stop. Then we had appearances to make at sponsor events, commercials to shoot for the products we endorsed, photo sessions, and media interviews. The price of ascending to the top rung of golf's ladder was virtually no downtime. So skipping the occasional tournament gave me at least four clear days in a row to recharge. I know it doesn't sound like boredom would be a problem, given the wave we were riding, but the days on the course during the tournaments felt nearly interminable. *Tedious, mind-numbing, stultifying, monotonous, tiresome,* and *exhausting* are other words that capture my experience on the course. Bobbie, the creative conversationalist, was my saving grace. Still, each four-hour tournament round felt like eight hours.

It was just after we'd finished the opening round of the BMW Championship in Pennsylvania. I had additional responsibilities during this tournament in light of my sponsorship deal with BMW. But I still found a moment to make the call from the front seat of the BMW 750Li assigned to us for the duration of the tournament.

"Lisa Griffiths," she answered.

"Lisa, it's Adam Coryell."

"Adam, I thought you'd be on the course right about now."

"We just finished for the day," I replied.

"How did it go?"

"Not bad, I guess. It was kind of slow out there, and it was really hot and humid."

"Actually, Adam, I meant how did you play. Are you in the hunt, as usual?"

"I'm not sure. I don't really watch the leaderboard when I'm out there, but Bobbie said we were clear of the field when we finished. There are still some threesomes out on the course, but I think we're doing okay."

"Carry on. You're making my life much easier," she said. "So what's up?"

"Well, I wondered if you could help me spend a little of my money. I'd like to do something nice for my parents."

"Happy to help. We have some of your assets in relatively liquid holdings so we can easily free up some money. What did you have in mind?"

"I was just thinking of buying my parents a new house, just to make sure they're set for retirement."

"What a nice son," she said.

"Well, I hope I am a nice son, but this was Bobbie's idea to give me something else to distract me from the tedium of . . . um, I mean, well, she just thought it would feel good to do something for them."

"Got it. Just let me know the details when you figure them out, and we can transfer the money electronically wherever and whenever you need it."

"That would be great. I'll keep you posted. And thanks."

I waited until after Bobbie and I had dinner to call. I figured they'd both be home then.

"Mom, it's Adam."

"Adam! How's my little golfing sensation?"

"Just fine, Mom. I'm in Pennsylvania for the BMW Championship. Because they're one of my sponsors, I had dinner on Tuesday with all the BMW dealers in the region. My face still hurts from smiling so much. Then I had to sign swag for all of them and do individual photos. So it's been a busy week, even before the tournament started today."

"That sounds tough, honey. Are you holding up?"

"Mom, given what BMW pays me, I'd have been happy to give each dealer a foot rub, too. They've been very nice and very generous."

"Your father's here, so I'm going to put you on the speaker."

"Hi, Dad."

"Hey, Adam. I just caught some of today's highlights on the Golf Channel. Beautiful approach on fourteen. You really stuck that one tight."

"I don't actually remember that one, but I'll take your word for it," I replied. "Hey, I was wondering how you would feel if I bought you a new house? I seem to have a great deal of money, and I'd like to do something for you just in case the wheels fall off this golfing thing."

There was a pause on the end of the phone, but I could visualize them mouthing messages to one another in the silence.

"Um, Adam, well, that's quite an offer," Mom started. "But really, our house is paid off. We love it and we love the neighbourhood and the neighbours who come with it. I don't think we'd ever want to move. You should just keep your money and let it grow. You'll need it in retirement."

"I've earned quite a bit, you know," I replied.

"I know, and we're very proud of you, but we're just fine. We love this house. It has so many great memories."

"Okay, so not a house. How about that Tesla you've always wanted, Mom?"

She paused just a little too long. Within the week, a stunning blue Tesla Model S 100D with all-wheel drive was sitting in their driveway. She feigned anger until she slid behind the wheel. Perhaps I should have bought one for Dad, too. I didn't tell BMW about my purchase.

Not long after, Bobbie and I were flying via private jet back to San Francisco. It was Ryder Cup weekend, but since that pits American players against European players, we had a respite from the weekly PGA grind.

"For someone who is now a multimillionaire many times over, living in a nice condo, with a very nice BMW in the underground parking lot, you don't seem very happy," Bobbie said.

"I'm just fine. I'm just a little tired of playing golf every weekend."

"You did hear what just came out of your mouth, didn't you?"

"I know, I know. But the rest of the week is taken up with sponsor obligations and media opps. It never stops. I just want to spend some time on my writing," I whined.

"There'll be time for writing after this initial flurry. You're the flavour of the month right now."

"If only it lasted just a month," I replied. "I guess it would help if I lost a few tournaments."

"Your sponsors who are paying you a whack-load of dough wouldn't be very happy, though, now would they?"

I sighed.

"I know it seems bizarre to complain," I conceded.

"Hang on, let's get to the bottom of this. Most people with several million dollars in the bank and the virtual certainty of many more millions just for playing golf on the weekends would think it's a pretty good deal. I taught for thirty-five years, and those last two tourneys you won made you more money than I earned in my entire teaching career. Plus, I actually made more money on my cut of your winnings—thank you very much—in those two tournaments than I did in my last three years of teaching. We both seem to be scraping by," she said. "What's not to like?"

"But I'm doing nothing to earn this money."

"Wait a second. You're winning almost every tournament you play. It's customary to pay the purse to the player who wins."

"I get that. I'm just saying, I haven't really won those tournaments, my one-in-a-billion physical shell won them. I am not responsible. I have no agency, no control. I'm just along for the ride. There's no personal satisfaction when I'm putting out no effort to contribute to my success."

"Well, you've turned yourself into quite a competent putter."

"Whatever. I just find it kind of boring following my golf ball around, thinking about anything but golf, and just swinging the club over and over again all weekend long."

"Yes, but the point is you're swinging your club less often than every other golfer out there. So you win!"

"But I have no agency."

"But you have a Beemer, a condo, the full range of Montblanc fine writing instruments, and me. Isn't that a fair trade-off?"

"I guess it seems more than fair. But . . ."

Chapter 10

I'D BEEN THE number-one-ranked professional golfer in the world for nearly two years. And I wasn't very happy. (Yes, I know, how ungrateful can one guy be? But happiness and fulfillment are delicate flowers.) I was famous. I was wealthy. I was healthy, at least physically. I was loved by my parents, by legions of fans, and in a comradely way, I suppose, by Bobbie. Was I content? Was I fulfilled? Not so much. Was I barely able to gather myself each week to play in yet another four-day golf tournament, even if I won, which I usually did? Able? Yes. Barely? Absolutely. But I tried to disguise it from the players and fans on the Tour, and even from Bobbie, too, and put on the face one might expect to see on someone blessed beyond all reason.

I actually didn't mind most of the appearances and promotions my publicist arranged for me. I got to meet semi-normal and generally very nice people, and I usually wasn't holding a golf club at the time. It did require me to smile and be nice and humble, but I like to think the latter two came naturally, and I became quite adept at faking the first.

I was holding it together pretty well and still trying to write in whatever time I could squeeze from a very crammed schedule. It was difficult. But who in their right mind could complain about my life? Who would listen? Bobbie was still having the time of her life. She was doing what she'd always dreamed of doing, except I was taking the shots out on the course.

Then I faltered. It never would have happened had Charlotte Sampson, the senior ESPN documentary producer, not fallen ill that day. Susan Maddocks and I had finally agreed to an in-depth, two-hour-long, one-on-one interview with Charlotte for an ESPN special presentation. I'd studiously avoided serious interviews while doing enough on-the-course scrums and banal talk show appearances to satisfy Susan, my sponsors, and golf fans. But it seemed ESPN would not relent. Susan negotiated long and hard with Charlotte to keep some topics, like my love life (non-existent), family (private), and how I really felt about golf (grateful, bored, ambivalent at best, and resentful at worst), off the table. Susan believed we could avoid any more substantive media interviews if I did this one ESPN piece, so I agreed.

We had three hours booked late on a Tuesday afternoon just before Bobbie and I were to fly to Dubai for a promotional appearance. This little three-hour window was the only possible time we could slot in the ESPN interview for the next few months. The Summer Olympic Games were quickly approaching and there just wasn't another time.

As luck would have it, Charlotte ate shellfish of questionable provenance at a restaurant for lunch, and was down for the count by four p.m. Curt Hammersmith, another, less seasoned host, was whisked into makeup and soon sat in the chair in front of me as his mic cord was fed down the back of his shirt. With so many other interviews behind me, I wasn't exactly nervous. But this was not your standard four-minute post-victory scrum.

Curt held a clipboard with Charlotte's questions written on it. All might have been well had he stuck to the questions. But he loosened up, and about twenty minutes in, as so often happens when you start to get comfortable and relaxed, he went off-script.

"I got to say, it's been interesting hearing you tell the story of Bobbie Davenport and her measuring tape and Professor Gunnarsson's theory, but it really is extraordinary just how good a golfer you are. How does it feel to be the undisputed number-one golfer on the planet?"

Uh oh. It felt like he was poised to go down the flattery path. I hated the flattery path. I wanted to look for Susan Maddocks or Bobbie. I knew they were there on the set, but the lights were so blinding it was as if a dark curtain had descended, enclosing Curt and me in this little cocoon so bright I could almost see the bones in my hands. So I just kept my focus on Curt.

"I mean, you must wake up every day and do a little dance of joy," he said.

"Well, I'm very, very lucky to have been introduced to Professor Gunnarsson and his theory by my high school phys ed teacher, Bobbie Davenport, who is now my caddie. Obviously, I'm very fortunate."

"*Fortunate?* That sounds like the understatement of the millennium. What's it like to know with considerable certainty that on nearly every Sunday afternoon, you're going to collect another win, another trophy, and another cheque for one or two million dollars?"

Then I did look off towards where Bobbie and Susan had been standing before the interview started, though of course I could see nothing. I feared I might lose it. I wasn't sure I could keep up the false front if he continued in this vein.

"It doesn't happen quite like that. There are a lot of good golfers out there. Anyone can win each week. But I'm certainly lucky."

It was time for him to stop with the praise. I could feel myself approaching the edge.

"And you're humble, too. You are the very best at something that is very difficult. You've broken almost every course scoring record on the Tour. You've won every major at least once. The only time you don't win is when you don't play. It is astonishing and miraculous. It must be just so satisfying."

I felt my resolve buckle beneath the weight of his platitudes. This was exactly what I'd hoped to avoid, but it was too late, he'd gone too far. I couldn't restrain myself. I tried, but I couldn't stop.

"Satisfying?" I said, in a far too disdainful voice. "You think it's satisfying. I'm sorry to burst the idyllic bubble you've conjured up, but there are many words I'd use to describe my relationship with golf, and *satisfying* is not one of them, nor is *fulfilling*, *rewarding*, *fun*, *exciting*, *interesting*, *exhilarating*, or even *happy*. Am I fortunate? Lucky? Blessed? Well compensated? Set for life? Absolutely. But is it satisfying? No. Not by a long shot."

Curt actually pulled back in his chair as if I'd taken a swing at him. "What? I don't understand, and I'm not sure our viewers and golf fans around the world will either. You've been given a gift that has made you rich and famous. Shouldn't you be grateful?"

I sighed. "Of course I should be grateful, and I am grateful. But that's not the same as being fulfilled or happy. I know it's hard to fathom, but let me turn it around and try to make my point in a different way," I started, searching for a way to make myself clear. "Okay, I'm making up a story here to explain this better. Let's just say when you were born, you had a birthmark on your lower back. Yeah, that'll work. And for whatever quirk of fate, whatever against-all-odds luck, your birthmark was a perfect portrait of, um, hmmm, let's say Elvis. So you're born with this beautiful Elvis birthmark on your back."

Curt furrowed his brow in concentration.

"I'm not sure I understand," he said.

"Stay with me, Curt," I said. "And I don't mean this birthmark has a passing and crude resemblance to a face that might kind of look like Elvis in a certain light, from a certain angle. No. Your birthmark looks like a brilliant, crisp, clear, pristine portrait of Elvis."

I could feel myself getting into the story and picking up speed. Now that I'd started, I couldn't stop. I didn't want to stop.

"As you grow older, it grows even bigger and clearer and more inexplicable. Now, as the years pass, you decide you want to fulfill your dream and become, um, let's see, maybe an opera singer. Yes, you want to be an opera singer. You're no Pavarotti, but you're quite good and it's all you've ever wanted to do with your life. Instead, your birthmark is discovered and before long, you're on talk shows and TV specials, you're doing public appearances and getting an agent, you get an audience with the Pope, you appear at the Rock and Roll Hall of Fame, and the money is rolling in. Then you open an exhibition hall in Memphis, and Elvis fans line up around the block day in and day out to pay homage to the image of the King on your lower back. You're rich beyond your wildest dreams, and a big celebrity. But there's no time for opera singing. Do you understand what I'm saying, Curt?"

"Well, I understand that I've got all the money I'll ever need and some fame, too. I'm not sure I'd be complaining," he replied with a chuckle.

Time for round two. I could feel anger and relief coursing through me at the same time.

"Then you really don't understand," I said. "Do you know how the story ends?"

"I open a nationwide chain of Elvis Birthmark waffle houses?" He guffawed.

"No, and it's not funny," I said, shaking my head. "No, that's not what happens. Instead, you get so tired of it all, and so hollowed out from never pursuing your operatic dreams, that one day, almost in a trance, you have a plastic surgeon remove the birthmark. People are shocked and horrified, but you've stopped caring. Pretty soon you're singing in a local choir."

Curt seemed to recognize that he'd caused something special to happen. He sat back, squinted a little, nodded his head, and urged me on.

I could feel myself getting more animated and energized as I told the story. I was waving my arms around. I was leaning forward in a chair that wasn't really built for anything but sitting back, relaxed. It was getting hot under the lights. I suddenly noticed that my voice sounded a little different. It was in a slightly higher register, and it was taut and tense. I also spoke much louder than I should have. But I was in no mood to stop now that the dam had burst.

"Then you finally get some voice training. You land a part in the chorus of a community operetta, and you pull it off. You do quite well. Then you audition for a minor role in a minor opera, in a minor company in a minor city. You get the part and earn good reviews for it. Finally, you snag a leading role in a big touring production and you find yourself on the road, with positive reviews in each city. Then do you know what happens?"

I realized I was standing now. I could hear people whispering in the dark beyond the lights. Curt Hammersmith shook his head, his eyes wide.

"There's a scar on your back that you'll always have, but for the first time in your interesting, strange, and blessed life, you're actually happy and fulfilled. You finally understand what being happy really feels like. You're not at Carnegie Hall. You're not at the big Italian opera house—what's that called again? La Scala or something. You're not at the Met in New York. You're with a touring production in Spokane, or Edmonton, or North Tonawanda. And you're happy—happier than you've ever been."

You might think that I sat back down then, but I didn't. I just stood there over him.

"Now do you understand?"

"I'm not sure."

"Really? Have I been that obscure in my explanation?" I said in an even louder voice. "Look, you said it earlier. I've been given a gift. I didn't ask for it. I didn't earn it. I can't even practise, or I dishonour the gift. So when I'm out there, I'm just a body, swinging without thinking, without working, without even understanding. I've done nothing. It's just my body. So your praise is misplaced when you pile it on for something I literally have had no role in earning. I am a vessel, an empty vessel. I didn't become the best golfer on the planet, as you so artfully put it, by endless study, hours of practice, and a deep commitment to excellence, where I sacrificed everything else in my life to achieve this lofty goal. No. Now, that would have been satisfying. No. There was none of that. I was born with legs, arms, and a torso that are freakishly well suited to golf. If I practise, I get worse. If I think too hard on the course, I get worse. If I make any effort at all to get better, I get worse. I don't deserve praise and accolades for my golfing prowess any more than you deserve praise for having nice, thick hair, a handsome face, and a square jawline. We both simply inherited our good fortune."

I was breathing hard as I headed for the finish line. It started to dawn on me that I'd gone completely off the rails. But you know what? I'd stopped caring.

"And eventually what has earned me riches and fame and all manner of worldly goods, well, it becomes a burden. I know, I know. It sounds almost contemptible to complain about such a gift. But hear me out. You're taught from a very early age to work hard for what you want, for what you love, to put out the effort and never give up, and maybe, just maybe, success will find you. And when it does, that satisfaction feels so good because you are solely, or at least largely, responsible for what you've been able to achieve. That, to me, is the story of a good life well lived. That is happiness. That is rewarding, fulfilling, and satisfying. That's the story of an opera singer, or maybe a writer. But that is not my story as a golfer."

With that, I walked off the set, pulling off my microphone and battery pack as I headed for the door.

The limo was outside the loading dock, waiting to take Bobbie and me to the airport.

"What the hell just happened?" Susan asked as the three of us climbed in. "Are you all right?"

"I'm not sure. I think so. I feel a lot lighter," I said. "But I'm really sorry. It was not the interview I was expecting after all our discussions with Charlotte. He just pushed the wrong buttons and I kind of floated out of myself. I'm sorry."

"And that birthmark story, where did that come from?"

"That was a clumsy and feeble attempt at metaphor, or at least an analogy," I replied.

"That, young Adam, sounded to me like a fable with a very clear moral," Bobbie said. "I didn't realize it had come to this. Are you really that miserable?" She looked very concerned.

"No, I'm not miserable. I'm just not happy, and there's no time to do what makes me happy," I said. "Sorry, I'm just a little overwhelmed right now. Maybe it's the looming Olympics. I don't know."

"Just try to relax, and don't do any interviews when you're in Dubai," Susan said. "I'll see if I can talk Charlotte into scrapping the interview, but I'm not hopeful. She knows she holds gold in those last ten minutes, even if she wasn't in the host's chair."

Bobbie was quieter on the flight than she usually was. Come to think of it, she'd seemed a little subdued for the last week or so. We were seated in our own individual pods on the first-class upper deck of the quite amazing Airbus A380. But we'd flown that way before, and she would always hover around for at least the first part of the flight and we'd talk about stuff. That night, she begged off, claiming she was a bit drained.

Susan had set up the Dubai promotion for Nike. I'd be driving Nike golf balls from the roof of the Burj Al Arab. You know the building. It's the one shaped like a billowing sail, perched right on the edge of the Arabian Gulf. It's one of the tallest hotels in the world, just a bit shorter than the Empire State Building. Conveniently, we were also staying in the Burj Al Arab overnight before returning to L.A. the next afternoon.

A small, raised platform had been built in the middle of the circular helipad on top of the hotel. We were instructed to stay away from the edge and the very low white railing that wouldn't stop a chihuahua from leaping over. When I ventured closer to the railing for a look down to the water, I felt a little queasy.

There were two stages of this shoot. First, the cameras would be set up on the helipad and they'd shoot me driving balls off the platform from various angles. They expected I'd be out there swinging for about forty-five minutes to get what they needed in video and stills. The second part involved a helicopter. The director, photographer, and videographer would take all their equipment, dash to a local helipad, jump into a chopper, and return for aerial shots of me hitting more balls. In this era, you really needed the de rigueur drone or chopper shots. The director didn't yet trust drones, hence the chopper. They would give me instructions via radio. Bobbie had been seconded to handle the walkie-talkie and relay directions to me.

Did I mention that it was about 270 degrees out there as we stood discussing the shoot, fully exposed on the helipad/driving platform? Now I understood why there were four changes of clothes, all the very same carefully chosen Nike ensemble, waiting in my hotel suite. It only took the makeup person about ten minutes to get me camera-ready. That made me feel a little better. Then we were outside in the blazing sun again. They were right. The shoot did take about forty-five minutes, and two of my four Nike outfits. It was kind of cool seeing the balls rocket into the sky and arc into the sparkling blue Arabian Sea below. But man, it was sweltering.

As the shoot team packed up their equipment from the first stage, the rest of us retreated to the air-conditioned bar— closed down for the shoot—to cool off and rehydrate. Bobbie had a beer, and I had an enormous glass of water and a Coke.

"I hope the aerial part doesn't take as long," Bobbie said as we sipped our drinks. "That many drives in quick succession seems dangerously close to practising. Professor Gunnarsson would not be happy."

"I'll try not to pick up any bad habits," I replied. "Don't worry, I'm not even thinking out there."

"That's my lad," she replied. "I think this promo is a tad too close to the Olympics. I'm not sure Susan should have booked it." She bowed her head and looked tired.

"Are you okay, Bobbie? You seem, I don't know, a little quiet lately."

"Just a little preoccupied, son," she replied with a weak smile. "Between the Olympics and a lovely blue vintage OMAS 360 with a cursive italic nib I've been chasing on eBay, there's a lot going on."

I nodded but decided not to push her any further.

The shooters and the director hustled by and said they'd be airborne and in position in about forty minutes. They'd radio when they were approaching.

After I'd changed clothes again, the makeup artist worked me over one last time. Her challenge was to keep me from looking as if there were rivulets of perspiration cascading down my face, when in fact there were rivulets of perspiration cascading down my face. The AC had me feeling just about back to normal by that stage. About fifteen minutes later, the security guard who'd been with us on set approached us.

"Okay, the director has just called on the radio to say they are earlier than expected and that we should go back up," he said.

"I didn't hear that on my radio," Bobbie said.

"Yes, we changed the frequency so we wouldn't disturb you," the guard explained. "The director also said that I should only bring you two outside for the helicopter shots. He doesn't want others with us to get in the way of the photos and video, yes?"

Bobbie nodded. "I guess that makes sense," she said.

"Fine with us," I replied.

"Okay. We should go now," he said.

The guard led us up the staircase to the door. He waved us through and back out onto the helipad, where my clubs awaited me. Then he locked the door from the outside, pulled an iron bar from behind a large planter, and pushed it through the double door handles. I thought that was kind of odd, and looked at him.

"We take your security very seriously, sir. Especially when you are here almost by yourself," he said, with a reassuring smile.

A couple of minutes later, I was giving my driver a few easy swings while Bobbie looked on. Then suddenly she looked past me with a puzzled expression on her face. I turned and saw the guard reach under a tarpaulin rolled up near the door. In what seemed like slow motion, he pulled out a rather powerful-looking rifle.

"Hey, what's going on?" Bobbie shouted as she moved over to where I stood.

He turned with the gun and trained it on us. He looked scared. He was bobbing from foot to foot and aiming the gun, first at me and then at Bobbie.

"You both shut up! No speaking! Now throw your phones and that radio over to me. Slowly! Do it!"

My heart rate skyrocketed. I felt my knees trembling. I looked at Bobbie.

"It's okay, son," she whispered. "Let's stay calm. Our friend is clearly shaking in his drawers, but we'd better do what he says."

She then looked at the guard.

"Just relax. We'll do what you say. Just be careful, please."

We slowly pulled our phones and Bobbie's radio out of our pockets and slid them towards him along the rooftop. He kicked them further away, towards the railing. He then reached into his jacket, struggling a bit to balance the gun with one hand. He pulled out two plastic tie-wraps and tossed them to us.

"Put these on each other's wrists. Quickly. Quickly! Do it now!" he screamed.

He kept sneaking glances up the coast, out into the distance.

Bobbie slipped the tie-wrap around my wrists and pulled it snug. Then I did the same for her. It was a little harder with my wrists already constrained, but we managed.

"Do not play with me!" he shouted. "Pull them tighter. I must see the skin being pinched. Do it!"

We tightened one another's tie-wraps so that we were both in some discomfort.

"See, it's cutting into my skin," Bobbie said, lifting her arms so he could see.

"Me, too," I said, mimicking Bobbie's moves.

"Okay, okay. Sit down on the floor over there so I can see you, and do not move."

Bobbie and I followed his orders and sat next to one another on the rooftop helipad, leaning against the wooden platform from which I was supposed to be driving golf balls. The guard —I guess it's safe to say he wasn't actually a guard—moved to the far edge of the helipad and, while still pointing that big gun at us, scanned the horizon and checked his watch.

"What's he looking for?" I whispered to Bobbie. "And why does he keep checking his watch?"

"Let's leave that question alone, shall we? We might not like the answer."

The guard continued to survey the clouds while checking his watch and aiming that big gun our way.

Bobbie leaned towards me.

"That, young Adam, is an AK-47," Bobbie said. "I'm sure you already know this, but the Kalashnikov, as it's affectionately known, was designed in 1947. 1947! It's older than I am!"

I tried to ignore her little assault rifle treatise, but after years alongside Bobbie, I knew resistance was futile. Oblivious, she prattled on with her little biography of a firearm.

"I mean, that weapon has played a defining role in so many revolutions across the last seventy-five years. It deserves credit and blame, in nearly equal measure, for most of the coups, terrorist acts, territorial skirmishes, insurgencies, and armed conflicts from one side of the globe to the other!"

"Bobbie," I whispered.

"A few years ago, I read a fascinating account of the Kalashnikov's pivotal place in world history, and . . ."

"Bobbie," I said a little louder.

". . . it would not be an exaggeration to say that governments were toppled and born, wars were won and lost, and national borders were drawn and redrawn, all on the trigger of the same gun that guy standing in front of us is holding right now."

"Bobbie!" I snapped in a voice that quite accurately reflected just how freaked out I was at that moment.

"What?" She looked genuinely puzzled.

"Bobbie, that's all very fascinating—actually, at this precise moment, it's really not—and I'd be pumped to learn more about this historically significant firearm were it not for the complicating fact that he's pointing it directly at us . . . on purpose . . . with malevolent intent and little chance of missing us should he decide to squeeze off a burst."

Bobbie fell silent for a moment, but not nearly long enough. "But look how the sun glints off it," she continued after a moment, shaking her head. The faraway expression on her face seemed somewhere between admiration and awe. "Quite stunning."

I lifted my eyes to the man standing about thirty metres away. He wore an expression that balanced rage and anxiety on a knife edge while brandishing what I now knew to be an internationally celebrated assault rifle.

"Yeah, and look how angry he is," I replied. "Quite frightening."

While his gun was pointed our way, his eyes were not. He just kept staring into the clouds.

Bobbie ignored me and turned to scan the horizon.

"Man, what a view from up here."

By this time, she seemed completely at ease. I was not. I was terrified—all-in, flat-out, and full-on. On the fear spectrum, I situated myself somewhere well past freaking and heading fast to fainting. If I knew of a stronger word than terrified, believe me, I'd be trotting it out right about now.

"Aren't you scared?" I asked.

"Quite," she replied. "But so is our friend over there."

I looked over at Mr. Kalashnikov, who kept his weapon trained on us while taking furtive glances into the sky and tilting his head like a dog hearing a sound we could not. Bobbie and I sat next to each other with our backs literally, and in every other sense of the word, against the wall.

"These things are so much more effective than handcuffs," Bobbie offered, examining the plastic tie-wrap that bound her wrists. The one that secured mine was too tight and dug into my skin. It hurt.

"I mean, they're strong, light, easy to carry, and just as effective as overbuilt steel cuffs against the modest power of the human forearm," Bobbie continued. "Plus, the pièce de résistance, there's no key to lose. Brilliant!"

She actually chuckled as she said "brilliant." I'm not kidding. With a bad man training an assault rifle on us, she chuckled. I felt like I might pass out, but Bobbie didn't notice. She continued her enthusiastic, even fawning, dissertation on the advances in personal restraint embodied in the lowly plastic tie-wrap, but the sound of my own pounding heart nearly drowned her out. Yes, I know. I plead guilty to the charge of cliché. I'm a writer—or at least I want to be a writer—so I'm programmed to hate clichés. But sometimes they're clichés for a reason. I had never really believed that old adage—that old cliché—that your life actually passes before your eyes in moments of dire peril, in that little space that exists between passed out and passed on. But you know what? It's true. Perfect memory fragments, intact, whole, pristine, flying at you almost faster than you can take them in. And with more detail than you'd ever recall without the catalyst of a life-threatening event. It's true. It's all true.

We heard it before we saw it. A helicopter. No doubt heading our way.

"Okay, now that is not a positive development," Bobbie said.

The sound of the chopper grew. Somehow, I knew it didn't carry the director, photographer, and videographer for our fun little promotion. Bobbie and I followed the chopper with our eyes as it grew from a speck to, well, to a full-sized helicopter. The guard still had the famous firearm aimed in our general direction, but he seemed more focused on the chopper as it approached and hovered above us. He motioned to the pilot to land the helicopter closer to the edge because of the wooden platform. We were buffeted by the downdraft of the rotor blades, but it actually provided some welcome relief from the oppressive heat. The noise verged on deafening. Bobbie suddenly leaned over until her mouth was almost touching my ear.

"Two things," she shouted.

I could actually feel the warm currents of her breath.

"First, in my hotel room, there's a big brown envelope in my suitcase. You must read what's inside."

"What? Why? I don't get it."

She shook her head. "There's no time to explain. Just read it. Second, if you make it through the next few minutes, promise me you'll stop living my dream and start living yours."

"What are you talking about?" I asked. "What are you doing, Bobbie?"

"Just promise me!" she shouted above the engine noise. I nodded but had no idea what was happening. Then she watched and waited until the guard turned slightly away from us and was clearly focused on the chopper. He was using one hand to communicate with the pilot as the helicopter hovered just above us. Then Bobbie pushed herself to her feet and started running.

"Hey! Wait! Don't. Bobbie!" I shouted. But she was gone.

She was surprisingly fast for a larger, stocky woman with chronic back issues. I wanted to push myself to my feet, but felt paralyzed watching Bobbie as she sprinted across the rooftop towards the guard.

He turned too late. She was already halfway to him. He looked terrified and opened his mouth, but the roar of the chopper swallowed his shout. Then I watched as he raised the rifle. There was a pop and a flash from the muzzle. Bobbie's left shoulder snapped back and something hit the wood above my head. Splinters landed in my lap. I ducked but kept my eyes on Bobbie. He'd winged her, but she was moving too fast and carrying too much momentum for it to matter much. She hit him squarely at full speed, just like she'd taught our high school defensive linemen to do when sacking the quarterback. Even with the impact, he still hung on to the rifle, but it was now aimed harmlessly out to sea. They were both moving as a single unit now. I was on my feet by then.

It was hard to process what happened next. It was like a mirage shimmering in the heat's haze. They both just disappeared over the railing. They were gone in an instant.

My heart felt like it stopped. My mind emptied. I realized I was moving towards the chopper. I could see the panic in the pilot's eyes through the windscreen. Something moved me then. Bobbie had acted. I had to as well, or I'd regret it later. I ran to my golf bag a few feet away and pulled out a four-iron. Even with my hands tie-wrapped together, I was still able to swing the club around my head and launch it at the chopper. It hit the windscreen club-head first, and bounced off harmlessly. But the pilot reacted as if he'd been hit by an Exocet missile. He jerked the controls and wobbled violently in the air. Anger swept through me as I realized that Bobbie was probably gone, I mean really gone. I just started hurling club after club. One hit the rotor and made a big noise, but didn't seem to do much damage. As rage consumed me, I was oblivious to any danger I was in and kept chucking golf clubs at the chopper. I think the pilot had had enough. He turned in the air, the tail rotor heading my way. He started to climb away from the building but I grabbed one last club, I think it might have been my pitching wedge, and threw it at the helicopter.

My wedge hit the tail rotor and made a sickening metallic grinding sound. A flash of flame shot from the tail and smoke billowed. The helicopter immediately began rotating. With each turn, I could see the pilot frantically trying to regain control. The tail bounced off the railing and the chopper somehow cleared the building. But it was no longer going up. It almost gently pirouetted down through the air, leaving a corkscrew of smoke in its wake, until it dipped out of my view. I moved closer to the railing to track the chopper's fall. I was suddenly aware of people screaming below as they watched the crash unfold. When the turning, burning helicopter hit the water, it was no longer such a gentle descent. It hit the waves upright, as if landing, but at much too high a speed. The sound reached me a second after the impact. There was no explosion. This was not a movie. The chopper turned on its side as the blades dug into the waves and snapped off. Then it was quiet as what remained of the helicopter bobbed in the sea.

My brain came back online. Maybe Bobbie's speed had carried the guard and her far enough out away from the building to hit the water. Could you survive a fall from that height into water? I rushed the rest of the way to the rail and scanned the sea below. I saw nothing. Then I looked directly below me. They hadn't made it nearly far enough out to reach the sea. They never could have. I could see their bodies on the ground, with little space between them. In the movies, the victims of such falls always have their limbs arrayed at weird angles. Not so here. Bobbie and the guard both looked like they might just be grabbing a quick nap. But even in my state, I knew neither would be waking up.

In the near silence, I could hear my own breathing and another noise, almost a moaning, that I realized was coming from me. I saw people below rushing towards Bobbie and the guard. Some of them looked up, but I couldn't even muster the resolve to wave. I felt so drained that I could barely move. Somehow, I lurched over to where my cellphone had come to rest on the roof. Despite my secured wrists, I managed to dial 911, without even knowing if it would work in Dubai. It did. I don't remember what I said, but it was enough. Then I sat back down and lowered my head between my knees to fight off the nausea that had come over me. It didn't work. I threw up and cried at the same time. It was so hot. I thought I might pass out. I knew Bobbie was gone. But it was so hard to accept that I had to remind myself every few seconds that it had really happened. That she had taken the guard over the rail to save me. Once, I even went back to the edge of the roof to confirm her body was still there below me. Then I guess I just curled up next to the rail in the heat and blubbered. I'm told that's how they found me fifteen minutes later when Dubai's version of a SWAT team burst onto the rooftop from a fire escape stair-well. Another chopper approached, circled briefly, and then departed. I learned later it was the director and videographer, ready to start the second stage of our little promotion.

IT TOOK NEARLY five hours before they let me back into my hotel room. It was very strange being there by myself, espe-cially because Bobbie and I had already opened the doors connecting our two adjoining suites. I knew what I had to do then, but I didn't rush. I didn't know what I'd find, so I was careful, and deliberate, and scared. While I had trouble remem-bering everything that had unfolded on the roof high over the Arabian Sea, I recalled my last exchange with Bobbie Davenport word for word.

I followed her rooftop instructions, even though it felt like such an invasion of privacy to be looking through her suitcase. I found the envelope. *Princess Margaret Hospital* was printed in the upper left-hand corner. I opened it. My fingers were trembling. To be honest, all of me was trembling. I just wasn't sure whether it was leftover stress and fear from the roof or new anxiety from what I held in my hands. The printed form looked so benign, but across the top it read *MRI Results Report*. Then I read the word. *Glioblastoma*. Just one word. *Glioblastoma*. I was sure I'd heard it before. I pulled out my iPhone, and Google helped jog my memory. A few years before, Gord Downie, the lead singer of the Tragically Hip, one of Canada's most popular rock bands, had endured a long, almost noble, and terribly wrenching public decline after his diagnosis with glioblastoma. The medical authorities on the Internet, whom we all seem to trust implicitly, apparently agreed on at least one aspect of this aggressive and often inoperable form of brain cancer: it was terminal.

This prognosis was reinforced by a brochure I also found in the envelope. It bore the cheery title *Medical Assistance in Dying and End-of-Life Decisions*. Finally, to tie it all up into a nice, neat little package of grief, Bobbie's will was among the papers she'd gathered in one place. It was a simple will leaving all her worldly possessions to a number of charities that supported writers and public libraries in Canada. Such a Bobbie thing to do. I should also note that I was named as her executor. I guess I shouldn't have been surprised.

That night, I slept like a baby. In other words, I woke up every two hours or so and cried for a while. By the morning, all the questions that had swirled in my head about Bobbie's rooftop charge were answered. It all fell into place. It all made sense to me. Bobbie would have deplored a slow and steady deterioration, likely accompanied by pain, not to mention the memory loss, confusion, and reduced brain function. She'd have never accepted that. What unfolded atop the Burj Al Arab was the Hollywood way out. It was perfect. It was Bobbie saving us both.

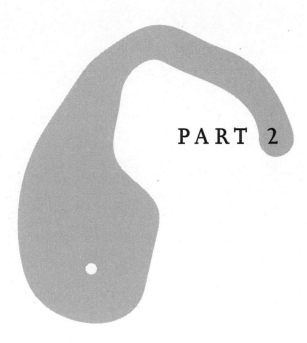

PART 2

Chapter 11

THE AUTHORITIES FIGURED it out pretty quickly, calling it a botched commercial kidnapping. It wasn't about religion, nationalism, ideology, terrorism, or territory. It was just about money. I guess I was a good target, given how much money I had amassed in so short a time. The pilot suffered only minor injuries in the forced sea landing and confessed quickly and completely. His co-conspirator, the Kalashnikov-wielding security guard who was supposed to protect us, died after his unscheduled flight on Air Bobbie. According to the chopper pilot, the plan had been to kidnap Bobbie and me, then kill Bobbie to convince me of their seriousness, and finally have me buy my own survival for a $10 million e-transfer. It would have worked, too, if they'd managed to get us onto the chopper and off that roof.

Finally, after another morning of repetitive meetings with the police, I flew to Toronto on a private jet arranged by the president of the United Arab Emirates and flown by the most experienced pilots in their air force. My parents had been ready to fly directly to Dubai after the story broke, but I persuaded them that I was okay to make the flight home alone. I'm not sure that was true, but I just wanted to get out of there. I wrote Bobbie's obit on the plane using the Conway Stewart Wellington she'd given me. There was no one else to do it. Bobbie's parents had passed on several years earlier and she had no siblings, so it fell to me. I was simultaneously honoured and anxious, and though the task was difficult, they were some of the most satisfying sentences I have ever written. I made sure Bobbie Davenport was seen as the hero she truly was. But everyone would know that soon enough, without the obit. The CCTV cameras from multiple rooftop angles provided all the dramatic and traumatic footage needed to secure Bobbie's place in the heroism hall of fame. When I was still in mid-flight, the sequence began playing endlessly on television and popping up everywhere online. I didn't need to watch it. I know what happened. I was there.

With the onboard Internet service, I also managed, via a series of emails, to arrange for a memorial service in her honour at Timothy Eaton, one of the largest churches in Toronto. I didn't think she was religious. We'd never really discussed it, so it was quite possible she was an atheist. But holding a memorial service in a big church was not about piety and devotion. It just seemed an appropriate and convenient location for a gathering to honour her memory.

They met me at Toronto's Pearson airport. With Dad at the wheel, my mother held on to me in the back of the Tesla all the way home. I've never felt safer and more secure than I did during that week or so at home with my family. For that brief respite, it was almost as if the last seven years, and the extraordinary events they had brought with them, had never happened. My parents wanted me to talk to a therapist or counsellor to make sure I processed and dealt with the grief driven by what unfolded on the roof of the Burj Al Arab. I didn't mind the idea in principle, but I managed to persuade them that it was all still too fresh. That I needed some distance and perspective before professional help would really be beneficial. And no, I hadn't processed and dealt with it all yet. I knew that much. But I had plans that could not be delayed.

A few days later, the church was packed. I had no idea so many people would come. Though Bobbie Davenport didn't have any living direct family, there was no shortage of students, colleagues, and friends attending her memorial service. A sizable contingent from the Ladies' Golf Club of Toronto was there, including Duke, who wept from the time he entered the church to the time he slipped out the door a few minutes before the benediction. I was very happy to see several of Bobbie's fellow PGA caddies and even a few Tour players in the church paying their respects. Even the commissioner of the PGA attended. Of course, Lisa Griffiths and Susan Maddocks both dropped everything to be there.

Professor Gunnarsson was not able to make the long flight from Australia in time for the service, but he did call me and express his regret at Bobbie's passing. I was impressed with the level of empathy he was somehow able to muster given his filter-free tendencies.

Three television satellite trucks were stationed in the parking lot, but with Susan's help, I managed to avoid doing any media interviews and instead issued a prepared statement that would have to suffice for the time being.

I didn't see her until I stood at the lectern at the front of the church for my remarks. She sat several rows back, right on the centre aisle. Alli was with her parents and gazed at me with such sympathy, support, and strength that I looked nowhere else until I was finished my piece. As it turned out, I didn't need my notes. I just needed the expression on Alli's face. With my eyes on hers, and a couple of deep breaths, I started.

"Bobbie would have been thrilled that so many of you are here today. But let's face it, she would have hated the idea of an event like this to celebrate her life. Well, too bad, Bobbie, we're doing it anyway."

The line earned a few chuckles from the assembly and that calmed me down a bit more.

"Bobbie Davenport was my teacher, my coach, my counsellor, my caddie, and most of all, my friend. An obscure Scandinavian kinesiology journal and a tape measure brought us together in the fall of 2013 and altered both our lives forever. Shortly after we first met, we discovered a few shared interests. We both believed that writing, storytelling, literature, and the power of words on the page could change the world. We both seemed to have been blessed with more than our fair share of curiosity. And on a smaller scale, our constantly inky fingers betrayed a common fascination with the esoteric world of fountain pens. Strange as it seems, golf wasn't one of those shared interests, though Bobbie Davenport was an NCAA star at Stanford and a perennial club champion at her beloved Ladies' Golf Club of Toronto. A wonky back kept her from greater golf glory, but she never lost her love for the game, even if I never quite gained mine."

I paused for a moment and looked out at the crowd. It had grown so quiet, I wasn't sure they were all still there. They were, all looking up at me. I breathed deeply to control the grief that sometimes distorted my voice.

"Yes, I confess, I still don't love the game of golf, though I know that sounds churlish and ungrateful in the face of what it has given me. My DNA bestowed the unlikely gift of a body that was almost perfectly suited for the game. But if I'm honest, neither my heart nor my head was similarly inclined, and they likely never will be. Not only did Bobbie Davenport, with the help of Professor Ingemar Gunnarsson, make the discovery that I just might have a future in golf, but she was there the whole way to help me seize it. You see, Bobbie Davenport was also a brilliant conversationalist—and that was a blessing. Paradoxically, she knew very well that the key to our success on the course was keeping my mind as far away from golf as possible. So we talked . . . a lot . . . about anything and everything. We talked our way around every course I ever played. I can't begin to tell you the broad range of topics that occupied us during tournaments. I don't know anyone else who could have carried me through all those rounds simply through the power of conversation. After all, as I have observed many times, golf is a game that takes quite a long time to play. Bobbie Davenport made the hours slip by, and I will be forever grateful."

I prattled on for another ten minutes or so and remember very little of it. I never mentioned the glioblastoma diagnosis. I just didn't think it was my place to reveal it. I do recall struggling to maintain my composure at a few points, but I managed to carry on, even if my voice quavered now and then. Several others spoke with great affection, telling stories from Bobbie's collegiate golfing days, her amazing reign at the Ladies'

Golf Club of Toronto, her teaching career, and her time with me on the Tour. I remember more of those remarks than I do of my own. I had no idea where I was on the classic journey through the stages of grief. But it felt like Bobbie's memorial pushed me at least a few more steps along the path.

Alli found me at the reception in the church auditorium afterwards. She enfolded me in her arms and just held me. She said nothing until the hug had gone on for quite some time. I almost lost it, but squeezed my eyes tight to keep them dry. Even when we pulled apart, she held on to my hands.

"Adam, I know nothing I can say will change anything, but I'm so sorry for everything. For what happened to Ms. Davenport. For what happened to you on that roof. It just seems unreal. It feels like a miracle you're standing here in front of me."

We talked for a bit. She told me she was heading into her second year of the master's program in creative writing at the University of Toronto. Good for her. It was wonderful and powerful to see her again and to be so close to her after so long. It felt like no time had passed. It felt like high school again. But it wasn't.

YOU MIGHT THINK I'd have withdrawn from the Olympics under the circumstances. No one would have blamed me— no one except perhaps Bobbie. She'd been so pumped when golf was declared an Olympic sport for the Rio games in 2016.

Only Augusta and the Masters meant more to her, and not by much. Our plan had been to fly to Tokyo early to get acclimated to the time change and play a few practice rounds on the Olympic course. So I went on my own. No one could talk me out of it. Not my parents, not Susan Maddocks, not Lisa Griffiths. No one. When I refused to reconsider, it was strongly recommended that my family accompany me to Tokyo to provide the support I needed so soon after my traumatic experience high above the Arabian Sea. But I said no, several times. I can't really explain why. I claimed they would be a distraction, that I really needed to focus, that I wanted to follow the plan Bobbie and I had carefully laid out, even if Bobbie wasn't there. I must have been persuasive, because eventually everybody backed off and I was permitted to go by myself.

It may sound like I've descended into the realm of greeting card prose, but I went to Tokyo for Bobbie. I suppose I was there to finish our journey, partly for me but mostly for her. She'd have never forgiven me if I'd missed this perhaps once-in-a-lifetime Olympic opportunity. Obviously, my parents were concerned about me going on my own, but I promised to check in with them every day. Additional security was assigned to me, beyond what other high-profile athletes were given. As well, I had round-the-clock access to the team's sports psychologist in case I decided to start processing Bobbie's loss when I was in Tokyo. Finally, the Canadian Olympic Committee assigned a "handler" just for me, to take care of anything I needed, twenty-four hours a day. A young staffer at the COC, Kerry Copeland, drew the short straw.

I had many offers from PGA caddies who had befriended and respected Bobbie to be on the bag for me in Tokyo. But I didn't want a new caddie. If Bobbie couldn't walk the course with me, I wanted to walk it alone. I carried my own bag on the PGA Tour anyway, with Bobbie always walking next to me. But the rules approved by the International Olympic Committee stated that "all athletes in the Olympic Games shall employ caddies for all practice and competition rounds."

Eventually a compromise was reached. I needed an official caddie, but I could carry my own bag. Kerry Copeland would pull double duty and serve as my caddie as well as my "handler." I briefed her when we met at Canada House shortly after my arrival in the Japanese capital.

My goal was to know the course very, very well by the time the Olympic tournament got underway. Course knowledge would ease my club selection decisions during the tournament now that I'd be without Bobbie's counsel for the first time in my golfing life. I played a few practice rounds at the Olympic venue, the Kasumigaseki Country Club, and walked it several more times without swinging a club. Kerry accompanied me each time and we practised her caddying skills as we went. I asked her to walk close enough to me to suggest she was my caddie, but not so close that she was a distraction. She took it well. She was a fast learner and never said a word to me on the course unless I said something to her.

The only thing I didn't practise during those pre-tournament rounds was talking to Bobbie. My plan was to picture her next to me on the course and to talk to her, in my mind, just as I would were she actually there. I had compiled a long list of topics to carry me through seventy-two holes of Olympic golf and I didn't want to squander them on my practice rounds.

The long days before the tournament left me tired and sad, though I didn't cry. I couldn't stop thinking about Dubai and Bobbie's heroic act. I couldn't stop thinking about what she'd said to me atop the Burj Al Arab. I couldn't stop thinking about how much she would have loved this Olympic experience. Once in a while I also thought about how stupid it was to be driving golf balls into the Arabian Sea from the roof of a luxury hotel.

Somehow, I made it through to the Thursday in the second week of the Games. Kerry performed her faux-caddie role to perfection. She followed instructions well and stayed far enough away so it worked for me and close enough so it worked for the Olympic officials. The commentators initially focused on our unorthodox approach, but after the first day it just became the norm. Kerry kept her eyes focused on me at all times and sustained the agreed-upon perimeter. She stood very still when I was shooting, with her hands behind her back, looking more like a Wimbledon ball girl than an Olympic golf caddie. Whenever I looked at her, she always responded in the same way. She would offer the first very faint traces of a smile and nod her head once, as though she were saying, You got this. It seemed to work.

I was nervous as the first round got underway. I played with Byeong Hun An from Korea and Nicolas Colsaerts from Belgium. I'd played with Nicolas once or twice before, but never with An. I was talking to Bobbie in my head as I lined up my drive on the first tee. I was silently expounding on my theory of fiction as the ideal vehicle for truth-telling, even better than creative non-fiction. It was a discussion we'd had often, so I could also hear in my mind her responses. It was kind of like watching reruns of shows I'd seen before. In the middle of this, I knocked a solid drive down the right side of the fairway, straight and true. And I was off.

When I watched the TV highlights in my room that night, I was surprised to see my lips moving as I lined up shots later in the round. Clearly my plan to keep my conversations with Bobbie completely inside my own cranium had eventually fallen apart. It looked like I was in the middle of a deep discussion with someone just outside of the TV camera's frame. Well, in fact, I *was* in a deep discussion at the time, and that's what got me around the course at four under par and near the top of the leaderboard.

I don't want to dwell on the remaining rounds themselves. I find it boring enough to play eighteen holes of golf. Describing the whole proceeding is even more mind-numbing. Suffice it to say, the combination of Kerry's silent support from a distance and Bobbie's spiritual presence from an even greater distance just seemed to work. It certainly wasn't the same as having Bobbie there in the flesh, as it were, but we adapted.

At the end of the fourth and final round, as my par putt disappeared into the hole, Kerry's cool and calm demeanour dissolved and she jumped into my arms. I was so shocked I almost dropped her. Without getting maudlin, when I stood at attention to the strains of "O Canada," the Olympic weight no longer on my shoulders but now around my neck, I cried. Many, even most, gold medallists cry on the podium. But mine weren't tears of joy, or national pride, or personal achievement. By the time the last notes of the national anthem died away, I knew what I had to do.

On the Monday morning after I returned to Toronto from Tokyo, Susan organized a jam-packed news conference at the King Edward Hotel. She'd spent the previous week or so dealing with my sponsors and calming them down. She told them my gold medal made their contracts with me even more valuable and that we intended to honour every clause in our agreements with them. Several of them wanted extensions to the terms of our contracts, but I was adamant. Susan was disappointed, as any agent would be in similar circumstances, but she understood. I'd declined all of the post-Olympic celebratory events hosted by the federal government and Canadian Olympic sponsors as graciously as I could. Almost everyone seemed to understand, even if I wasn't yet sure I did. Don't get me wrong. I was certain of my decision. I just wasn't sure I could explain why.

Just before the news conference was to start, my cellphone chirped.

"Hello?"

"Adam, I think you are being an idiot. You just won the Olympic gold medal. Please do not do this."

"Professor Gunnarsson, so you obviously got my message," I said. "I'm sorry I couldn't reach you directly. Your office said you were at a conference."

"You have so much more to do, so much more fame to gain, so much more money to make. Do not do this. It defies logic."

"I never really wanted the fame, at least not this way. And I've already socked away quite a bit of money and more is on the way, at least until my endorsement deals expire. I mean, how much money do I really need?"

"As much as you can get."

"I'm sorry, professor, but my mind is made up. Bobbie agrees with me, or rather, agreed with me, and helped me see the light," I said, as I noticed Susan frantically signalling me.

"Oh, sorry, professor, but I really have to go now. We'll talk again. Bye for now."

"Okay, it's time," Susan said when I reached her in the small anteroom. "Are you sure about this? Because I can shut this whole thing down right now."

"Thank you for everything, Susan, but I'm as sure about this as I've been about anything in my relatively short life."

She smiled and nodded. "I know you are," she replied. "Okay, you're on your own up there until you finish your statement, and then I'll take the podium to direct the Q&A. Now, don't forget to make eye contact, particularly with the cameras on the risers at the back of the room. Your real audience is watching through those lenses. Be yourself and don't get drawn off track. This is a short and simple story, so keep it short and simple."

"Got it."

When she opened the door, I walked to the skirted table at the front of the room and sat behind the single microphone. I'd made notes and they were folded in my pocket. I knew I wouldn't need them. I was calm, even serene. That's how I knew I was doing the right thing.

"Thank you all for coming on short notice, and I thank my agent, Susan Maddocks, for making all this happen this morning. Some of you may have already guessed what this is all about, but to make it official, I'm here to announce that I am giving up professional golf as of this moment. The Olympic Games was my final tournament."

There was no gasp from the reporters. They'd put it all together before I even opened my mouth. That's their job.

"It is important to me that you all understand that today's decision was not driven by the trauma in Dubai just a few weeks ago, though it is certainly not an unreasonable theory. I've actually wanted to do this for a while now, but just felt I owed too many people—the fans, the sponsors, Ingemar Gunnarsson, Bobbie Davenport—and that I somehow had a duty to make the most of the strange gift I was given at birth. My parents' combined DNA created a physical body that allowed me to excel at a sport I'd never even played until Bobbie Davenport put a nine-iron in my hands less than seven years ago. As you all know, my rise in the golf world was just as swift as it was inexplicable. And I felt a lot of pressure to use the gift I'd been given. But Bobbie said something to me on the top of the Burj Al Arab that changed my view and, in a way, liberated me. I have her to thank for so much, including the last insight she ever shared with me."

Most of the reporters were looking right at me, but some were taking notes as I spoke. Susan was watching me and smiling for support. I took a deep breath and headed for the home stretch.

"It's the right time for me to take a break from golf and figure out my life. I'm grateful for what this game has given me, and I'm painfully aware that it's given me a lot, including the financial security to take this step, a luxury not many enjoy. But I'm going to seize this moment after completing the Olympic journey that Bobbie Davenport cared so much about, to move on to the next stage in my life. Don't bother asking what my plans are as I don't actually know, but I'll now have the time, and I hope privacy, to figure that out.

"To close, may I express to the whole country what a privilege it has been to represent Canada and to have our national anthem played and our flag raised with a gold medal hanging around my neck. It was all I could ever have dreamed of. Beyond the gratitude I owe Bobbie, I also offer my deepest thanks to the people around me, including Lisa Griffiths, Susan Maddocks, Professor Ingemar Gunnarsson, my last-minute Olympic caddie, Kerry Copeland, and of course my parents, who have always supported me unconditionally.

"Thank you again for coming."

After the Q&A, I did a series of pre-arranged satellite interviews with media in other parts of the world, and then I escaped. I thanked Susan for everything and then eluded the hordes of reporters in the lobby when I slipped down a back stairwell, out a side door, and into my mother's Tesla. Then, the very next day—after many hours of shopping and preparations—I

again eluded the hordes of reporters still dissecting my decision when I slipped out of town under cover of darkness.
Actually, I pulled out around eight p.m., so it was more like
under cover of dusk. The point is I slipped out of Toronto,
unnoticed and alone.

Chapter 12

IT TOOK ME nearly four hours to drive from Toronto to North Bay. I pulled into the Pinewood Park Resort just before midnight. I was rocking more than three days' worth of beard growth, a Toronto Maple Leafs ball cap pulled low, and glasses that did nothing for my vision and less for my appearance. I'd made the reservation under my standard pseudonym, Adam James, just to minimize the likelihood of my whereabouts being discovered. I need not have worried. The young and very sleepy guy staffing the late-night reception desk barely lifted his eyes to mine as he passed over my key. He probably wasn't a golf fan anyway. I crashed as soon as I got to my room. I was still wallowing in melancholy about Bobbie and all that had happened, but for the first time since Dubai, it was balanced by a sense of excitement and anticipation about what might lie ahead for me now that I'd severed my ties with the golf world and essentially killed the goose that laid my golden egg. So what did lie ahead? I honestly didn't know. That was the point of my little sabbatical.

The next morning I drove up Highway 11 in my rental car. By midmorning I pulled in to a marina on the shores of a familiar lake.

Temagami is an Ojibway word meaning "deep water." It's no coincidence that Lake Temagami is a very deep body of water. My many summers at camp on this lake, the wonderful weekends spent at Alli's cottage, and the utter isolation from civilization made it the perfect place to contemplate my next act. No obligations. No schedule. No couriers delivering important papers. No one seeking autographs. And no reporters waiting outside my door. In fact, the only door I'd have would be a zippered panel on my tent. I'd be truly alone. I was interested in how I would handle the seclusion and a few weeks of monastic living. To be clear, I wouldn't be stuck in the Stone Age. I'd packed my laptop, my mobile phone—a cell tower had recently been erected on Bear Island—my iPad, and a high-end solar battery charger. I planned to be isolated from the world without the world being isolated from me.

It took about twenty minutes to finalize my canoe rental. The guy at the marina encouraged me to rent an aluminum boat with a twenty-five-horsepower outboard, but I wanted the physical strain and the thinking time that paddling would give me. I knew the lake well and had canoe-tripped through most of it in my youth. So I was headed for familiar territory, the Southwest Arm. Arguably the least populated part of the lake. It would be a full day's paddle on a calm day. Two days against the wind and waves. Mercifully, the lake was like glass. I loaded up my gear and shoved off as quickly as I could. It was not uncommon for the wind to come up later in the day.

It was so tranquil and serene, and I loved the dull ache that gathered in my shoulders as I paddled. I kept up a steady pace and only referred periodically to the GPS on my phone. For the most part, I knew where I was going. I remembered all of the major landmarks, including Bear Island, the old Wabun Lodge, Camp Wigwasati, and Cattle Island. Near the end of the journey, I recognized an island we'd always called Birch Island, though I don't think that was its official name. Courtesy of a very dry summer and a lightning strike in the early part of the last century, the island had burned pretty well to the ground. As nature took its course thereafter, the deciduous trees—mainly birch—grew much faster than the more dominant red pine, giving the island a much lighter shade of green than the mainly coniferous islands and shore-line around it. The colour difference really made the island stand out. And it became a guidepost for trippers navigating the lake. It marked the end of another leg in my journey that morning.

Paddling for several hours straight naturally lends itself to thinking, whether you're ready for it or not. For a good part of my journey across the lake, an idea flitted in and out of the mists in my addled brain. It wasn't fully formed but it hung around, knocking over other thoughts and generally making a ruckus. I wasn't quite ready to focus on it in any depth, but it was there, orbiting, trying to land.

I made it to my destination late in the day, with very little left in my muscles and bones. I was exhilarated and exhausted. Back when I'd spent so many summers on Temagami, we'd always called this spot Silverbirch. It was a lovely and large campsite just a half hour's paddle from the boys' camp. It was often where we'd spend the last night of canoe trips before the easy paddle home the next day. Thankfully, it was uninhabited, at least by humans. I beached my canoe around the small peninsula, where the water was even calmer. I had some difficulty walking after so many hours kneeling in the canoe and paddling, but I eventually found my feet and managed to haul my gear, food pack, cooler, and tent up to the decrepit picnic table that still featured my initials, carved into one of the legs along with those of my cabin mates when we were eleven years old.

I really wanted to rest for a bit, but feared if I didn't pitch my tent right then while I was still upright, it wouldn't happen at all. So I did that, then inflated an air mattress and unrolled my sleeping bag and mini camp pillow. If you're thinking it sounds more like "glamping" than camping, well, you might be onto something. But I wanted to be comfortable. Camping wasn't the point of the canoe trip. I was there to think, to take stock, to make a few life decisions, to remember Bobbie, to grieve, and to write.

I found that writing often helped order my scattered thoughts. When I developed characters, mapped out their movements, charted their lives, it somehow made it easier to do the same things in my own life, without it being such a big deal and so intimidating. It happened more by stealth. I could sneak up on those important challenges in my own life by wrestling with them in my characters' lives. In hindsight, that was clearly the whole point of the antiphonal novel I'd been writing with Alli all those years ago.

I'd brought enough food and freezer packs to last for my first four or five days before I'd need to switch to meals cobbled together from cans, dry mixes, and the lake's still-pure water. That night, I just cooked hot dogs impaled on a sharpened green stick I'd cut from a birch tree. It was one of the most satisfying meals I'd had in recent memory. Hours of paddling always made simple food taste so much better. By the time the sun was sinking, I was just about comatose. I maintained consciousness long enough to secure my food for the night. I used enough duct tape and shock cords that I doubted even Houdini could break into my cooler, let alone escape from it. Then I stumbled into my tent, zipped the flap closed to prevent death by mosquitoes, and collapsed onto my sleeping bag. I sank into a very heavy sleep, too deep for dreams.

The next morning, the call of a red squirrel in a nearby tree woke me up, along with every other living thing trying to sleep within a two-hundred-metre radius. It's hard to believe that the cute and cuddly, fur-bearing, forest-dwelling, nut-hoarding, garden variety red squirrel has mastered such a loud and obnoxious noise.

My cord-enwrapped cooler was intact and unmolested, though I suspected raccoons and other creatures were conspiring in the woods. On a whim, I launched the canoe into the lake. The surface was like glass. Not a ripple in sight. I just paddled around the inlet, protected by the peninsula of the campsite. It was so quiet and peaceful.

A loon, male by the colouring, surfaced about a hundred feet or so away from the canoe, and I stopped paddling just to watch him. What a glorious creature. He rode low in the water, the white flashing on his neck and wings in stunning contrast to his black head and body. Beautiful. And then came his melancholy, lonely, otherworldly call in high-fidelity, stereo, Dolby surround sound. It was awesome, in the true and traditional sense of the word. I was transfixed, drifting, my paddle across the gunwales. Then the loon looked right at me before disappearing beneath the surface. I kept my eyes on the water. Suddenly, this black and white torpedo streaked right by me about a foot below the surface. If I'd reached into the lake, I could have touched him. I could see him so clearly. Only the bubbles in his submerged wake betrayed the water. I'd never seen anything like it. I was startled and knocked my paddle into the lake. Then it was over. He surfaced quite a distance away and moved around the point, out of sight. I figured nothing was going to top that experience so I retrieved the paddle and headed back to the campsite, exhilarated.

I started a fire and cooked up eggs and bacon. I'd forgotten to bring scouring pads to clean the frying pan, so I reverted to a technique we had employed back in my canoe-tripping days. I scrubbed out the pan with moss. It actually worked quite well. I called my parents to reassure them that all was well and that I hadn't taken leave of my senses. Then I sat at the picnic table in the morning sun with a Rhodia notebook and my beloved Miguel de Cervantes fountain pen, a beautiful limited edition in Montblanc's Writers Series celebrating literary luminaries in history. Such a smooth writer. It had been an early indulgence after my first PGA victory.

The idea that had taunted me the day before, darting in and out of my cerebral shadows, was back and bolder that morning. I played with it for a while, turning it over in my head and seeing how the light of day danced over it. It soon took centre stage in my mind, shouldering other thoughts aside and insisting first on prominence and eventually on dominance. I wrote some notes, the smooth, wet blue-black line of Iroshizuku Shin-Kai ink flowing so effortlessly onto the slick paper. I wrote out the idea as it came to me. It wasn't so much an epiphany or revelation that struck without warning. It felt more like a very slow and methodical advancement of a notion rooted in logic and efficiency, designed to target at least two birds with one stone. I wrote it out again with a little more detail as I answered my own questions and filled in my own blanks.

I didn't let the proposition bully me into surrender. I didn't embrace it instantly. I approached it warily, with questions of logistics, goals, and motivations. To help my thinking, perhaps even to slow it down, I launched my canoe again and paddled aimlessly around the lake near the campsite. I found that doing something physical freed up my brain. My arms, shoulders, and knees protested at being summoned again so soon, but the paddling helped.

An hour later, I was back at the picnic table creating a list of pros and cons. There were more pros than cons. I decided to stop thinking about it for a while, worried that I was going too far, too fast. So I jumped in the lake. I swam in the cool, soft water for about half an hour. My paddle-weary muscles thanked me. I just floated around for the most part. I could actually sit and rest on a rocky shelf a ways out from the shore. It was lovely and restorative. I spent the afternoon reading. In addition to my iPad stocked with literature, I'd also brought a few old-school trade paperbacks, including a thick one by Mark Helprin set in Paris. I pulled my air mattress and sleeping bag from my tent and positioned them in the sunshine beneath the sprawling red pines. And I read. I read for a very long time. It was pure escape, and took me completely out of my own mind and matters. It helped restore balance and perspective. I needed it.

That night I slept deeply once again and opened my eyes to the sunlight pushing through the nylon walls of the tent. I could hear the water lapping on the rocks and the breeze passing through the pines. I also discovered upon surfacing that my decision seemed to have been made sometime in the night, while I slept. It's not that it was made without me. It just felt like the right call in the morning. Any reservations I'd had the day before had packed up and left the field. I felt serene and secure again—always a good sign.

I revved up my laptop and went to the website. I read everything I could. It seemed tailor-made for me. It was flexible and interesting, with a broad range of offerings that would allow me to indulge my broad range of interests. I studied all the requirements and descriptions and then made a tentative wish list.

I was excited. I hadn't expected clarity and comfort to arrive quite so early and easily. I briefly wondered if I were rushing it and if perhaps my sudden enthusiasm might be shutting down other options I should be considering. But I didn't think so. It didn't feel like that. The stars seemed to be aligning so nicely —that is, until I noticed that the final application deadline had passed quite a while ago. My heart and hopes sank. It seemed like the perfect solution, a return to my first love in more ways than one. I decided to call. Perhaps the deadline wasn't of the drop-dead, forever variety.

I found what I needed at the bottom of the webpage. Then I had to remind myself what day of the week it was. Would they even be open? I was relieved when my iPhone confirmed it was Friday.

"University of Toronto," the receptionist said.

"Hello, could I have extension 2356, please?"

"One moment, please."

"English department, Melinda speaking."

"Hello, this is Adam Coryell . . ."

"Yeah, right, and I'm Taylor Swift," she cut in.

"Sorry?" I said. "I mean, um, actually it really is Adam Coryell speaking."

"Uh oh. Are you really *the* Adam Coryell, you know, gold medal and all?"

"Yes, I really am. And I was hoping to speak with Professor Moore."

"I'm so sorry. I really thought you were pranking me," she said.

"No worries," I replied. "I get that a lot."

"Okay, please hold while I put you through to the department chair."

I waited.

"Evelyn Moore."

"Yes, professor, this is Adam Coryell, and I'm calling about the application process for the M.A. in English in the Field of Creative Writing."

"Hello, Mr. Coryell. So you're back in Canada?"

"Yes, I am, but please call me Adam," I said. "I'm actually camping on Lake Temagami right now, trying to think a few things through after a rather eventful few years."

"I'm so very sorry about everything that happened before the Olympics," she said. "And congratulations on an amazing performance in Tokyo, under the circumstances."

"Thanks so much. Yes, the golfer in me seemed to perform quite well, notwithstanding."

"So how can I possibly help the world's most famous golfer?"

"Well, I'd really love to apply for the M.A. program with a focus on creative writing starting this September. But I know that applications closed quite a while ago."

"You're right. The deadline passed some ways back."

"Is there even the slightest chance of applying now and getting in for September? I know it's very unusual and well outside the normal application procedures."

"It is unusual, even unprecedented, but strangely, the door may have opened a crack. First of all, we are not quite at capacity on the creative writing side of the program. Had you been interested in straight English lit, it would not be possible. Secondly, we actually just had a student defer her admission for a year."

I could feel my heart pounding but couldn't think of anything to say.

"So, Adam, the rare opportunity to apply for the program at this late date is really only part of the equation. Do you have a relevant undergraduate degree and the academic achievement you would need for a master's? I'm afraid I only know you as a golfer."

"Oh yes, right. Yes, I have a four-year B.A. in English and creative writing from Stanford, with distinction," I added.

"That's an excellent school with a respected program," Professor Moore said. "You'll also need writing samples, as well as a couple of academic references. Do those requirements pose any problems?"

"No. I have plenty of writing samples from Stanford, and I'm quite sure I can secure at least two recommendations from my professors."

"Well then, Adam, I'd encourage you to get started on the online application. We'd need it in the next forty-eight hours."

"That is just wonderful news. I'll get it done. Thank you so much," I gushed.

We talked for a few more minutes, but I was eager to get moving on the application and to call Stanford for their part in the process.

Miraculously, everything was in order by late afternoon. Stanford had sent my transcript, which I'm proud to report featured very strong marks, to U of T by noon. By 2:30, three of my ex-professors had agreed to provide academic references, including Amy Edwards. I'd finished preparing the online admissions forms by 4:15. Then I worked my way through my own pieces to select what I thought were my best writing samples.

When I had it all assembled and ready to go, I took a break. I wanted to give myself just a bit of distance before reviewing it all again with a fresh mind and pushing the big green "submit" button.

I was just about finished eating the steak I'd cooked up when something on the lake caught my eye. It was a black blob bobbing in the water, but clearly moving across the channel towards the campsite. When it was still quite far away, I first thought it might be a loon. But I could see no flash of white around the head and it really wasn't moving like a loon on the water. Then I decided it was a beaver. There was a beaver lodge in the small, calm bay created by the peninsula of the campsite. But as it moved closer, it seemed too large for a beaver. Because they're so industrious, overweight beavers are rare. I didn't believe in lake monsters, so that left one other possibility that didn't make me happy.

The black blob was heading closer. It swam around the point and started crawling up on shore. That's when I finally made a positive identification. The swimming black blob was a swimming black bear. They were quite common on Lake Temagami. And apparently, I wasn't the only one who thought my steak had smelled wonderful when sizzling over the open flames.

I moved fairly quickly when I finally realized a bear was about to invade my campsite. And when I say I moved fairly quickly, I mean my feet barely touched the ground as I sprinted for the canoe, shoved it into the water and leapt aboard. Thankfully, my paddle was still rattling around in the bottom of the canoe. It certainly makes it easier to control the canoe if you have a paddle. With a few powerful strokes, I was a couple hundred feet offshore as the bear hauled himself up onto land. He shook off the water and then stood up on his hind legs, his nose aimed high. He moved quickly to the frying pan, which was by then cool and resting on the picnic table. A small piece of steak and a strip of fat I'd cut off were left in the pan. They weren't in the pan for long. The bear then spent a few minutes licking out the frying pan. I couldn't have cleaned the pan any better with a hot-water pressure washer. Luckily, the bear didn't seem that interested in the cooler—but he did eat a whole pound of butter, an entire box of Multi Grain Cheerios, a full bag of all-dressed potato chips, and a Tupperware container filled with brown sugar. This took him about forty-five seconds.

His next stop was my tent, and because I hadn't zipped up the entrance flap when I'd last emerged, he walked right in. At one point he was lying down on my sleeping bag with his head stuck outside the tent. Eventually, with no more obvious food to eat, the bear lumbered out of the tent and back over to the picnic table. He actually placed his two front paws on the bench to give him better access to whatever was sitting on top. It finally dawned on me that the bear was now positioned very close to my laptop. Then he actually shifted to the left so that he hovered directly above my keyboard. He looked as if he might just reach out and type an email. That's when the bear raised his right paw above his head. This looked to me like the wind-up for a devastating swipe intended to knock my precious laptop not just off the table, but quite possibly all the way into the lake.

Naturally, I hadn't yet formally submitted my application for admission, and the bear seemed to know this somehow. So I stood up in the canoe—rarely a good idea—and emitted the loudest, longest, and freakiest noise my lungs and vocal cords could muster. It was somewhere between bloodcurdling and inhuman. The sound scared me—and I made it. The bear stopped in mid-swipe and was clearly startled. I knelt back down and kept up my sound assault while paddling straight towards the campsite and the bear. Between strokes, I banged the paddle as hard as I could against the gunwales to add a different noise to the mix. The bear seemed a little perturbed by my performance. He slipped off the table and hustled back towards the water on the other side of the campsite from whence he'd come.

I carried on my earsplitting scream concerto and paddle-banging. The bear was just about back to the water when I leapt ashore, grabbed the frying pan, and banged it incessantly with a steel pot. It added another horrible, deafening sound to the clamour. The bear splashed into the water and swam back across the channel. I sustained my rhythmic banging and vocal raving at the water's edge until I saw him wade ashore on the other side and disappear into the woods. Only then did I stop my caterwauling and pot-pan percussion. I was exhausted and my throat really hurt. When I regained my faculties, I rushed back up to the picnic table. My iPhone was on the bench— the screen was cracked, but it still seemed to be functioning properly and providing the essential hotspot Internet connection. My laptop monitor was dark. But as soon as I nudged the touchpad, the screen flickered to life, the U of T application submission page still beckoning.

Upon closer scrutiny, the computer seemed fine except for a large globule of black-bear drool on the flat metal area bordering my keyboard. A piece of paper towel dealt with that quickly enough. Before an earthquake or meteorite could interrupt my mission, I quickly reviewed my entire application again and reread my writing samples. I didn't catch any new mistakes or make any last-minute changes. I hit the "submit" button and it was done. An "application received" message appeared on the screen, and there was a confirmation email in my inbox.

I stayed that night to finish up another writing project I'd been avoiding. Then I cried for quite a while. I'm pretty sure it was about Bobbie. Having my immediate future sorted out seemed to liberate my mind to wrestle with other issues. Clearly, I hadn't fully processed Dubai. It actually felt good to let go emotionally. But I was on a schedule, so I pulled myself together the next morning, cleaned up the campsite, gathered dry wood for the next person, loaded the canoe, and paddled hard all the way back to civilization.

I drove through a good part of the night and arrived home around midnight. My parents had waited up and were thrilled to see me. There'd been no word from U of T while I'd been paddling and driving all day. But I heard from them the next morning. The email was from the Office of the Registrar, and the subject line told the tale: *Acceptance to the Master's Program in*

English in the Field of Creative Writing. I was very glad I'd not been driving when I heard the news.

There was a lot to get done in the short time remaining before my program started. But I was pumped. I was back. Winning the Masters was great. Being accepted into the master's program was better.

PART 3

Chapter 13

"THANKS AGAIN, Professor Moore, for taking a chance on me," I said, when I phoned her the following week. "I'm grateful."

"Well, you deserve to be in the program. Your application was outstanding, as were your writing samples and your references. In the end, it was a very easy decision."

"Wow. That's great to hear," I said. "Um, I know I'm pushing my luck, but I have another unorthodox request that I hope you'll consider."

"That sounds interesting. Carry on."

"Well, there is a thriving cottage industry amongst media types devoted to figuring out exactly what I'm doing next with my life. I understand that news of my enrolment at U of T will eventually get out, but I'd really like to delay that for as long as possible. As well, I really want to be treated like any other grad student, particularly by my classmates. With that in mind, I wonder if my name on the class list might simply be Adam James, my first and middle names. That was the name I used when submitting poems and stories to publications while at Stanford to ensure I'd be judged on my writing and not on my golf."

"Hmmm, that is highly unusual, but I suppose so are these circumstances. I'll have a discussion with the registrar, but I think we can make something happen," she replied. "As I understand it, the only official documents that require your full name are your admission application, your transcripts, and your degree, should you complete the program. I think I can get him to agree to this if I position it as a measure that is in your academic interest."

"That would be amazing. I'm not sure I'll be readily recognized, as I've let my hair grow long, I'm now sporting a beard, and I'm wearing glasses. If you can't, well, then you can't. I get it. We'll deal with it. But it would be nice to have a bit of breathing room."

"I wouldn't count on your true identity remaining a secret for very long, but we can try to support you on that front."

"Thank you very much. And yes, I agree. The news will break sometime. But even if I can be Adam James for a few weeks or months, that would help me get out of the gate cleanly."

A lot happened that first week of September. After spending a lot of time online and on the telephone, I managed to shut down my life in San Francisco, repatriate everything I had down there, including my car, sort out Bobbie's affairs, and buy a great condo at the corner of Yonge and Bloor in the heart of downtown Toronto. It was a 2,800-square-foot corner unit in the upper reaches of a two-year-old luxury high-rise building. Lisa Griffiths handled the financial part of the transaction. No need for a mortgage—we paid the full price through a certified electronic bank transfer. After an amazing interior designer worked her magic in record time, I moved in the Friday before classes started. And I confirmed that my name on the class list would be Adam James. We would see how long my secret would keep.

I hadn't shaved since the Olympics. I'd had no idea I could actually grow a beard, but apparently I could. I let my hair kind of do what it wanted. As it grew out, it became a little unruly —not quite curly, but at least wavy. To avoid looking too scruffy, I at least kept my newly grown chin spinach neatly trimmed. Standing before the bathroom mirror, I was quite surprised at how different I appeared. But that worked just fine for me. This was part of the plan. Despite a raft of sports reporters charged with discovering where I was and what I was doing, I don't think many people knew I was even back in Toronto. I'm sure a few of my neighbours knew, but generally, I could walk around the city wearing a ball cap and no one really gave me a second glance. I certainly wasn't going all out to hide my true identity. I knew my anonymity would be fleeting, but I was enjoying it while it lasted.

I spent the weekend enjoying my new condo, doing some grocery shopping, cooking dinner for my parents to inaugurate the kitchen, and generally psyching myself up for my first class on Monday. It was a short-story workshop course. In preparation, the professor had already emailed the class and attached a short story written by one of my fellow grad students. Our assignment was to read the story and be prepared to critique it on Monday.

I didn't love the story. Nothing really happened in it. It was entirely the disjointed interior thoughts of a young man as he walked along a remote highway after his car ran out of gas. I thought it needed something, but I wasn't exactly sure what or why. I wondered if it reflected Hemingway's iceberg theory, in which much of the story is unstated but clearly lurking below the waterline. Maybe I wasn't seeing what was really happening beneath the surface. My plan was to keep my ears open and my mouth closed during the class, at least until I found my feet.

When I arrived on Monday, there were only about a dozen students, mainly women, seated around a very large table. The numbers forced me to rethink the mouth-shut part of my classroom strategy. A few of them close to where I sat introduced themselves and I reciprocated. I tried to keep track of their names—Bethany, Shannon, Stephen and Kaz, I think. They all seemed nice. I liked Professor Keller. He was youngish and looked like a struggling writer in his faded jeans, sandals, and flannel shirt. His chaotic hair and beard made it appear as if we shared a stylist. He talked for a while about the course and how much more difficult short stories were than novels.

"Some of you seem surprised. Some of you probably thought starting with short stories is the logical way rookie writers begin, before eventually finding their feet and graduating to the big leagues and writing novels," he said. "Not so, in my mind. Think about it. Novelists can stretch out on their massive canvas, indulge in digressions, and generally pad their writing to reach their word count. They can get away with prose that is a little flabby when it's against the backdrop of a one-hundred-thousand-word manuscript. But a short story writer has no such luxury. Every single solitary word must count. Every single solitary word must be right. Every single solitary word must be perfect. Many novelists edit chapters, pages, paragraphs, and sometimes sentences. Short-story writers, well, we edit right down to clauses and words. We have no space for superfluous verbiage. We must distill our prose until it is pure and powerful."

He let that sink in. No one said a word, though there was some vigorous head-nodding.

"So I'm one of those who thinks novels, despite their length, may well be easier to write than short stories. And don't get me started on the difficulties inherent in pulling a collection together, finding the theme that links the stories, and ordering the pieces to maximize impact. In comparison, writing novels is a walk in the park."

"Then why do story collections get no respect out there?" asked a woman sitting next to me. "Novels still seem to be literature's gold standard."

"Because so few people, critics included, really understand how short stories are crafted and what they truly demand from the writer and the reader," he replied. "But that's why we're all here. So, on that happy note, let's dive in. I circulated Stephen's story last week. I'm going to make the dangerous assumption that you have all read it and given it serious thought. That's what this course is all about. You owe it to each other to commit as much to reading and critiquing your colleagues' work as you do to writing your own. That's what a workshop class is all about. Let's start with Stephen's ambling-down-the-highway piece. Who'll start us off?"

Stephen put his hand up.

"I just want to give some context for the story," he said.

Professor Keller held up his hand like a stop sign.

"Sorry, Stephen. We only hear from the writer at the end. Your readers will seldom have the benefit of a set-up from the author. So you must set context in the story itself." He looked around the classroom. "Okay, who's up?"

"Well, I read it twice and I still don't know what it's supposed to be," said a young man at the end of the table. "A guy runs out of gas, has no cell signal, and so is forced to walk along the shoulder, sharing his random thoughts. And man, does he think a lot, and all over the map, too."

"Okay, you've just made an observation about the story," Professor Keller said. "But we need more than that. What was Stephen trying to get across? What was his point?"

"I wondered if it was a meditation on the impact of technology and how little time we all have in today's hectic society to think, to really think," said a woman seated across from me.

"Okay, now we're getting somewhere," the professor said. "That's digging in a bit. That's what we need to do. Who else?"

"I kind of thought he might be a little ADHD. His thoughts were flying in from all directions on countless topics. I wondered if his search for gasoline was a metaphor for his own search for peace, stability, and order."

"Good. That may not be what Stephen intended, but you're getting underneath the prose and that's good," Professor Keller said. "Who else?"

"Well, I just thought the writing was pedestrian, while the empty-gas-tank metaphor was too obvious. It's clear that the guy in the story is tapped out in his life and looking for something to save him. But the running out of gas thing is cliché and overdone."

This comment came from a clean-cut student sitting at the end of the table. He shook his head and even rolled his eyes while sharing his little hatchet job with the rest of us.

Stephen blanched. I blanched. A few of the other students blanched. Safe to say there was blanching.

"Whoa!" the professor said. "Let's remember that your story is going to come up for critique in the coming weeks. The point is to be constructive in our criticism. Give the writer something they can consider, something they can act on, something they can salvage. Perhaps I should have spent a bit more time on what we're looking for when critiquing our colleagues' work."

"Sorry, but it's just bad writing. I don't even know where to start with it," the student protested.

"Look, it's simple. In your critique, be thoughtful, be considerate, be empathetic, be understanding, be gentle," the professor said.

"In other words, don't be a dick," Stephen said.

"Right. Inelegantly put, Stephen, but true," agreed the professor. "Don't be a dick. But also, as writers, we need to have thick skins and learn how to take criticism. Even in sharply worded rebukes, there is often a kernel of truth. Our job is to not take it all so personally that we fail to see the value lurking in the sometimes unnecessarily harsh criticism. Readers don't mince their words on Amazon or Goodreads, and frankly, neither will some of your editors and beta-readers. So don't take criticism personally. Listen, consider, and decide for yourself whether to act and what to act on. That's our job as writers."

The clean-cut guy at the end of the table, who was forever after known as Dick, scowled but said nothing more.

Much to my relief, none of my fellow grad students seemed to recognize me, although Professor Keller had nodded his head knowingly, almost conspiratorially, when we shook hands at the beginning of class.

While I had seen Allison around campus a few times, particularly in the library, I hadn't yet spoken to her, and I didn't think she'd yet seen me. I hadn't really figured out how to approach her, and decided I should just let it happen. So on Thursday afternoon that week, I walked over to the library bearing my precious cargo in the hopes of seeing her.

I slipped up to the mezzanine level, which yielded a good view of the tables one floor below. And there she was, hunkered down at a table, writing in a well-used notebook. Even from where I stood, I could see she was still using the vintage orange Parker Duofold I'd given her years earlier, on the day we broke up. She looked good. She looked great, in fact. Her hair was a little shorter, and her jeans and hoodie screamed out *student*. Seeing her did something to me. I was just happy to be in the same room with her again.

Why wait? I headed back down the stairs, carrying our antiphonal novel with my new chapter newly inked.

My last act at the campsite on Lake Temagami—which seemed like months ago, not days—had been to write the next chapter in our long-neglected antiphonal novel. As you might expect, it featured a reconciliation, after several years, of the young woman—by then in Toronto—and the itinerant hockey player. I didn't know if Alli was seeing anyone right then. For all I knew, she was in love with someone else. She could even be engaged to the good-looking dude from Christmas a few years ago. But I had to try. I had to know.

I wasn't moving in slow motion, but it sure felt like it. She looked up when I was still some distance off. I could feel my knees wobbling from sheer anxiety and expectation. Our eyes met for an instant before she turned away again. Ouch, that hurt. Then she paused and snapped her head around to find me again. She was out of her chair like a shot and came to meet me. Her hug was long but there was really no way to tell exactly what kind of embrace it was. It could very well have been a "Great to see you after so long, Auntie Irene" hug.

"I didn't recognize you at first," she said after pulling back from the hug but holding on to my hands. "What are you doing here, Adam?"

"I figured I was long overdue to deliver my next chapter. Sorry it took me seven years."

I handed her the notebook. She took it and beamed at me. I wish I could have bottled that moment.

She led me back to her table and pulled around the chair from the other side so it was next to hers and we both sat. She then reclaimed my hands.

"Seriously, where have you been, and how are you doing?" she asked.

"Well, I've just spent some time camping on Lake Temagami, sorting out a few things—you know, figuring out my life and what comes next," I said.

"I can't believe you were in Temagami. I wish I'd known. You could have gone to visit my parents."

"Well, I think I really needed the alone time. The lake has always been a special place for me, for several reasons. Just being there always helps me think. It was where I made decisions on the next chapter in our novel, and I guess in my life," I continued. "And as for how I'm doing, well, I think I'm okay. What happened to Bobbie and then the decision to leave golf was a lot to process. I'm sure I'm not finished dealing with it all, but I was certainly feeling a lot better paddling out of Lake Temagami than I was paddling in."

"Well, your 'Goodbye, golf' news conference was a shocker."

"Really?" I asked.

"Hmmm. Well, not to me. But to the rest of the world, I mean," she replied. "And what are you doing here? Are you living at home again?"

"Well, funny story. And I hope you're okay with this, but at the last minute, I was accepted into the master's program, you know, here, in creative writing. I started on Monday."

Her eyes widened and she stood up, still holding my hands. It felt so good to be in physical contact with her. Her hands were soft and warm.

"Yay, Adam, that's fantastic! You'll love it. The profs are stellar. This is going to be amazing. We're getting the band back together!" she said. "I can't believe I haven't seen you yet. Then again, maybe I have but just didn't recognize you. But I'm digging your new back-to-the-land look."

She reached up and held her hand against my cheek when she said it.

"Well, I'm trying to fly a little under the radar to give myself some space and time. In fact, as far as my fellow grad students know, my name is Adam James."

"You mean they don't know? They haven't recognized the famous golfer who brought down a chopper and then won a gold medal?" she asked.

"Well, the administration and the profs know, and I expect

the students will know soon enough," I said. "Oh, and I bought a condo at Yonge and Bloor so I won't be freeloading off my parents."

"In that newish, really tall building on the corner with the cool wavy-shaped sides?"

"That's the one."

"Nice," she said. "Okay, I can't wait any longer. Can you sit for a bit while I read?"

"Sure," I replied. "I'll sit here as long as you like."

She finally released my hands to grab the notebook and turn to my chapter.

I watched her closely as she read. If she were to roll her eyes or shake her head, I'd be done for. But she didn't. She smiled as she read. She looked over at me often. I thought I even saw her lip tremble once, but that might have been wishful thinking. When she finished the chapter, she flipped back to the start of it and read it again.

When she closed the spiral notebook, she leaned forward again in her chair so she could reclaim my hands, which I'd conveniently left within reach.

"I loved it," she opened. "Your writing is stronger, more mature, more fluid. It's good."

"Thanks," I said, wanting more than a writing critique.

"And I like where the story is going, too," she said, and squeezed my hand.

We talked all afternoon and a good part of the evening, too. It was like we'd never been apart. We talked writing, fountain pens, what we'd been doing with our lives. We covered a lot of ground that afternoon. Maybe we really were getting the band back together. It felt the same as it had when we were teenagers, but different, somehow. Deeper, somehow. She was quite busy and really trying to focus on the novel she was writing for her master's and, she hoped, for publication.

We touched on our love lives, or in my case, the lack thereof. She wasn't involved with anyone either, and hadn't been for a while. I don't think she noticed the cardiac cartwheels I turned while sitting across from her. It seemed she was giving me green lights at every intersection. We both agreed we wouldn't rush into anything, though right then, I would have happily rushed into it. I was ready to rush. I'd been ready to rush for six years or more. Rush, rush, rush. But I played it cool. I was in for the long haul.

THE NEXT MONDAY, one of my stories was up for critique in the workshop class. I was excited and terrified but couldn't tell where one ended and the other began. My story was about a man born with a very special birthmark that scarred not just his body but his life. The key points hadn't changed from my original, televised rendition, but I'd added brushstrokes to fill out the details and make it feel real. At least, that was the plan.

I'd actually honed it a bit on Lake Temagami. Was it ready? Was it finished? Was it exactly where I wanted it? I had no idea. But I felt a connection to the story and genuinely wanted the group's feedback.

"Okay, Adam's story, 'The Birthmark,' is up today. Who will kick us off?"

I sat there with my TWSBI Vac Mini poised above a Rhodia Heritage notebook. *Here we go.* Stephen jumped in first.

"I liked the overall arc of the story and the message it conveyed, but I think it could be improved in a few ways."

"Okay, how?" Professor K. prompted.

"Well, the protagonist doesn't feel fully fleshed out. We know more about his birthmark than we do about him, how he thinks and feels, who he really is. He just feels a little flat. I thought we'd learn more about him as the story unfolded, but we didn't really."

I could feel myself nodding in agreement as I took notes.

"Who else felt that way?" the professor asked.

Several hands were lifted high.

"You don't have to raise your hand, too, Adam. It's your story."

"Sorry, but what Stephen says actually makes sense to me."

"Okay, who's next?"

"I liked it. It made me think about life and happiness. But I had some issues, too," Bethany said, taking the floor. "I know it's a bit cliché to say this, but I thought there was a lot of telling going on in the story and not enough showing. Rather than just having the narrator tell us stuff, Adam could have made those points through dialogue, or action in the story. I think it would help the pacing and make the whole piece, I don't know, more animated, more dynamic than it is right now."

"Wow, that's awesome advice," I said. "I see what you're saying. Thanks for that."

Trudy shot me a puzzled look. "Are you being sarcastic?"

"What? No, of course not," I protested. "I mean it. I think your critique is sound and really helpful."

"Well, while we're being so receptive with the constructive criticism, I have a thought on the dialogue that's already there," chimed in Kaz. "There are about six different characters who speak to the narrator in the story—old, young, men, women, rich, poor—all of them are different. But if you read the dialogue, they all kind of sound the same. I think you need to reflect how different the characters are by making them sound different in dialogue."

"Holy shit, you're right," I said, shaking my head as I thought about what she'd just said. "This is great stuff."

Kaz furrowed her brow.

"I'm serious," I pleaded. "As soon as you said it, I saw it. You're right."

Then our friend Dick, who we had learned was actually named Brad, raised his hand and Professor Keller nodded his way.

"I just don't think it's realistic that someone could have a birthmark that looks exactly like Elvis. It's too far-fetched. You're asking readers to suspend their disbelief so dramatically, so extremely. It just doesn't fly for me."

"I hear you, Brad. And thanks for that," I replied. "But I think of this story as more of a fable, or maybe a parable. The birthmark is symbolic, metaphorical, and I hope readers understand that."

"How many of you took it as metaphorical?" Professor K. asked.

Everyone's hand went up except Dick's—I mean Brad's.

I was still taking notes when the class broke up. I'd taken in a lot of really good advice. I didn't agree with all of it, but most was constructive and gave me a clear path to rework the story. When I looked up from my notes, only Professor K. and I were left in the room.

"Well, I got to say, I have never in my teaching career seen anyone take a heap of criticism in such a warm, welcoming, and grateful fashion," he started. "So that was really all on the up and up?"

"Why does everyone think I was putting on an act? I thought the comments were extremely helpful, and most of them were rooted in sound analysis."

"Most writers don't take criticism so well," he replied. "I certainly don't."

I thought for a moment before I responded.

"I understand that, but let's just say that in my earlier life, I never received thoughtful and constructive criticism from anyone, I suppose because I was pretty good at what I was doing. But I don't have the same gift for writing. I have the desire and the drive and I hope the discipline to be a writer, but not the innate talent. So I desperately want to improve. The feedback will help me get better. I enjoyed the critique today because I need and want it so much so I can develop and improve. Does that make sense?"

"Oh, it makes lots of sense, and I commend you for your enlightened view. I just don't know many writers who can pull it off."

I worked most of the night revising the story based on the class's feedback. It was wonderful. I loved it. The changes seemed so clear to me. I'd just needed a nudge in the right direction. My ability to critique my own writing was improved by the exercise. I started to see other minor issues, which I tweaked and hopefully resolved.

The next night, Alli came over. We hugged when she came through the front door, but no kisses were exchanged. Perhaps she might have planted one on me had she not been immediately distracted by the condo and its amazing wraparound corner view to the south, right down to Lake Ontario.

"Oh my gosh, this is beautiful," she said, turning slowly on the spot. "And the furniture and the rugs and everything else are stunning!"

I led her to a closed door next to the master bedroom. I waited till she was standing right next to me before I opened the door and ushered her in.

She said nothing, but the look on her face sufficed. The library was not a large room. I didn't want it to be large. I kind of wanted to feel as if I were wearing the room. The wall of glass faced west, where the sun was setting, turning the clouds and the sky a lovely shade of vermilion. Except for the door, dark wooden floor-to-ceiling built-in bookshelves made up the other three walls, and they were filled with the books I'd collected over the years. There was room for more books. A glass-topped desk, on which rested my laptop, abutted the window. A small wooden cabinet under the desk held my fountain pens. Finally, a deep, dark-brown leather chair rested next to the desk for when the need to write gave way to the need to read.

"It's perfect," she whispered, taking in the whole room. "Perfect."

"I'm glad you like it," I said.

"I could write some serious prose in here."

"Anytime you wish."

I asked Alli to read my original version of "The Birthmark" and then the revised story. I watched her out of the corner of my eye while she read. I could tell before she opened her mouth that I'd made progress with the revisions. She nodded her head almost imperceptibly throughout the new and improved edition.

"The second one is much better," she said. "Please tell me it's the revised version and not the original."

"Yes. The changes were driven by the great feedback I got from the rest of the class. Almost all of their comments made sense to me, and I just ignored those that didn't. When I have a sound diagnosis, I think I can prescribe the right treatment and carry it out."

"This revised draft is strong. It's more lyrical and literary than your earlier work. I really like it."

"I find the writing easier when I'm telling a story that means something to me," I replied.

"Well, it's not hard to see how personal this story is," she said. "This is what came out of that bizarre TV interview you did just before Tokyo, right?"

"Guilty."

"Don't say guilty, like it's a bad thing. I think the best stories come from our own lives. That's how we write with real authenticity and conviction. It's a good thing."

"I've been thinking. I've only ever written short stories. Now that I understand just how difficult they are, I'm thinking I might like to try messing around with a novel," I said. "What do you think?"

"I think you should. In fact, I think the way you write, speak, and think might even be better suited to longer-form fiction," she replied. "What's the story?"

"Well, it feels a little like the short story you just read, but it's not the same. I had this idea to write in the voice of a youngish man who's been blessed with an extraordinary singing voice. He sings beautifully and powerfully, and catches the attention of record executives. He soon finds himself at the top of the pop charts, on top of the world, living a life he'd never imagined. He is respected, revered, and brings joy to so many people around the world."

"But . . ." Alli prompted.

"But he's not happy. He's not satisfied. He's not fulfilled. It all leaves him strangely cold. And he has another calling."

"Don't tell me. He wants to write."

"Nope. He's obsessed with astrophysics, and is proficient in that realm, though he falls somewhat short of gifted."

"So he's torn between the fame, money, mansions, fast cars, and women that come with pop stardom, and the esoteric, monastic, often impoverished life of an astrophysicist studying the universe. Kind of like choosing between star or stars. I like it," she said.

"Star or stars," I repeated. "Hmmmm, that might be good title."

"I have absolutely no idea where you could have picked up that storyline," she said.

"Me either."

Then she slipped her arm around my waist as we watched the western sky cycle through various shades of orange.

Chapter 14

I WAS SPENDING quite a bit of time with Allison. It felt so good to be back in her orbit. I was careful not to make any assumptions or try to move too far, too fast. This was too important to me to mess it up. So we just took it slowly, which required all the self-restraint I could muster. When it felt right, I had one more card to play sitting in a wooden filing box on the floor of my bedroom closet.

Late one afternoon in early October, Alli arrived at my door with a big smile and an even bigger envelope.

"It's finished," she said, handing it to me. "I'm finished."

"What, your novel?"

"No, I've been secretly building a Death Star all this time and I'm ready to blow up my first planet," she replied. "Yes, Adam, my novel. I really think it's done, or at least it feels like I'm done with it."

"That's fantastic! Congratulations," I said and, seizing any opportunity for bodily contact, went in for a hug. "When can I read it?"

"You're holding it in your hands right now," she said, pointing to the envelope in my clutches. "Would you read it and tell me the truth about it? I'm so immersed in it, I don't even know if it's a novel anymore. I don't know if the story hangs together, if the characters are believable, if the pacing is there. I just have this faint inkling that it's finished."

"Of course," I said. "If you could assume a low profile and keep the noise down, I'll start right now."

"Thanks, Adam," she said, and leaned over and kissed me on the cheek. I just barely resisted the juvenile temptation to turn my head at the last second to take it on the lips. "I can't stay. I've got my second-year American Lit marking to do. Be honest on the novel. I can't hand it in if there's something wrong with it, but I'm too close to see it right now."

"I promise honesty. Now, let me get to it."

I shooed her out the door, stealing a parting hug, and then ripped open the envelope. I put the stack of manuscript pages on the coffee table, stretched out on the couch, and started reading. It was 3:45 p.m.

There was no title yet for the novel, but it was a ghost story. Or perhaps it wasn't. You don't know, even when you've finished it, whether there really is a ghost or if the narrator is not fully stable mentally. I looked up from the manuscript once at about 8:15 to go to the bathroom. At 2:30 the next morning I read the final page.

There was no way I could have read her novel in anything other than one sitting. I had no choice. I was bowled over. My fingers could barely work my cellphone. It rang quite a few times before she answered. That's when I realized it was nearly three in the morning.

"Adam, is that you?" she asked in her groggy sleep voice. "Are you okay?"

"I'm so sorry, Alli, I just realized what time it is."

"Well, when the little hand is almost on the three, and it's dark outside, it's sleepy time."

"I know. I know. I'm sorry. But I just finished your novel."

I'm pretty sure I actually heard her sit bolt upright.

"What, you finished it? You read the whole thing. You're done?"

"Yes, all of those things," I replied. "I just wish you were here right now so I could, I don't know, maybe hold you while I told you how utterly spellbound I've been for the last nine hours or so. I loved it. To descend to cliché, I could not have put it down if our building were on fire. I'm so proud of you."

"Well, when you put it that way, I wish I were there, too."

"That novel is going to be an international bestseller. You heard it here first."

"Whoa, cowboy. Let's not get too far ahead of ourselves," she replied. "My thesis supervisor hasn't even seen it yet. And then there's that minor obstacle of finding a publisher."

"I've never been more certain of anything in my life. This manuscript will soon be a published novel with a stunning and haunting cover, and it will fly off the shelves in staggering numbers."

We talked for an hour. I'd read her manuscript as a reader and as a writer. So I gave her chapter and verse about the novel's many virtues so she knew my praise wasn't just puffery.

"I like having you around. You're good for my confidence," she said.

"Oh, I'm good for more than that."

ONE MORNING ABOUT a week later I was on my way to my morning class, walking west along the south side of Bloor Street, when I noticed someone on the north side of the street taking my picture. The shooter was subtle about it, but I caught it. When you've seen it as often as I had in the previous five years, it's easy to pick out. I didn't let on that I'd seen him and his camera, but just carried on walking. Courtesy of shiny and clean store windows next to me, I could see that the photographer, still on the other side of the street, was following me. I had quite a good view of him in nearly every window I passed. I just looked like I was window-shopping when I was really tracking the shooter's every movement as he tracked mine. I should have been a spy.

One block later, the photographer got into a white car that pulled up beside him. They sped away down Bloor. I kept one eye on them as they pulled a U-turn at the end of the block and headed back towards me. The closer they came to me, the more clearly I could see the long lens of the camera poking out the passenger window. I casually cut down a side street and into a building filled with stores. It was futile. I saw the car four more times that day. I was pretty sure my cover was blown. In a way, it was somewhat of a relief. Anticipating discovery is almost as exhausting as avoiding it. And it really had been just a matter of time. It seemed my time was up. I turned off my cellphone.

My suspicions were confirmed on my walk back from the university that afternoon. The white car was no longer tailing me. They'd probably already got what they needed. I'd avoided the Internet all day and didn't know whether my photos were already circulating in cyberspace. I visited Laywine's in Yorkville on my way home. I hadn't been in for a while and wanted to see what fountain pens they had on sale, and maybe pick up some ink and notebooks. I was a little anxious about leaving the store so I ended up spending more time and money than I'd planned.

I bought some more of my favourite paper, and a couple of Rhodia dotPads. I also stocked up on some ink, specifically Iroshizuku Ku-Jaku, which in technical terms is kind of bluey-greeny. When I finally came out of the store, a camera from Sportsnet was waiting for me. I'd been so focused on the white Chrysler that I had failed to notice the Sportsnet satellite truck. Well played.

"Hi, Adam. I like the new look," the reporter said. "Can I just ask what you're doing now that you've left golf?"

I really had only one option.

"Um, I'll be issuing a statement later this afternoon and I'll make sure you get a copy. Thanks so much."

Then I bolted, trying very hard not to look like I was bolting. I headed in the wrong direction—away from my condo—cut through an underground public parking lot, walked back up into a neighbouring building, and after carefully scanning the area, slipped back to my building without being followed.

Alli was waiting for me when I came through my front door. I'd given her a key the week before so she could write in my little library when I was in class.

"I tried to call you," she said. "I'm sorry, Adam, but you're busted."

"I figured, so I turned off my phone."

I opened my laptop and typed my own name into Google. Several news sites had the shots, and everyone else piled on soon after. I looked like a desert island castaway in the photos, and at least one sportscaster tweeted that I must be living in my car.

"Well, I guess in this day and age, staying undercover for five weeks ain't too bad," I said. "But now there's really no point in carrying on this charade any longer."

"Does that mean you can shave?" Alli asked.

"I thought you liked the beard."

"I do like the beard, but it kind of makes you look like the Unabomber living in the backwoods."

I shaved right then and there, and got a haircut next door after clandestinely exiting my building via the ramp from the parking garage. Susan issued a statement on my behalf over the wire explaining that I was now living in Toronto and enrolled in graduate studies in creative writing. She also managed the deluge of interview requests. We declined them all. The tabloid photos of me looking like a nineteenth-century homesteader would have to do.

Later that evening, Alli and I were just lounging on the couch watching the lights of the city sprawled out below us. We didn't dare turn on the TV.

"Are you okay?" she asked.

"I think so," I replied. "I knew it wouldn't last, but it was nice while it did."

"Yes, it was nice."

"Maybe it might have been better to have been open about my post-golf life right from the very beginning, rather than letting the media fascination bubble away until it eventually boiled over. If I'd been forthright from the outset, maybe it all would have blown over in a couple weeks and I would never have had to grow my beard."

"There's no point in second-guessing now," she said.

"Right. Sometimes hindsight can be very annoying."

It occurred to me just then that perhaps now was the perfect time to play my last gambit in Operation Alli.

"So, now that the big charade is over and my true identity is out of the closet, as it were, there's something else in the closet I figure I should bring out," I said.

"Uh oh. That sounds deeply psychological," she replied with what sounded like trepidation.

"Well, even though we are lying on a couch, it's not deeply psychological at all. In fact, it's quite literal. There is actually something in my closet I want to show you."

I moved from horizontal to vertical and disappeared into my bedroom. When I returned, I placed the wooden box on the coffee table in front of her.

"Nice box," she said.

"I'm glad you like it, because it's yours."

She looked at me as she leaned forward. I nodded and she lifted the lid. Her eyes widened when she saw all the letters sealed in envelopes, fully addressed in my hand with whatever fountain pen I had in rotation at the time. She sorted through them a bit.

"Wait, are all of these to me?"

"Every one of them."

"How many are there?"

"Well, let's see," I said as I reached into the box. "They're stacked in reverse chronological order, and I numbered each one where the stamp would normally go to make it a little easier to keep track. It's not exactly the Dewey Decimal system, but it gets the job done."

I grabbed the top letter in the pile to check its number, even though I already knew what it was.

"One hundred and one over the last six years. I wrote you every three weeks or so, as if we were still together. I wrote this last one while in Temagami in August."

"But you never sent them."

I just shook my head.

Then she buried her face in her hands, stomped her feet— almost as if she were running on the spot while still seated— and released a long, low moan. It took me a second to realize it wasn't really a moan, but a word. Sort of a word-moan.

"Nooooooo."

It dawned on me that perhaps it actually hadn't been the perfect time to play my last gambit in Operation Alli. Since I couldn't really follow my instincts right then and curl into a fetal position on the floor, I just sat next to her saying nothing and doing nothing.

"Noooooooo."

Again with the moan and feet-stomping. I worried about my neighbour one floor below. But it passed.

Alli suddenly turned and hugged me so tightly, breathing was difficult. She snuffled into my neck and I could feel the wetness of her tears.

The suspense was killing me and I couldn't wait any longer.

"Um, I don't want to interrupt the moment, but what's wrong?"

She pulled back and gathered herself. She wiped her eyes, sniffed a few times, ran her fingers through her hair, and then sobbed for another five minutes.

"I'm sorry. I didn't think you'd react this way," I said, closing the lid on the box. "Clearly I misread the situation. I don't want you to feel any pressure. I just . . ."

"Stop," she mustered. "Just give me a second."

I thought I should maybe stroke her arm or her shoulder in a comforting, overtly and infinitely platonic way. But I just sat there as one might in the electric chair.

It took ten more minutes, but she calmed down.

"Sorry about that. I'm just so upset that you did that and kept it up this whole time."

"Well, I don't know why it would be upsetting," I said. "I'm sorry if I've made a mess of this. We can just forget it happened. I don't want . . ."

"Stop!" she repeated. "I'm not being clear. I'm upset because I wrote to you as well, about the same number of letters."

"You did? Well, that's just awesome!" I said, shocked and tingling all over. "Can I read them? Where are they?"

"Ah, yes, well, um, now we're finally getting to the point," she explained. "You see, the letters I carefully wrote you and filed away are all currently residing in, um, a landfill site somewhere north of Toronto."

"I don't get it," I said.

"I kept them for a very long time, thinking we might have a moment like this at some point in the distant future. But about a year ago, you were winning everything on the Tour. You were on television every weekend. Your face was on magazine covers. You'd won every major at least once and were obviously on track to play in the Olympic Games. Well, the odds of getting back together again just seemed so remote. So I bit the bullet. I stopped writing you and I threw out all the letters. I didn't even recycle them. I didn't want them coming back in any way, shape, or form. So I threw them in the garbage."

"Ouch," I said. "I know how committed you are to the environment." It hurt a little, but I sensed we might be heading for a happy ending.

"I'm sorry. If I'd ever thought we might be with each other again, I would have kept them. But it seemed hopeless. I thought I needed closure. I needed to move on. I'm sorry I threw them out. I shouldn't have."

"It's okay. Thanks for writing them," I said. "You know, I saw you once at the Eaton Centre when you were doing Christmas shopping that first year I came back from Stanford. Anyway, I kind of watched you for a bit," I blurted. "There, I said it."

"You did?"

"Well, even from afar it was just so good to see you, and we'd agreed we wouldn't contact each other. But I wasn't stalking you. I just watched until you disappeared into a store and then I left. I thought I should tell you. Oh, and I'm sorry."

"It's okay. If I'd seen you, I'd probably have watched you for a bit, too."

"And remember when I went over to your house during your family Christmas party?" I asked.

"I remember."

"Yeah, well, sorry about that, too."

"That was hard," she said. "I was so surprised to see you. I just wanted to talk to you all night. And then what's-his-name came out and got all proprietary and touchy-feely."

"Robert Usher," I said.

"Right! Robert Usher. Wow. It's a little weird you remember his name. But it's really nice, too."

Alli stayed over that night, and all was right with the world —I mean, other than no longer being able to move so freely around it without being recognized.

When I walked into my poetry workshop the next afternoon, my beard gone and my hair cut, everyone knew who I was. The story of my surfacing in Toronto had been running on all the networks since the previous afternoon. I don't mean it was the lead news story. There were far more important things going on in the world. But it certainly led the sports coverage on Canadian channels. My fellow grad students all seemed to take it in stride and were actually quite nice about it. There were no avid golfers in the class, or I suspect they would have known much earlier.

"Welcome, Mr. Coryell," the prof said. "Nice to see you again for the very first time."

"Um, thanks. And look, I'm sorry if I seemed deceptive, but I really just wanted you—all of you—to treat me, and my writing, as you would any other student. I just wanted to be a normal grad student."

"Well, you're not a bad writer for a pro golfer," said Shannon, who was sitting next to me.

"Well, um, thanks, but I'm here because I'm a much better

golfer than I am a writer. The problem is I really want to be a writer, and not a golfer. So I need your help."

"This is a much better look for you," Bethany said from across the table, pointing vaguely to the general vicinity of my head.

"Thanks."

A FEW DAYS later, my cellphone rang around lunchtime. It had been ringing nearly constantly since news of my whereabouts broke. I had been rejecting all of the calls from numbers I didn't recognize, but I knew this one. So I answered.

"Professor Gunnarsson."

"No, you can't be Professor Gunnarsson, because I am," he said.

"No, no, it's Adam Coryell, but I knew you were calling."

"What? How did you know I was calling when I didn't even know until just before I dialled?" he asked.

He sounded a little different, but I couldn't put my finger on why.

"Right. Well, I mean your name appeared on my phone when it rang, so I knew it was you."

"Well, it still seems a little presumptuous."

"Professor, are you in Adelaide?"

"Of course I'm in Adelaide. I'm always in Adelaide. I'm marooned here in Adelaide. I will never escape Adelaide."

"I see. But by my calculations that would make it about two o'clock in the morning where you are."

"Well, where I am is at my kitchen table with a good friend. And yes, you are correct, it is just about two o'clock in the morning."

"Oh. Right. Well, it's nice you've got a friend to talk to."

"I've been with two friends tonight, but neither is very talkative. Jack Daniel's ran out a little while ago, so now I'm with Jim Beam. They both are very staunch friends when my hate for this godforsaken land gets too much for me."

I'd never heard him under the influence. I didn't even know he drank.

"Ahhh, okay, now I understand. Well, um. I'm sorry you had to resort to those two particular friends. They may not seem like friends in the morning."

"It is the morning already. And I still like them."

"Right. Professor, what can I do to help? I'm a long way from Adelaide, but I'd like to help if I can."

"I know you're a long way from here. You're in Toronto. I saw it on CNN tonight. The big mystery is solved! You've exchanged your golden golf clubs for a pauper's pen," he said, his voice building. "If you really want to help me, throw the pen away and go back to the PGA. It is a crime against golfers everywhere and against your own potential to give up the game you play better than anyone else before you. Stop this nonsense and go back."

"I'm not really sure how to respond to that," I replied, a little annoyed. "Why is it so important? I've proven your theory. The algorithm works. It kind of feels like it's actually a good time to move on and do something else, something that really makes me happy."

"You are wrong and possibly stupid, too. Interest in my pet PIPP theory is in fact waning, because despite the publicity around your success, we have never found anyone else with a ninety-plus G-score. I can no longer bear to call it the Gunnarsson number. I go with G-number now. That is what it has come to."

"You mean in the whole world, there's no one else above ninety in any sport?"

"Of course there are. There must be. We just don't know who they are. Oh sure, we have a few prospects. There's a twelve-year-old boy in Bogota who comes in at eighty-nine for the discus. If he grows proportionately in the coming years he could break ninety, but it's for the fucking discus. Who cares about the discus? I'll tell you who. Nobody! Why couldn't it be soccer, basketball, American football, or baseball—you know, where the real money is?

"There is also a woman in the Philippines who is already fifty-seven years old and for some reason has a Gunnarsson number of eighty-eight for bloody platform diving," he continued in an over-the-top theatrical tone.

"Well, that's promising, isn't it?" I said, trying to cling to anything that faintly resembled hope.

"Adam, please try not to be stupid. It is many things, but promising is not one of them. It is quite likely that her G-number was over ninety when she was in her twenties. So we are already going backwards. But there is more to cry about in her case. You see, she lives with a deeply rooted fear of water after a traumatic duel with the undertow at a local beach when she was six! But being afraid of water is just not enough. She also is scared of heights. So we have a potential world champion ten-metre platform diver who is scared of water, scared of heights, and too old to compete anyway. That is cruel, almost as cruel as this godforsaken Adelaide. I haven't been back to Stockholm in two years and it will be the end of me. Jack Daniel's and Jim Beam understand. But no one else does."

I wasn't insulted by his continual reference to my stupidity. He couldn't help it.

"I'm so sorry, professor. I'm sure you'll find someone else. It's just a matter of time."

"Just go back to golf. That will help until the next Adam Coryell arrives."

"I'm really sorry, professor, but I just cannot go back to the game. I just can't do it."

"I know," he replied, and hung up.

I was alone in the condo. Alli was doing final editing on her novel with her thesis supervisor. Now that Operation Alli was complete, it was time to consider Operation Ingemar. I just sat there and thought for quite a long time. With only a stunning view to distract me, I found I could actually think quite well. Something emerged in my mind. It was a bit hazy, but enough to describe to others. I liked it. So I called Lisa Griffiths and then managed to conference in Susan Maddocks, and Operation Ingemar was soon underway.

Chapter 15

SOME MAY HAVE thought it was the approach of Christmas—
you know, the season of giving—that triggered it. But I knew
better. Or maybe it was just my subconscious still trying to deal
with the trauma. Whatever the reason, I had another idea. The
more I thought about it, the more I liked it. It seemed the perfect fit. I did a little research online and started to crunch some
numbers. If I wanted to make any kind of impact, it was going
to take a significant investment. Coincidentally, I was fully able
to make a significant investment and still never have to work
another day in my life if I didn't want to. And of course, that
didn't even take into account the unspeakable riches that would
surely come if I ever became a fully-fledged published Canadian
writer. Ha! You know the old story. If you want to make a small

fortune, start with a large fortune and become a novelist or open a bookstore, or better still, both. Anyway, the point is I could afford to pursue this new idea I'd just come up with and still maintain a lifelong residence on Easy Street.

After another long call with Lisa and Susan, they both agreed to work with me on the initiative, provided I agreed to stop proposing new and interesting ways to part with my money. They were just looking out for my best interests. But Lisa confirmed that even after underwriting my latest brainchild, I'd still be forever fine financially. So with their blessing, I met on my own with the Canadian Association of Public Libraries to discuss the proposal in broad terms. To put it mildly, they were ecstatic. It wasn't every day someone walked in off the street and offered to throw money at them. So I wasn't surprised they were delighted, but it's always nice to have your ideas embraced. Nothing was etched in stone that first meeting, but the good folks at the CAPL needed no encouragement to take our discussions to a more serious level, where I'd bring in Lisa and Susan to support me and they'd bring in a team of professionals on their side. A solid start.

I loved almost everything about the master's program—my courses, my professors, almost all of my fellow students, and what I was learning. The smaller class sizes and predominantly workshop format seemed to concentrate and almost purify the teaching experience. And I was absorbing it all like a parched sponge. I was nearly obsessed with assimilating the comments and advice my fellow aspiring writers shared when my work was critiqued. Don't misunderstand me. I didn't accept every suggestion, but I considered every one, and edited my work accordingly. But I could almost feel myself growing stronger and more confident as a writer. I was learning my craft.

In addition to constant tinkering with a growing collection of short stories, I'd also started mapping out the novel that had been steeping in my mind for several months. I felt the stories were getting close. Each time I worked through them, I made fewer and smaller changes. Restructuring became reworking became revising became refining, until it felt like they were nearly ready for prime time.

My second time around with Alli could not have been progressing more successfully. Since the night I had popped the lid on the box of unsent letters, we'd been together almost constantly when we weren't toiling on our respective master's programs. I was happy . . . very happy. Always a dangerous observation, but there you go.

It was about a week before Christmas. Alli and I were having a rare dinner out at a Chinese restaurant nearby. Eating at a restaurant was seldom intimate and romantic for us, even at a really nice one. Eventually someone would approach us.

"I can't believe you're right here in this restaurant," it would start. "I've been a huge fan from the beginning. I followed you at the Players last year. You played amazing. Oh, and the gold medal. Wow, that was incredible. We were all so proud. Um, would you mind autographing my napkin? The restaurant is letting me take it. Sorry about the pasta sauce. Makes it authentic, right?"

This scene played out at least once each time we tried to have a quiet dinner out. It was almost always with fans who approached us apologetically and said really nice things. But not always. A few weeks earlier when we'd dined at a restaurant in Yorkville, a short walk from the condo, a young, athletic-looking woman had approached our table and she did not look happy. There was no *Excuse me* or *Hello* or *I'm really sorry to interrupt your dinner*. She just cut right to her point while cocking her finger at me like it was loaded.

"You have been given a rare gift and you are wasting it. That is an offence against your nature, an offence against your family, an offence against golfers like me who work so hard to improve, and an offence against the game."

"Oh, I see. Well, thanks for sharing your thoughts," I replied, trying to turn down the heat.

"You should be ashamed of yourself. You could have achieved so much. But instead you've just sucked a whack-load of money out of the game and walked away."

"Well, I'm not sure that's quite fair . . ."

"I'm not finished," she cut in. "All I ever wanted was to play on the Tour. Any tour. It didn't even have to be the LPGA. But I'm just not quite there, and it looks like I'll never quite get there. So it really pisses me off when someone with your natural talent and skill squanders it, when I'd give anything to have half your ability. It's disgusting."

She spat out her last declaration with such venom, I started to worry and eye the exits.

I didn't even notice Alli stand up, but in an instant she was standing right in front of my tormentor, in close enough proximity to trigger anyone's personal-space alarm. Alli had a fierce look on her face but spoke in a quiet yet intimidating tone.

"It's time for you to get out of his face and go back to your table. I've never seen anyone behave so rudely in my life. Adam doesn't owe you or the game or anybody else anything. So step away now, and don't you ever pull such an insulting stunt again. Am I coming in loud and clear?"

The woman was caught off guard, but probably not as much as I was. Her mouth was agape, matching mine. Eventually she gathered herself, closed her mouth, glared at Alli, and took a small step back.

"Fine. I was finished anyway," she said as she turned and walked away.

"Oh, you're finished all right," Alli replied, holding the perimeter until the other woman was back at her table.

Then Alli sat back down and smiled sweetly at me.

"Sorry about that," she said. "Where were we?"

"Well, I was just about to say that I'd gladly go off to war with you, but I'd never want to go up against you."

"Sorry, she just made me very angry," Alli replied. "She just found out that if you want me to unleash the beast, start abusing someone I love."

And there it was. She stopped when she realized what she'd said, her eyes on the table. Then she lifted them to mine with a very tentative, even fearful, look. The beast was gone.

"Sorry, I could have phrased that differently," she said.

I reached out and cradled her hand.

"I'm glad you didn't. I love you, too," I said without thinking.

Then I briefly started thinking. *Uh oh.*

"I mean, assuming you were using that word in the same way I was. Um, if you meant love in the familial or friendship sense, and that would be fine, I guess, but then I'd be sitting here feeling a little exposed and . . ."

"Shhh, please," she said. "Don't ruin it."

I shut up fast.

We'd avoided going out to dinner for a while after that, but had mustered the courage again after a few weeks. Only one person dropped by our table that night, as we cracked open our fortune cookies. Alli tensed up a bit, but she need not have this time. The older woman stopped only briefly.

"I won't delay you," she started. "I just wanted to wish you well with your writing. Higher callings are very few. Honour it."

Then she nodded and left. We left soon after.

When we arrived back at the condo, I stretched out on the couch. Alli reached into her bag and pulled out a familiar spiral notebook.

"Okay, the next chapter is finally finished," she said, waving the book about. "I was up writing it last night into the wee hours."

"Well, as we now know, higher callings are very few," I replied, and held out my hands for the notebook.

While I read her neat and lovely cursive, she sat in the chair across from me. She pretended to read, but I could see she was watching me much of the time.

In the antiphonal novel, the relationship was heating up. It was a really nice chapter, so well written, and quite moving in the portrayal of two young people in love. But the last paragraph triggered a sudden and unexpected inhalation that Alli would have had no trouble detecting. The chapter ends with the young woman gently and tentatively proposing that she and her boyfriend move in together.

I looked up at her and caught her eyeing me over top of her book. I sat up and faced her.

"Really?" I said. "Are you serious?"

"What?" she replied.

"You know very well what," I said. "Are you serious? Are we ready?"

"Well, I'm not sure *we're* ready, but I feel like I'm ready," she replied, almost in a whisper. "But if you have reservations . . ."

"Reservations? I've been ready for months, but wasn't sure you were. We should really talk more often," I said, standing up. "This is wonderful. I'm thrilled. Um, when can we start?"

"Right now, I guess, if you're sure."

"I'm sure."

"This is the best Christmas present you could have given me," I said as I crammed myself next to her in the chair that was really only designed to accommodate one.

"Well, you're an easy mark if you think me invading your luxurious space is a gift to you."

"If you're worried about this place not feeling like your space, I can sell it and we can move somewhere else, you know," I said.

"Adam, I love all this. It's beautiful," she replied. "Besides, you've haven't even finished unpacking your boxes yet. It feels like we're still moving in anyway. But I need to make one thing clear. I'm paying my share of the expenses."

"Oh, well, it's already paid for in full. So there's no mortgage or rent."

"That's not the point. I'll be paying, even if I'm paying you. I insist."

She moved in within the week.

JANUARY 2021

"Hello?"

"Adam, this is Ingemar," said the voice on my cellphone.

"Oh, hi, professor. How are things in Adelaide?" I asked, sustaining the charade.

"That is an excellent question. I am very pleased to inform you that I am not in Adelaide. I arrived in Stockholm today and hope never to leave again."

"Oh, well, that's great news, professor. You've gone home. Congratulations."

"Thank you, I am extremely happy. I cannot tell you how happy I am. There is no measurement device in all the sciences that could quantify my happiness," he said. "But you already knew all of this."

"I'm sorry?" I replied.

"Why ever are you sorry? I hope you have no regrets about what you have done."

"What? I'm sorry, I'm not really following you," I stammered.

"Let us drop the theatrics, shall we? You are the only person on the planet with the knowledge and wherewithal to fund the new chair in my name at my home university," he said. "The powers that be here insist it is an anonymous donor and they refuse to divulge the benevolent person's name. But they don't have to. I wanted to say thank you. You have delivered me, and I thank you."

I paused to think, but further sham protests seemed pointless.

"Professor, you changed the course of my life seven years ago. I am very comfortable, living in a condo that I paid for in cash, pursuing what really makes me happy. You and your PIPP theory made all of this possible. Anything I might have done to help get you back to Stockholm is a very modest expression of my gratitude. But please do keep this between us."

"As you wish," he said. "Again, I am grateful to be home and to be able to continue my research. And I am learning to be nice to everyone around me, which I do not find at all practical or easy, but I will not imperil the new program through my own actions and behaviour."

"That is good to hear, professor," I said with some relief. "I'm sure there are a few ninety-plus G-scores out there in the world, and you will find them. I know you will."

MARCH 2021

You have to give them up at some point, and it was time. I'd worked on them for so long. Each time I reviewed them, I'd find something I wanted to change, but the significance of those edits eventually declined to insignificance. I'd debate with myself over the placement of a comma for an hour or so before removing it. Then I'd put it back in on the next pass. It was time.

I remained committed to having the stories considered strictly on their merits. I was well aware that I'd have absolutely no difficulty finding a publisher, and a major one at that, if I sent out the manuscript under my own name. The way celebrity works in this early part of the twenty-first century, when you have a certain amount of fame—and regrettably, I still had a lot —what you have created is not nearly as important as the fact that it was you who created it. In my case, objective literary criticism of my writing really wasn't important. Publishers knew there was a welcoming consumer market for anything written by gold medal golfer and kidnapping trauma survivor Adam Coryell. I was not interested in that. I'd spent seven years in the golf world with no real agency over my success. I refused to have my celebrity remove any agency I had over my writing life.

So I'd decided to submit my short-story collection to publishers under the pseudonym MacGregor Wilson. It was a subtle inside joke for golfers. MacGregor and Wilson were the names of two older and now lower-profile golf equipment manufacturers. Was it a bit cheeky on my part? Maybe. But I didn't think it would ever become known. And even if it did, it would at least show I had a sense of humour, though perhaps not a well-developed one.

My plan was to avoid literary agents, as they would obviously insist on meeting me before agreeing to represent me. This limited my opportunities to smaller publishing houses that

accepted unsolicited manuscripts. And I had to land a publishing deal while maintaining my anonymity. It was an uphill
battle to find a publisher at the best of times. It was an even
steeper climb when a pseudonymous manuscript was your
only asset. I drafted a cover letter explaining that for personal
reasons, I was submitting my short-story collection under a
pseudonym and that I could not reveal my own identity, even
to publishers. I tried to assure them that it was not for any
untoward or unsavoury reasons. It was just a personal choice,
to allow me to be judged on my art alone. I felt compelled to
note, though Alli advised against it, that even if it were published, I wouldn't be able to make any appearances to promote
the book publicly in my own true name. I wondered briefly if
maybe such a scenario would intrigue publishers and even
enhance my shot at a book deal. Probably not, but I was looking for silver linings in a sky filled with dark clouds.

Over the course of two weeks, I sent out customized query
letters and my manuscript to dozens of publishing houses in
Canada and the United States. It didn't take long to hear from
some of them. The swift rejections that rolled in to the fake
email address I had created leaned on one predictable rationale.
They simply weren't prepared to consider a pseudonymous
submission without knowing the identity of the author. They
were protecting themselves from the unknown. I probably
would have done the same thing. But I was protecting myself,

too. I only brought Alli, my parents, Lisa Griffiths, and Susan Maddocks into the MacGregor Wilson tent.

In the days and weeks that followed, I found myself checking my MacGregor Wilson Gmail account every twenty minutes or so, and found an empty inbox almost every time. When there was a rare response, it was always a rejection. I'd been warned that the publishing industry seemed to move in geological time. So I waited, and waited.

When I wasn't checking my email and waiting, I worked on my novel. I used Alli's line *Star or Stars* as the working title. I learned quickly that I didn't really know how to write a novel. It seemed daunting. But as I mapped out the arc of the story and began to identify major plot developments and key events, I felt much more confident. I kept breaking the story down into smaller and smaller segments, adding detail as I outlined. I prepared character sketches of all the major players in the novel and invented plausible backstories for them. Then I determined my settings and learned what I could about them. I could really feel the freedom offered by a novel's larger playing field. I resisted the temptation to start writing the manuscript until I really felt like I understood the story. Finally, I wrote a rather detailed chapter-by-chapter outline in bullet-point form. I discovered that uncertainty was the enemy of my writing. The bullet-point outline reduced my sense of uncertainty to negligible levels. It felt like it was time to write.

With only about fifteen hours of classes each week, I had plenty of time to sit in my library, look out the window at the city sprawled out before me, and write. It was quite straightforward to write a chapter when guided by four or five pages of bullet points. Writer's block was never an issue, so the chapters piled up. Of course, I still constantly checked my MacGregor Wilson email, with demoralizing results.

Alli was about a month away from completing her master's when it happened. She'd just arrived home. I was cooking chicken thighs, rice, and carrots for dinner. I not only golf and write, but I can also hold my own in the kitchen. I'm no culinary savant, but if there were a Gunnarsson number for cooking, I think I'd score reasonably well.

"Hey," she said as she came through the door.

"Hey, how was your day?" I asked.

She didn't reply, but kicked off her boots and hung up her coat. She had a strange, kind of flushed and concerned look on her face that I couldn't remember ever seeing.

"Alli? Everything okay?"

She walked towards me and sat on one of the leather bar stools at the kitchen counter.

"Yes, sorry, everything is fine," she replied. "But we do need to talk. I got some news today."

She said it the way you might if you'd just been given a terminal diagnosis, or your mother had died.

"Alli, what's wrong? What's happened? We'll get through it."

My heart was pounding.

"Um, well, I just signed a publishing deal for my novel with a big New York house," she said, still in her stage-four-cancer-diagnosis voice.

While it would have been the Hollywood thing to do, I didn't drop the wooden spoon I'd been using to stir the rice. But I easily could have. She'd only recently started sending out queries to publishers. They didn't usually move this fast.

"Sorry, did you just say you signed a big New York publishing deal?"

"No, I signed a publishing deal with a big New York house. It's not quite the same. The book will be released first in Canada, and then shortly thereafter in the U.S."

"Is there an advance?"

"Well, um, yes, there is," she replied.

"And?"

"And, it's quite satisfactory."

"Okay. Are you comfortable sharing the magnitude with me or should I continue wriggling in anticipation?"

"Right. Well, the advance is sixty thousand dollars."

That's when I dropped the wooden spoon.

"But it's against royalties. So in a way, I still have to earn it," she said. "And it was an auction, so the number is artificially inflated."

"Alli, this is fantastic! You've hit a home run on your first trip to the plate! Wooohooo!"

I was jumping up and down by this stage, grains of rice flying off the wooden spoon I'd just picked up off the floor. One grain landed on Alli's cheek. She reached up to wipe it away.

"This is wonderful, stunning, glorious news! This is what you've always wanted and now it's happened! Congratulations!"

The counter separated us, or I'd have grabbed her and danced her around the room. But it wasn't just the counter that stopped me. She still looked bereaved.

"Alli, what's wrong? You're not reacting at all like someone whose dreams have just come true."

It took me a long time to wrestle it out of her. Turned out she was so reserved because I'd also been waiting to hear some good news from publishers, any publisher, but hadn't.

"Wait. Let me get this straight. The only thing holding you back from ripping off your clothes and doing naked celebratory handsprings around the room is your concern that I don't yet have a publishing deal?"

"Well, the wraparound wall-o-windows also makes the naked-handsprings manoeuvre unlikely."

Then I did walk around the counter to her and put my arms around her.

"Alli, please, I could not be prouder of what you've accomplished. I knew when I sat up all night reading your novel that this moment would come. This is about you. It is your moment. It is a time to celebrate. This is not about me. It's about you. And anyway, I'm hoping that someday I'll find someone to publish me. But your awesome news does nothing but inspire me and fuel the fire in my belly to be a writer. This is what we've worked for. We were never going to sign publishing deals at the same time. The odds of that are astronomical. So do not waste any more time, energy, and emotion worrying about how I'll react to your fantastic news because now you know. I'm so happy for you and proud of you. So enjoy it. I insist. You deserve this. You've earned this."

Then she cried as she held on to me. I was learning that Alli was easily brought to tears, often in a good way. I'm pretty sure this was good crying, happy crying. Eventually the details came out. It was an imprint of Penguin Random House in New York. The deal was for world rights and the advance was very generous for a debut novel from an unknown Canadian writer. They were planning to publish it in the fall. She'd done it.

JULY 2021

In mid-July, when I checked my MacGregor Wilson Gmail account for about the sixth time that morning, an email was waiting for me. It had arrived a few minutes earlier and was from ProsePump, a very small publishing house. I vaguely remembered sending them a package back in March, but I'd heard nothing from them, or from many others, since. Every time I'd received a response from my spring outreach, it was a short, terse, direct, clear, even resounding, rejection. So I steeled myself for yet another and clicked on the email.

Dear MacGregor,

ProsePump is a small literary press based in Peterborough, Ontario, with a focus on short-story collections, particularly by writers just waiting to break through. I founded the press nearly thirty years ago and remain one of our lead talent scouts. I have read and reread "The Birthmark" and have been entranced by its quirkiness and inventive writing. I think these stories deserve a broader audience and I also believe Canadians will enjoy them. With that in mind, I'd like to offer you a publishing deal with our humble house. While we do not have deep pockets, we are committed to our authors and we'll do whatever we can within our modest means to put your prose in front of people.

I can offer an advance of $500 against royalties at a rate of 10 per cent of the cover price. We don't publish hardcover books, so this will be a trade paperback on first printing, with national distribution. I foresee an initial run of 3,000 and we'll see what happens from there. If we need a second printing, all the better. I'd welcome your ideas for the cover, but we have several very accomplished designers in our pool, one of whom will come back with a beautiful look for your debut collection.

I fully understand that MacGregor Wilson is a pseudonym, and I accept that your decision to preserve your anonymity in no way exposes ProsePump to negative publicity or liability should your identity at some point in the future be revealed. We take you at your word. I also understand and respect your desire to conduct our business via email. We agree.

If this is satisfactory in principle, please reply accordingly. Then I will forward a publishing contract reflecting the general terms outlined herein. We hope and expect that this partnership will serve your interests and ours. We await your response.

Sincerely,

Edison Hull

Publisher

ProsePump

I was actually very calm reading the email through the first time and the second. However, the next five times I read it, I grew increasingly agitated. It was a mix of excitement, ecstasy, and panic. I didn't realize until the seventh pass that I'd been chewing on the corner of one of the couch's throw pillows. I'm not sure how long I'd been masticating, but judging from the damage I'd done to the unsuspecting throw pillow, it had been a while. I freed it from my dental clench and let it fall to the floor.

I quickly researched ProsePump online and was relieved to learn it was not one of those fly-by-night pseudo-self-publishing operations that require the writer to pony up their own dough. Rather, it was a very small but well-established and respected literary publishing company. There were also several positive references to Edison Hull. Yes!

As for the terms he proposed, as far as I knew they were in keeping with current practices. The five-hundred-dollar advance wouldn't cover the cost of an oil change on my BMW, but I didn't care.

You'd think after winning an Olympic gold medal and the Masters, I might have some passing understanding of the heights of excitement and achievement. Apparently not. I was shocked, not just at securing a publishing deal but at the extraordinary and unprecedented feeling it engendered. Winning the gold had not even approached how excited I was with the ProsePump deal.

I sat on the couch in silence and looked out over the city as a sense of calm settled over me. I was going to be published. Finally, finally, after a seemingly endless cascade of rejections, I was going to be able to walk into a bookstore and see my story collection on the New Releases shelf. It was then that I realized I hadn't yet responded to Hull's offer.

I hit "reply" on his email.

Dear Mr. Hull,

Thank you so much for your very welcome email and kind offer to publish "The Birthmark." I gladly accept the terms you outlined and look forward to signing the contract as soon as you can send it. As for the $500 advance, if it's acceptable to you, I'd rather you keep that money and devote it to additional marketing efforts. I'm content to wait for my royalties. I'm grateful that you understand my rather unorthodox request for anonymity. I assure you that if my true identity were ever to be known, it would not affect ProsePump in any deleterious fashion—in fact, the opposite may well be true.

Thank you again. I can scarcely believe it.
MacGregor Wilson

Chapter 16

ON TUESDAY, SEPTEMBER 14, 2021, Alli and I arrived at the main branch of the Toronto Public Library at nine-thirty a.m. The event was to start at ten. I hadn't wanted to be there for it, but they insisted and I'm not very good at saying no to nice people, particularly when they're toiling in and advocating for the public library system in this country. So I agreed.

A small stage of sorts was set up on the ground floor and rows of chairs had been arranged. Alli sat near the front while I was whisked into the little side room off the stage. The platform party, as I learned our presenting group was called, was small. The head of communications for the Toronto Public Library would emcee the announcement. The president of the

Canadian Association of Public Libraries and I would sit at the skirted table on the stage.

When we received the signal that it was showtime, we filed out of the side room and up onto the stage. Our host went directly to the podium while the CAPL president and I settled into our chairs at the table. A large monitor stood behind us, kind of between the podium and the table. I looked up to see a packed house filled, I was told, by library board members, the Friends of the Library, the staff of the main branch hosting us, and other library supporters. I found Alli in the second row and she made funny faces at me in an effort to relieve my nerves. It worked a little, I think. Across the back of the room, several cameras on tripods stood on a riser. A number of reporters stood impassively, steno pads at the ready. The room fell silent.

"Good morning, I'm Tessa Conway, the director of communications here at the main branch, and I'm pleased to welcome you to our library and to this important and very exciting announcement. My role is simply to introduce the important people to my right and to wrap up when we're done.

"We'll be hearing first from Sonia Smythe, the president of the Canadian Association of Public Libraries, and then from our very special guest, Olympic gold medallist and pro golfer Adam Coryell. Please welcome Sonia Smythe."

Sonia rose and walked to the podium while Tessa stood off to the side.

"Good morning. I am so pleased to be here with Adam Coryell to make a very important announcement that will strengthen public libraries across the country and bring a love of reading to more remote regions, particularly indigenous communities that currently have very limited access to public library services.

"It is entirely through the generosity and vision of Adam Coryell that we are able to make this announcement this morning."

Of course, everyone always assumed this was all driven by my unbridled generosity. It probably looked like it from the outside. But it all made me a little uncomfortable.

"I'll present the major components of this new investment and then Adam will offer a few additional details. Most smaller and more isolated communities in Canada do not have brick-and-mortar public libraries. Infrastructure funding is just not available. But we have always wanted to serve these areas, and have done so in the past using mobile libraries. As the name suggests, these are modified vans, buses, and other vehicles that tour more remote communities on a weekly basis, bringing books and other services directly to them."

Alli kept her eyes on me and smiled, as did many of the other members of the audience.

"Unfortunately, over the years, funding for mobile libraries has not kept pace with the need. Many mobile libraries are now off the road, having been either put up on blocks or sold for scrap. But today, we begin a new era in mobile libraries in this country, thanks to a significant two-part donation by Adam Coryell.

"Adam has generously donated eight million dollars in capital funds for the purchase and modification of thirty brand-new mobile libraries, or bookmobiles, to bring books, reading, and the library to rural and remote indigenous and other communities."

The monitor on the stage flickered to life with an artist's rendering of the newly designed mobile library. It was painted in wild colours and the words *Bobbie's Bookmobile* were emblazoned across the side. It really looked cool. I got a little choked up when I saw it and was pleased with the oohs and ahs from the crowd.

"But buying and outfitting the bookmobiles is only part of the story. To ensure we keep them on the road for the foreseeable future, Adam has donated an additional five million dollars to create an endowment fund to service the vehicles and keep them running in tip-top shape. We've already purchased the stock vehicles, and the modifications are being made right now. We hope the first of the new bookmobiles will be on the road as early as next month.

"This is an extraordinary gesture by an extraordinary donor. Ladies and gentlemen, Adam Coryell."

The audience—except for the bored-looking reporters at the back—stood and applauded. There were a few whoops from the more enthusiastic library supporters in the audience. At that moment, I really wished I'd been stronger in resisting this kind of public event. I reached to shake Sonia's hand as I made my way to the podium, but she drew me in for a hug. Eventually, I made it to the mic and the crowd settled.

"Thank you for coming out to this. It isn't how I normally spend a Tuesday morning. In fact, I'm missing a class right now."

The audience chuckled and I relaxed a little bit—just a little bit.

"But I'm very pleased to be here. This is important. I owe Bobbie Davenport a great deal. It was she, armed with a measuring tape and an academic paper by a Swedish professor by the name of Ingemar Gunnarsson, who first suggested that I just might have some natural ability in a game I'd never played before. From the moment Bobbie Davenport put a golf club in my hands for the first time, my life was never the same, and neither was hers. She was my teacher, my counsellor, my coach, my caddie, and above all, my friend. Without her, there is no way I'd have been lucky enough to play professional golf, to win a few tournaments, and to represent Canada in Tokyo. And not to dwell on it, but as most of you will know, a year or so ago on a rooftop in Dubai, she gave her life to save mine."

The room was silent. I could hear myself breathing between sentences. I kept my eyes on Alli.

"As you can see from the screen behind me, this mobile library program is literally undertaken in Bobbie's name. When she was very young, she lived in a small community on the north shore of Lake Huron called Thessalon. She was an only child and, as she tells the story, her life really began the day the bookmobile rolled into town. It changed her and, as much as anything else, helped chart her course in life. She became an English and creative writing teacher, as well as a phys ed teacher and coach. She was also a very accomplished amateur golfer."

Almost there now. Wrap it up.

"So this donation is made in her name, in her memory, and in her honour. I don't really think of this as a donation. I consider it to be an investment. And when these thirty bookmobiles start to change lives the way one changed Bobbie Davenport's many years ago, we will all reap the returns on this investment. Thank you again for being here."

Alli led the standing ovation that followed. I'll have to check my files, but I may never have been quite as uncomfortable as I was sitting at that library table under the lights as the applause carried on for much too long.

It was all over shortly after that. The media asked a few questions, I did a few stand-up interviews for the reporters who had come, and then I gently extricated myself, grabbed Alli, and started walking back to the condo, just a block south.

"You were great," she said, squeezing my hand. "Just about perfect. Bobbie would have been very proud."

"Thanks. I was just glad to get out of there. I'm not sure I could have handled one more person commending my so-called generosity."

"That's because they don't know you the way I do," she said. "You are a very kind person, but I think what you did today was not just exercising generosity. It was just as much about assuaging guilt."

I stopped and looked at her. "Guilt about Bobbie?" I asked.

"Of course not," she said. "Guilt about the wealth you so effortlessly amassed."

I nodded and we walked on.

It was an all-Bobbie-all-the-time kind of day. At about four-thirty, Alli and I drove out of our underground parking lot to begin the drive north to our next destination.

The Ladies' Golf Club of Toronto looked just as it had on my first visit almost exactly eight years earlier. It felt a bit odd but still nice to be there again. It was the first time I'd ever been there with Alli and without Bobbie. The event had already started when we made our entrance. It wasn't my idea to make an entrance. But my presence caused enough commotion to boost it to "entrance" status. Duke saw me from the other side of the room and headed my way.

"Adam Coryell, so good to lay eyes on you," he said, gripping my hand and shaking it. "Welcome back to where it all started."

"Thanks, Duke. It's great to be back. The old place looks pretty much the same to me."

"We don't like a lot of change around here. It was a very big deal last year when we decided to move the tee blocks back on fifteen. So change isn't really our thing."

"I saw you at the service for Bobbie and I'm sorry we didn't connect afterwards," I said.

"Ahh hell, I was a mess that day. I'd have been pretty terrible company anyway, so I bailed just before the minister brought the curtain down."

"Yeah, but you came. That meant a lot."

"Well, Bobbie meant a lot to me." Duke's eyes glistened.

"If I could have your attention, everyone, we're going to begin," said an older woman in her outside voice. "If you could make your way out into the hall at the entrance to the restaurant, we'll get started."

It took a few minutes before the crowd assembled. The older woman running the show stood in front of the entrance, where a blue drape concealed something on the wall.

"I'm Shirley Crosby, president of the club this year. Thank you all for coming. This won't take long," she said. "Our executive has been struggling with how to memorialize Bobbie Davenport, in light of her important contributions to the club and outstanding performances on the course as a near-perennial club champion in her day. Well, we tried not to over-think it and we hope you all approve. I should also say how thrilled we are that her protégé, Adam Coryell, is here with us this evening."

Duke led a cheer that melted into applause. I smiled, nodded, and gave a rather anemic little wave.

"Adam, would you mind joining me here for the unveiling?"

I didn't know about this, but figured it didn't sound too onerous. I made my way up and stood on the other side of the drape from Shirley.

"Okay, we've never really had a formal name for our restaurant. And I know Bobbie really enjoyed sharing a meal with friends right here. So, ladies and gentlemen, from this moment on, the dining room will be known simply as . . . if you could help me, Adam."

We both grabbed our respective corners of the blue drape and pulled it away.

"Bobbie's!"

A plaque of sorts was revealed. The word *Bobbie's* in flowing script angled along the top of the plaque. Below was a photo of Bobbie and me taken at Augusta during the Masters. We were standing together on the tee at twelve, the par three in the middle of Amen Corner. She looked so happy in her classic Augusta white coveralls. Beneath the photo was a brief bio detailing her exploits at the club, on and off the course. Seeing the photo gave my heart a little lurch, but I took a deep breath and covered my tracks. Just above the photo it read,

> In honour of Bobbie Davenport and her many years of service and success at the Ladies' Golf Club of Toronto. Tuesday, September 14, 2021.

Alli was a trouper and stayed with me while I spoke to everyone. Several club members extended standing invitations to host me any time I wanted to play a round for old times' sake. I thanked them all and promised to get in touch if I ever felt the urge. I was quite sure I wouldn't feel the urge to play golf again anytime soon, if ever.

OCTOBER 2021

In a strange coincidence, Alli's novel, *Ghostly*, and my short-story collection, *The Birthmark*, were published in the same week. But that was just about the only common ground our books could find. *The Birthmark* seemed to sneak onto book-store shelves quietly, with little or no fanfare. It's difficult to gain any kind of profile for a new book, particularly a short-story collection, when the author is completely unavailable for any promotion and publicity.

On the other hand, Alli's publisher laid on a big launch event at a large independent bookstore in downtown Toronto. A rare midweek book review appeared in the arts section of the *Globe and Mail*, and to call it a rave seemed to shortchange the word. Alli's novel had buzz before it even hit bookstores, so her launch was packed. It wasn't broadly known in publishing circles that Alli and I were together. So I wanted to stay in the background at the launch and not shift any of the attention from where it belonged—squarely on Alli. Don't read any con-ceit into my concern. It was just a reality of celebrity culture, even though Dubai and Tokyo were more than a year in the rearview mirror. Unfortunately, Alli couldn't get through her launch remarks without thanking me and pointing me out standing in the shadows at the back of the room. But it didn't really matter. There were no reporters in the house. There seldom were at book launches.

Alli smiled through the entire event. Both her publisher and editor spoke in glowing terms about the novel. They gushed and Alli blushed. There were blurbs on the back cover from three of Canada's most respected and revered novelists, two of whom attended to show their support. Alli spoke very well and then read a section that aptly captured the tone and voice of the novel. During the reading, the audience was utterly silent as they sat in the palm of Alli's hand. After the formal part of the proceedings, Alli assumed her position at the signing table as the line snaked through the entire store. It was Toronto rush-hour traffic brought to life in a bookstore. I watched Alli engage with each of the excited attendees as she patiently and gratefully signed their books. She was a natural. She was made for this world. And I was pleased to discover just how happy it made me feel. Writers are a competitive lot. Yet I could not discern within me even the faintest traces of envy, jealousy, or resentment. I have no doubt I'd have felt differently had it been anyone other than Alli. I guess that's love.

Three days later, *Ghostly* opened at or near the top of virtually every bestseller list in the country. There were multiple reviews, all of them positive and some ecstatic. And her publisher reported that the first week of sales was off the charts with no sign of slowing. The U.S. launch the following week showed a similar trajectory, including a very favourable review in the *New York Times Book Review* and a place on their extended bestseller list. Hollywood could not have scripted it better. Speaking of Hollywood, a big studio optioned the novel's film rights for a healthy sum. It didn't get much better than that.

Edison Hull at ProsePump kept me apprised of how my collection was doing on its journey into the published land. In
summary, our market penetration was modest at best. Not all
bookstores are so keen to stock story collections, as they seldom sell as well as novels. *The Birthmark* was stocked in about
30 per cent of bookstores. In the first two weeks, five copies
were sold. As for sales in the U.S. and other countries, well,
that was easy. Zero. The collection was only published and
available in Canada, at least for now. ProsePump was doing its
best to promote the book, but that really amounted to some
social media posts, a giveaway of one copy on Goodreads, and
a launch news release that nobody picked up.

But I did like the cover they came up with. No, it didn't feature
an Elvis birthmark. That would have been too literal. It was more
of a contemporary and colourful collage of shapes that really
caught the eye. There were two blurbs on the back, with a partial
of one of them on the front, offered up by two other ProsePump
authors I'd never heard of. But I was grateful and emailed them
both in my MacGregor Wilson persona to thank them.

There were a few reviews in more obscure publications.
Based on the critical reaction to the collection, I was happy
there weren't more reviews. There were some positive comments in the critiques, but it was hard to find them amongst
the ambivalent and negative comments. As usual, when I read
them I ended up agreeing, at least to a certain extent, with the

criticisms. I clung to the most laudatory comment I could find in the reviews: "Wilson is a competent stylist." I assumed it was related to my writing and not my fashion sense. ProsePump added it to my sparse bio page on their website.

Alli took in stride all the attention her book was getting, and was even somewhat reserved about it at home.

"You seem utterly unaffected by all of this," I said one day as she was about to leave for the airport for another stop on her book tour. "Aren't you thrilled by what's happened? I certainly am."

"Adam, of course I'm thrilled. Inside, I'm over the moon and quivering twenty-four hours a day. But I try not to get swept up in it. When I write the next novel, I want to be the same person who wrote this one, because that seemed to work well. So I'm just keeping it chill."

"As long as that's the only reason," I replied.

"Now, what do you mean by that cryptic comment?" she asked.

"I just wouldn't want you to be tempering your enjoyment of all this because you're worried about how I might be feeling, given that my humble collection isn't exactly flying off the shelves—not that it's on very many shelves in the first place," I replied.

"Well, I just don't want all this to change anything with us," Alli said, holding both of my hands. "Your book is wonderful, and soon people will realize it and it will start to sell more and more. Remember, collections are always tougher, and you're hobbled right out of the gate by remaining anonymous. I get why you did that, and I respect that, but it does make it harder to market the book."

"This is not about us. We're fine. I'm so proud of you I could pass out at any moment. Not only are *we* fine, but *I'm* fine. I'm really happy to be a published author. And I'm even happier to be in a serious relationship with the newest literary rock star."

While she was on the road, I worked hard on my novel. It hadn't turned out to be quite as painful a process as I'd feared. After I'd fully outlined the story, I actually really enjoyed writing the manuscript. Guided by my outline, I found I could write with purpose and confidence simply because I knew the story so intimately. I figured I'd be in a position to send ProsePump the manuscript early in the new year, if the editing and polishing went well. Edison Hull had expressed a desire to see the novel when it was ready and had even included a first-right-of-refusal clause in the publishing contract for *The Birthmark*. So I was on a mission to move from short-story writer to novelist. I hoped my collection's lacklustre reviews and sales wouldn't prompt a change of heart in Edison Hull.

I checked my email and found a message waiting for me from Google. I'd set up Google Alerts on the name MacGregor Wilson to monitor the online world for mentions and reviews of the book. Yes, I ego-searched my own pseudonym. I clicked on the link in the email notice and was taken to a book blogger's website. It seemed she had read and reviewed my collection for her blog, known as LitLog. My heart started racing as I recognized the cover of my book at the top of the most recent post, published just an hour before. I quickly read through her review. I then contemplated cancelling Google Alerts. It was not a favourable review, though I did discover another damning-with-faint-praise line I could use on my website alongside "He's a competent stylist." The line was "He's an okay writer . . ." I left out the second half of the sentence, which began with but.

Then, feeling the need to torture myself, I made the horrible mistake of visiting Goodreads, where I looked up my book. I had a momentary surge of pride when I saw that in the three weeks since it had been released, twenty-three readers had finished the book. I say momentary because I almost immediately noticed that the average rating for The Birthmark was 2.49. To be clear, the rating is out of 5. I briefly considered rating my own book with a 5 to try to nudge the aggregate score above the 2.5 threshold. But it just didn't feel right. Wisely, but with some effort, I decided not to read the comments reviewers had left.

I checked in on BookRanker, a site that listed all current titles in the Canadian market in order of sales. On the home page, I saw that Alli's novel was still ranked number one in the

Canadian Fiction category. Fist pump. I typed my name, or rather, MacGregor Wilson's name, into the search bar and up came my book. Then I shut down my computer. My ranking was 189,765. Go Team MacGregor!

Chapter 17

I CLICKED ON the email from Edison Hull, and I was not calm as I did it. The subject line read *Your fine novel.*

Dear MacGregor,

Thank you for sending your manuscript a few weeks ago. I can genuinely report that the only relief I've had lately from the stress of running a small press in this economy was reading your novel, Star or Stars. It has some parallels to the title story in your short-story collection but digs much deeper. I think the novel form might be in your wheelhouse. Your writing is stronger in SoS and the characters more fully realized. I also like that your sense of humour seems to emerge more often in the novel. I know I'm keeping you in suspense here, but I did want you to know how much I enjoyed the story.

So, to end the suspense, we'd like to publish it. We're dealing with a few issues here that may delay our production schedule, but we'd like to aim for a fall release, this year. We think we can make that happen. The sales of The Birthmark were not what we'd hoped, but there were extenuating market factors in play unrelated to your collection. We have faith in your writing. We can offer a $1,000 advance against royalties at a rate of 10 per cent of the cover price. Like The Birthmark, the novel will be published as a trade paperback.

Well done, MacGregor. Hearty congratulations. If this is acceptable, please let me know so I can forward the requisite paperwork.

Edison Hull
Publisher
ProsePump

As you might imagine, I replied in the affirmative almost before the pixels of Edison's offer had fully materialized on my screen.

APRIL 2022

Alli was still doing quite a bit of travel to promote *Ghostly*. There were several spring launches in quick succession, including London, Edinburgh, Berlin, Paris, and Rome. The novel was very popular in translation and was still selling strongly in North America. Alli seemed to be in her element. But I missed having her around. I was a month away from finishing my master's, and my thesis was not only in the hands of my supervisor but would be published in the fall. So both Alli and I had reason to feel very good about our writing lives. Okay, maybe Alli had more reasons than I, but I was happy.

Six-month sales of *The Birthmark* were 253, including the 24 copies I'd purchased online. I didn't really know much about the publishing world, but even my rudimentary math skills told me ProsePump was taking a very big bath on my very small book. There were over 2,700 copies of the collection still out there in bookstores across Canada. I just had to figure out how to move them from the fiction shelves to the checkout counter.

It was while Alli was touring in Calgary, Edmonton, Vancouver, and Victoria for a week that I heard again from Edison Hull. I read his email as the sun sank behind the Toronto skyline.

Dear MacGregor,

I am truly sorry to be the bearer of bad news, but alas, I am the only one here. ProsePump has always existed on, or just above, the line that separates viability from insolvency. It is a familiar story for small presses everywhere. Well, I regret to inform you that a confluence of unfortunate events has finally pushed us below that iconic line for the first time. Moreover, there is next to nothing I can see in the future to restore our fortunes and keep our doors open.

Rooted in this reality are at least two implications for you. Firstly, the entire 3,000-copy print run of The Birthmark is in the market. But should there ever be a need for a second printing—and I hope one day there might be—I'm afraid another publisher will need to step in. Secondly, and more importantly, I'm so sorry but I must tell you in good conscience that ProsePump cannot honour the contract we signed with you for your novel, Star or Stars. In fact, we will cease to exist —much like the famous dead parrot in that Monty Python sketch— in a matter of weeks. The die is cast, save for a Hail Mary miracle.

So I hereby officially liberate you from our existing contract so that you can take your novel to other publishers and get it in the hands of Canadians. They deserve to read it. Please keep this email as formal notice that our contract is null and void.

I regret that we were never able to speak to one another, but I respect your desire for anonymity. I truly hope our paths cross again.

Edison Hull
Soon to be ex-publisher
ProsePump

Shit. And things had been going so well. I felt terrible for Edison. He'd taken a chance on me, invested in publishing my collection, and had not earned back anywhere near what he'd put in. I doubted the dismal performance of my book was solely responsible for pushing ProsePump into the lower reaches of the red, but I still felt like at least some of this was on me.

Ideas ran through my head. Since my book had hurt ProsePump's bottom line, what could I do to help save them? Well, there were options, and I was certainly in a position to move on them.

One idea was to buy ProsePump, clear their debts, and inject adequate cash to keep them going. I could do this as MacGregor Wilson, a silent, anonymous partner, or I could even do it in my own name. Money wasn't the issue. I suspected the required investment was denominated in six figures rather than seven or eight. No, the problem was that I just didn't want to buy the company that was publishing my own novel. It was tantamount to self-publishing. I have nothing against self-publishing. But I'd worked hard to earn my ProsePump publishing contracts and I didn't want to take what seemed like a step backwards.

That's when the big idea circled and then landed. I kicked it around for an hour or so, getting used to it and thinking through the implications. It would not have been my first choice. But unfortunately, it seemed like my only choice. I stepped out on our balcony in the twilight to clear my head. Twenty minutes later, when I had thought it all through, the big idea still worked but seemed even more unpalatable than it had a first glance. But I felt an obligation to act. Best of all, the plan would help the situation quickly—perhaps even resolve it completely. My course was clear. It was also unfortunate and unwelcome, but unavoidable.

I didn't call Alli. I didn't call Lisa or my parents. I didn't even call Susan, who was probably in a position to help. I knew what had to be done. I started by creating another fake Gmail account: breakingbooknews@gmail.com. Then I created a fake Twitter account: @BreakingBookNews. There, the infrastructure I needed was in place. I scrolled through the contacts in my mobile phone and made a list of sports reporters I'd dealt with while I was on the PGA Tour. I was surprised that the list numbered twenty-three. Then I spent about an hour online gathering email addresses for book columnists, book editors, book reviewers, and a few prominent book bloggers who might be considered literary influencers.

Then I wrote the following short email message:

Dear _____,

This is too juicy to keep to myself. I have just learned that the author of the recent short-story collection The Birthmark, published by ProsePump, is none other than Adam Coryell. Yes, that Adam Coryell. He used the pseudonym MacGregor Wilson to protect his anonymity. Don't believe me? I've attached a scan of a poem Adam Coryell published in the Stanford Daily newspaper in 2017, using his collegiate pseudonym Adam James (his first and middle names). I've also attached a scan of

page 172 of The Birthmark, where the poem makes a return appearance. Also, compare the lead story in the collection with that famous
ESPN interview Coryell did just before the Dubai tragedy. See any parallels? And let's not forget that for the last two years, Adam has been doing
his master's in creative writing in Toronto. See how it all fits? Finally,
wouldn't you agree that Adam was a little too cute choosing the names
of two golf equipment manufacturers as his pen name? I mean, really.

Just thought you'd want to know. You're welcome.

A friend

That should do the trick. I sent the same message and two scans
to twenty-three sports reporters in Canada and the U.S., and
ten Canadian book reporters. By that stage I felt no hesitation.
As Edison had said, the die was cast. Then I did call Susan, to
tell her what I'd done. As I'd expected, she was thrilled. She
was programmed to support anything that elevated my profile.
And this surely would. We agreed on key messages and talking
points to use when reporters called. The idea was to not cave
early, but rather to drag it out, to build anticipation and public
interest. Finally, I picked up the phone and for the first time
dialled Edison Hull.

"ProsePump, Edison Hull."

"Hello, Edison, my name is Adam Coryell."

"As in the golfing great, the gold medallist? That Adam
Coryell?"

"Yes, sir. And I can assure you, this is not a prank call. I actually am Adam Coryell."

"Well, it's great to speak with you, though I confess I can't figure out why you might be calling."

"Well, you also know me as MacGregor Wilson," I said, and then waited.

"Really! Seriously! Good lord, that is just incredible," he gasped, apparently stupefied. "You, Adam Coryell, famous golfer, wrote *The Birthmark?*"

"I did, and I remain so grateful that you stepped up to publish it when no one else seemed interested in the least."

"It deserved to be published," he said. "I can hardly believe it."

I briefly explained what I'd done and how I proposed to handle what came next. We also agreed on some lines he could use when the media inevitably called him. In short, Edison would only confirm that MacGregor Wilson was a pseudonym but would not reveal the identity of the author. That would give the story enough air and fuel to keep it crackling for a while.

Edison sounded like a great guy. I was not surprised. He was quite excited by the end of our chat as the implications of my big reveal began to come into focus.

About thirty seconds after I ended my call with Edison, my phone rang. I didn't usually answer reporters' calls, but today was a very big exception. It was ESPN. I took a deep breath. This would have to be played carefully.

"Sean, is that you?" I opened.

"None other," he replied. "Thanks for taking my call, Adam. It's been a while."

"Well, I was surprised to see your name flash on my screen after all this time," I said. "So what's up?"

"Someone is peddling a pretty convincing case that you are the author of a collection of short stories called The Birthmark, published last October by a small press known as ProsePump. Is it true?"

"Ridiculous. Who's pushing that story?"

"It came in over the transom anonymously, but a lot of what was in the message checks out and seems plausible. So is it you?"

"You're following up on a single anonymous source? Sean, it's a ludicrous notion."

"So you're denying it."

"It's a crazy idea."

"So you're denying it."

"I'm not even going to dignify it with a response."

"So you're denying it."

"I seem to have a lot of calls coming in, Sean. I'm going to have to let you go. I think you've been taken in by someone who isn't playing with a full set of clubs. Gotta go."

Similar exchanges unfolded with two-thirds of the reporters I'd surreptitiously contacted. They all called within an hour of my email. I spoke with Edison and Susan to compare notes.

They'd both responded to several calls. Edison seemed in favour of coming clean and getting the truth out there. But I argued that we could make the story bigger and the impact greater if we didn't fess up for at least another twenty-four hours. Susan agreed, and together we persuaded Edison to stay the course. It would be worth the wait.

I surfed from channel to channel to watch the story spread. It started on the sports networks: ESPN, Fox Sports, NBC Sports, TSN, the Golf Channel. But by about eight-thirty that evening, it had migrated to CNN, CBC News Network, CTV News Channel, and virtually every other network. Apparently, the public's appetite for celebrity gossip was insatiable. Each hour, the story persisted, airing late in the broadcast and sometimes with new information. They weren't confirming that I was the author. That was hard to do since I hadn't yet confirmed it. But as the hours passed, the story became more plausible and more convincing as the evidence piled up. Some networks actually played clips from my infamous ESPN interview as I created the bones of the birthmark story. The online news sites were all over it as well, adding tidbits their enterprising reporters and researchers had dug up to make it even more persuasive. By that stage, I couldn't reasonably have denied the story, so I turned off my phone and went dark for the night.

This was going exactly as I'd planned. I felt kind of like the Wizard of Oz working the levers behind the curtain. Though I still wished it hadn't come to this. For some reason, I slept well that night, though not for very long. I'd turned in quite late. Despite the two-hour time difference, I had managed to reach Alli in her Calgary hotel room. She was frantic. She'd been in a TV studio for a live interview. Just before her segment was to start, the sports anchor had led with my story. She claimed it knocked her off her game a bit, but she survived. After I told her the whole story, she thought my little master plan for world domination was brilliant. We agreed that if anyone asked her about the whole affair, she'd simply say they'd have to talk to me.

By the time I turned off my iPad, the world seemed convinced the erstwhile Masters champion and gold medallist was also a published author. Right on schedule.

"ALL RIGHT, TIME for phase two of Operation ProsePump Resurrection," I said.

I was on a conference call with Susan Maddocks and Edison Hull.

"Well, it's been quite a day so far and it's only nine-thirty," Edison replied. "But I can tell you that sales of The Birthmark have skyrocketed in the last twenty-four hours. I've had calls from the warehouse, my distributor, and even directly from retailers frantically searching for more copies. Orders for at least another five thousand copies have come in. That alone has restored access to my credit line. So we live to fight a little longer."

"That's great news, Edison," I said.

"Well, you did it, young man," he replied. "It was all you and your well-executed stratagem."

"I think we need to move quickly to close this circle and let the media drive even more book sales. We can't wait another day," Susan said. "So here's what I've set up for this morning, based on our discussions yesterday."

"I'm ready," I said.

"Adam, we're going to deal with sports first, and then move to news. So you start in an hour at TSN for a taped one-on-one with Connor McSweeney. Then they're going to put you at an anchor desk, and you'll do six eight-minute segments in a row via satellite with sports shows throughout Canada and the U.S., and one in England. After that, you're going to the CBC Broadcast Centre for a taped interview on *The National*, and also an interview for their books webpage. And everything is embargoed until noon, when all hell will break loose."

"What about CTV?" I asked.

"They'll get the TSN feed. So they're covered," she replied.

"Sounds like a plan," I said. "It's almost as if we know what we're doing."

"Well, I'm going to sign off now. I have to get on to our printers to start burning up the overtime. It sounds like we're going to need a ton of copies of *The Birthmark*. Keep me posted." With that, Edison hung up.

Susan and I conferred a bit longer to make sure we both knew what I was going to say. The questions were quite predictable. And we agreed that I'd simply be as forthright as I could be. Pull no punches. Apply no spin. Just be direct. That made it all easier.

I dressed up a bit, trying to look like a cross between a pro golfer and a newly published author. I made sure I had my entire schedule on my phone before I walked out my door. Susan had arranged a car to ferry me where I needed to go for the day. It was a black Range Rover. Of course it was. That was Susan's go-to limo.

At TSN, I was whisked into makeup and then into a chair on an elevated platform, where I sat facing Connor across a low table. The lights were bright and hot.

"Okay, Adam. This is great. Thanks for coming in. Of course, we're really focused this morning on the book, now that we understand that you did in fact write it. At least, that's what your rep told us. Are you good with that?"

"Yep. And thanks for doing this. I'm ready when you are."

Connor touched his earphone, likely listening to his producer in the control room.

"Okay, we're good to go," Connor said. He paused for a few seconds before starting off.

"We're really pleased to have Canadian golfing great Adam Coryell in the studio. Thanks for being here. It's been a while."

"Well, thanks for having me, Connor," I said with a smile.

"It was about eighteen hours ago that a story started circulating that you'd added published writer to your impressive résumé. And the rumour is that you are actually the author of this collection of short stories called *The Birthmark*," Connor said as he held up the book he'd had in his lap. "The author's name on the book is MacGregor Wilson. The publisher confirms that it's a pseudonym. So, Adam, are you MacGregor Wilson?"

"Well, if you'd asked me that yesterday, and many did, I would have tried to weasel out of the question without giving you a definitive answer. But I think we're a little too far along in the story for that to work. So the answer is yes. I can confirm that I am MacGregor Wilson and that I wrote those stories."

"Why didn't you use your own name on the book the way most authors do?"

"It's quite simple, really. I wanted my writing to be considered objectively and be judged on its merits, without my profile as a golfer influencing it in any way."

"But if you'd put your own name on it, maybe you wouldn't have been published by"—he stopped and flipped open the book—"ProsePump, but could have landed a huge book deal with a huge advance from one of the huge publishing houses."

"Well, Connor, that may well be true, but then I'd never really know if I was actually a writer, or just a famous golfer who writes. And I've wanted to be a writer for a very long time, long before I ever picked up a golf club."

It was quite hot under the lights, but I felt a strange, almost serene calm descend on me.

"So this is obviously not about the money. You want to be seen as a writer. And that seemed unlikely, perhaps impossible, if you were to use your own name."

"Well put. You just said it better than I could," I replied. "Perhaps you should be a writer." I smiled when I said it.

"But why admit to it now?"

"Well, I think the evidence pointed quite clearly in my direction. It seemed a little churlish, even silly, to carry on with the charade."

"At least this should be good for sales, right?"

"For my publisher's sake, I hope you're right," I said. "It's often tough for small presses in this country to stay afloat. The folks at ProsePump are wonderful and they publish very good books, notwithstanding their questionable decision to publish mine. But if there is a bump in sales, ProsePump could certainly use it, and I think they deserve it."

"Some might say you've come forward now knowing that revealing your identity will sell thousands of books and put thousands of dollars into your pocket. What do you say to them?"

I hadn't really expected that question, but my synapses seemed to be firing on all cylinders right then. I paused very briefly before responding.

"Well, Connor, for me, it's not about money. In fact, I'm donating all of my royalties from this book to the recently announced Bobbie's Bookmobile program, an initiative to put more mobile libraries on the road, in honour of Bobbie Davenport. The goal is to bring the joy of reading to more remote Canadian communities. Bobbie would have loved the idea. So I can assure you, if someone hadn't leaked the story yesterday, I wouldn't be here today."

"I understand that you have a novel finished that's in need of a publisher."

"I'm not sure where you heard that, but it is true that I have written a novel and it's possible that my current publisher will be bringing it out, but nothing is certain at this stage."

"A final question. Did you make a mistake choosing the pseudonym MacGregor Wilson, two names synonymous with golf?"

"Hindsight is a wonderful thing. I never thought this book would ever gain enough profile for the pen name to matter at all. But now that you've raised it, if I were doing it all over again, I think I'd probably choose a name that had no connection at all to what I used to do for a living."

And that was that. I used the same general lines in the rest of the interviews, whether they were for sportscasts or news-casts. I was exhausted by the end of it all. As I flopped on the couch late in the day, Alli texted me a photo she'd taken in the bookstore in Edmonton where she'd been signing that after-noon. It showed a stack of my books on a prominently posi-tioned table near the front of the store. A sign propped up on the table said,

The Birthmark

by Adam Coryell writing as MacGregor Wilson

That was encouraging.

MAY 2022

Never underestimate the power of celebrity, even when it's a reluctant celebrity wielding the power. Sales of *The Birthmark* took off, as I'd hoped, and ProsePump reaped the benefits. A month after the story broke, the collection had sold over 150,000 copies and there was no sign of it slowing. It had also been published in at least a dozen other countries, boosting sales even more. There were several high-profile reviews that followed, keeping me in a state of high anxiety. Interestingly, many in this new crop of reviews were fairly positive. Not effusive, but more positive than the first batch had been. I suspected literary expectations were lower for professional golfers, so I had an easier ride. I wasn't thrilled about that, but the goal of this entire escapade was to keep ProsePump's doors open. And we were successful on that front. They were very happily hopping, trying to meet the continuing demand for a short-story collection penned by yours truly—you know, "a competent stylist" and "an okay writer." I'll take it.

Immediately after that first TSN interviewed aired, all of the mainstream publishers starting rolling out the red carpet. They wanted a crack at my novel and were not shy about it. They were so persistent that I pushed them all to Susan, who collected the offers. By this stage, Edison Hall was keen to continue our relationship, and even though our original contract for the novel was no longer valid, he presented a revised offer and upped his advance to $5,000, leaving the rest of the term sheet as it had been originally.

I called Susan.

"So, how goes it with all our new publishing friends?" I asked.

"It's like the old days," she replied. "You are back to being a hot commodity."

"Yeah, for all the wrong reasons. They haven't even seen the manuscript yet."

"Well, they're ready to sign anyway. Let me give you the

highlights. We have fourteen publishers in play. I'll dispense with those whose offers can't really compete with the big boys. So we're really left with two. Penguin Random House tops the list with a $6.2 million offer, with HarperCollins in hot pursuit at a paltry $5.9 million.

"Hello, Adam, hello?"

"I'm here. Did you say $6.2 million and $5.9 million?"

"I did."

"Wow. Did Edison talk to you?"

"No, he said he'd speak directly with you. Did he call?"

"He sure did. We had a great chat. ProsePump bumped up their offer to five."

"Wow. I can't believe Edison was able to come up with five million dollars," Susan said.

"Ahhhhh, no. I mean five thousand dollars, which, I might add, is five times more than his original offer. He's never given an advance higher than three thousand dollars, so this is unprecedented."

"Well, good for Edison, and three cheers for ProsePump, along with a yellow ribbon for participation," she said. "But now to the real business at hand. We know the offers and we know the companies," Susan said. "So what do you think? Penguin Random House or HarperCollins?"

"Well, it's an easy call for me," I said. "Let's go with ProsePump.

"Hello, Susan, hello?"

I SPENT THE next few days, while Alli was still out west, phoning in my schoolwork—though it was all well in hand anyway—and just thinking. I thought a lot, for hours at a stretch. And I wrote. It had been such a crazy time that I really hadn't had much time to be with myself to think, ponder, meditate, cogitate, and generally reflect on the state of my life. My trip to Lake Temagami nearly two years earlier may have been the last time I'd been able to shut everything else down and just commune with my own thoughts. Now I could, at least for a day or two. As it turned out, I decided or discovered —I'm not sure which—that I'd never been happier.

"Let's not be apart for that long ever again," Alli said when she came through the door from the airport.

We held on to each other for quite a while with the door open and her bag still in the corridor. Some things can't wait.

Twenty minutes later we were leaning in to one another on the couch. At my insistence, Alli gave me a day-by-day play-by-play of her tour. There was a lot of talking into microphones, signing, reading, and shaking hands, punctuated by less-than-stellar hotels and mediocre restaurants. Then I gave an abbreviated version of the hairy events of the last week.

It seemed like the right time. I was prepared. I was also nervous. I pulled our antiphonal novel out from under the couch where I had hidden it.

"So, with all my spare time lately, I've written my chapter," I said, handing Alli the tattered spiral notebook.

"You didn't! I can't believe it," she said. "For the entire flight home I was thinking all I wanted to do was see you. Then I thought maybe you'd written the next instalment when I was gone. We are so simpatico."

She opened the coil notebook to the right spot and folded it over so it was easier to hold.

"Nice. That looks like Montblanc Corn Poppy Red. Am I right?"

I nodded. Then she fell into it without another word. She was a deep reader. Nothing short of mortar fire could distract her when she was inside a story. It was as if I were no longer in the room. I couldn't see her face, just the notebook in front of it and the last page of prose she'd turned over. This made it easy to track her progress. We were close now. I slipped my hand into my pocket and got myself ready. Soon, now.

Right on schedule, I heard her very sharp intake of breath. When she dropped the notebook in mid-paragraph, her eyes and mouth were very wide. When she saw me, they opened just a little bit wider, which was quite an achievement. I was in front of her on one knee. Yes, yes, I know, I know. I talk a good game about rejecting clichés. But sometimes they work. It took another split second for Alli to see what I was holding out to her.

I had a few lines ready, but I didn't even say a word. I had no chance. She hugged me hard and burst into tears, again. I'm pretty sure they were good tears. Happy tears.

ACKNOWLEDGEMENTS

WHEN I WAS IN grade eight, I took boys' golf as an option. (I also took boys' cooking, but that's another story.) Every Tuesday, my golf classmates and I would swing nine-irons on the soccer field and occasionally make contact with the Wiffle ball on the grass in front of us. I've played golf ever since, experiencing the alternating frustration and elation all golfers understand. Unlike most pastimes, in golf, you seem to need only a little elation—one good shot—to offset a heap of frustration—a dozen bad shots. But despite initial appearances, this is not a novel about golf. It's about life. Most authors would let you arrive at that conclusion on your own, but I just didn't want to leave it to chance.

I'm indebted to my McClelland & Stewart family, who have stood by me for seven novels. In particular, my editor, Bhavna Chauhan, has made this a much better book than it was, and for that I am grateful. My thanks to Erin Kern for her eagle eyes through the copy-edit stage where she caught things I'd never have seen, and to my stalwart publicists, Dan French and Kaitlin Smith, who helps keep me in front of book-lovers across the country. Beverley Slopen, my wonderful literary agent, has always been there for me. And Doug Gibson, who gave me my start at M&S and guided me through my first six novels, still provides wise counsel and constant encouragement. I think of Doug as my editor emeritus, as well as my friend. My twin brother, Tim, is often an early reader of my manuscripts, as he was for this one. His insights are helpful and appreciated.

As always, my wife, Nancy Naylor, and our two sons, Calder and Ben, continue to encourage my writing life despite the various sacrifices it entails. I'll endeavour to make it up to them, and will likely fall short. In many ways, they are why I write.

Terry Fallis, Toronto, January 2019